CHILDREN OF GOD

Lars Petter Sveen

Translated from the Norwegian by Guy Puzey

Graywolf Press

This publication is made possible, in part, by the voters of Minnesota through a Minnesota State Arts Board Operating Support grant, thanks to a legislative appropriation from the arts and cultural heritage fund, and a grant from the Wells Fargo Foundation. Significant support has also been provided by the National Endowment for the Arts, Target, the McKnight Foundation, the Lannan Foundation, the Amazon Literary Partnership, and other generous contributions from foundations, corporations, and individuals. To these organizations and individuals we offer our heartfelt thanks.

NORLA This translation has been published with the financial support of NORLA.

Published by Graywolf Press
250 Third Avenue North, Suite 600
Minneapolis, Minnesota 55401

www.graywolfpress.org

Published in the United States of America

ISBN 978-1-55597-820-4

2 4 6 8 9 7 5 3 1
First Graywolf Printing, 2018

Library of Congress Control Number: 2018934488

Cover design: Kapo Ng

Cover art: Shutterstock

And there are also many other things which Jesus did, the which, if they should be written every one, I suppose that even the world itself could not contain the books that should be written. Amen.

John 21:25

CONTENTS

CHILDREN OF GOD

1 ||| LITTLE CHILDREN

It was in the days of Herod the Great, in Bethlehem, and we were on the lookout for a little king of the Jews who'd been born. The stars were out, and we'd come to kill him.

Tuscus barged through the door ahead of Cato, who took the lead, sword in hand, while I followed. Celsus stayed outside. An old married couple were kneeling in the small room. A weak oil lamp cast a flicker of light on the pair. Cato pointed his sword at them. He was in charge; he was our officer. He opened his mouth, but instead of saying something, he doubled over and threw up on the floor. Tuscus took a step away.

"Cato," I said, but he paid no attention to me. The old couple stared at Cato and at all the vomit pouring out of him. I walked toward them with my hand resting on the hilt of my sword. If anything happened, I would have to take over; we'd trained for this. A dog, or something like it, howled outside. My breath smelled rotten. Cato vomited once again. His sword made a groaning sound as he let it scrape along the floor. It was too much for him, all these babies. How many boys had we killed just to get one little one?

I looked at the old couple. I looked around at what little they owned.

"Are there children here?" I asked.

The old man shook his head. "No children," he said, his wife beginning to cry.

"Celsus," I shouted. Celsus appeared at the doorway.

"We're coming out. We're finished here," I said. Celsus looked at Cato, nodded, and hurried back to his position outside. Tuscus turned around, touched what was left of the door he'd torn down, and muttered something. I went over to Cato and helped him up. Cato looked at me. His eyes were red and slaver was hanging from his mouth.

"I'm sorry, Capito," he said. "You shouldn't have to see me like this." He got up, sheathed his sword, and spat on the floor.

"Come on," he said, and we went out.

We changed formation. Cato and I went in front, with Tuscus and Celsus right behind us. Tuscus's large hands swayed back and forth in a strange rhythm. Celsus, with his blond hair gleaming in the night as if he'd been sprinkled with dust from that bright star.

Celsus just stood outside each door, listening and pushing back inside anybody who tried to come out. "Oh Celsus," said Cato at one point, his eyes bright and a strange warmth radiating from him. "You're always the one holding the fort, Celsus." To which Tuscus added: "The only thing he's holding on to is his dick. We're the ones who have to do the dirty work."

Our orders were hopeless. We'd been summoned from our base in Caesarea to serve in Jerusalem, and then, out of nowhere, we were asked to put together a small elite unit—only purebloods—and travel to Bethlehem. There was talk of some Jewish king having been born. King Herod wanted to put an end to the rumors. He hired us, paid us to do his bidding. We were to kill all boys in the town aged two or younger. King Herod couldn't trust Jews to do such a thing to their own people, but it was hard even for us. How many were there in this city? Who knew where the baby boys were? We broke into houses where people couldn't understand what we were saying. When we found children, who knew how old they were? We asked their mothers, who screamed back. We asked their fathers, but they refused to answer. Cato said we were to kill every single one we found, no more questions, just get it over and done with. As the night went on, Cato spoke more and more, his voice getting higher and weaker.

He hailed us after we came out of each house, telling us General Pompey would've been proud of us.

"They'll hear of us in Rome. We'll get our own section in the victory procession after this feat."

He carried his sword in his hand, never stopping to dry the blood off it. The men we shoved aside didn't dare look at him, while the women stood against the walls, whimpering their children's names and the name of their god.

But we were getting tired. We'd started off counting all the children, but I lost track of the number as the night went on. Our orders were hopeless: this wasn't what we were fighting for. How long had we trained, how much had we practiced with sticks, with those damned wooden swords, how much had we yelled at each other? We'd been trained for major battles, we'd been trained to be powerful opponents, but instead we'd been sent to this place at the edge of the Empire, where everything was so mixed up, so confusing. The enemies didn't line up with their armies on the battlefields; it was impossible to keep track of all the groupings and all the factions. Herod ruled as a client king by the grace of Emperor Augustus. Some people supported Herod and cooperated with him, while others moaned and grumbled. We were sent a number of times to clear out insurgents, whether they were poor people with no weapons or small gangs hiding in the hills. We often had to help those who despised us, going on patrol to chase away thieves, getting only angry looks in return, before being ordered to move back into the same areas to suppress revolts among the very people we'd been helping. All those small rural places were like a tinderbox ready to be set alight.

"We're done for this evening," said Cato. He spat and asked us to find water. He stank. We all stank. The stars were burning in the sky, one more brightly than the others. None of us had ever seen anything like it.

"It's cold," Tuscus said in a hushed voice, while Celsus said he wanted to sleep. A woman started wailing behind a wall just next to us. Cato looked sleepily toward the noise. Several lights were lit. I asked the others to check if they had all their kit. Tuscus answered that he did, Celsus too. I reported to Cato, who nodded. His face was dim in the night, like dying embers. The sounds of howling cut through the cold air.

"Dogs," I said. Cato turned toward me.

"What have we become?" he asked. I asked him what he meant.

"Let the dogs come," he said. Tuscus and Celsus were standing behind us; I could hear them breathing.

"I beg you, dogs," said Cato, his voice lower but facing out into the night. "Come and help yourselves so all this can be over."

"Cato," I said.

"Come on, dogs," said Cato. "Come on."

"What are you talking about?" said Tuscus.

"Nothing," I said, as more screams rang out. It was like a song dissipating between the buildings, before suddenly striking up again like a vast, displaced choir.

"Let's go home," I said.

"Home," said Cato, the word taking a strange form as he said it.

"We're going back," I said. Cato nodded vaguely. Tuscus looked like he wanted to say something, but he kept it to himself. Then he did open his mouth after all, but I told him to shut up.

"Let's head back," I said. "We need to rest."

None of us had been home in ages, but I didn't want to talk about it then. I cursed myself for using that word. There in Bethlehem, we were supposed to stay a few nights in an empty building on the edge of the small town. It wasn't far from Jerusalem, where we'd been quartered in the Antonia Fortress. But I liked it best in Caesarea. It was right by the sea, and on clear days I would try to see all the way across the water, all the way home to our own land. I could see home when I closed my eyes to sleep or when I smelled the plants damp after the rain, but it was happening less and less. I didn't think I was doing anything important for the Empire being where I was. It wasn't where the battles would be fought. All we did was wait and do our duty. Something bigger would come our way, I was sure of it.

But it was night, Cato was ill, and it was my responsibility to get us back after we'd completed our mission.

The chorus of wails had not died down and could still be heard like a wind blowing from the wilderness. I thought of the dogs that always came to scavenge the bodies of people we hung up, and the others we left lying, and I thought of the noises they made as they fought for their food, but this was something different. It wasn't snarling or howling; it wasn't the sound of four-legged animals. It belonged to the wind or the rain or the sea or whatever grows in the depths below. I had no idea how I'd get to sleep. None of us had any idea how we'd get to sleep. We did whatever we could to put off having to shut our eyes and be left alone in the dark.

Cato got undressed and stood there, naked in front of the small square opening in the wall that led out to the night. I lay down on the floor and tried to stretch my back. Tuscus and Celsus kneaded each other's muscles while they stared into space.

"It wasn't right, what we did," Cato mumbled. "We shouldn't have accepted this mission, it wasn't worthy of the Empire."

"I thought we would fight for Rome," said Tuscus. "Not go around sacrificing Jewish babies."

Celsus lay down and rolled over. Cato scratched his genitals as he went on muttering to himself. He was getting on my nerves. What was wrong with him? He was supposed to be a leader. He was the best among us; I could never beat him when we fought or trained together.

I asked how he was doing and whether his touch of sickness had passed.

"Shut up," said Cato. "I'm not sick, it's gone now."

"Are you sure?" I asked. "I don't want that damn stuff all over me tonight."

Cato came across until he was standing over me.

"Young or old, who cares?" I said. "I wasn't the one who started throwing up like a girl. Shit, you've probably caught some Jewish disease."

Before I could even get up, his punches hit me on both sides of my face. I pinched my nose and felt around to see if any teeth had fallen out in my mouth. Cato told Tuscus to bring me the washbowl.

"Get yourself cleaned up," he told me.

I called him a damn fool, a wet rag.

"Shut up and get washed," he said. I took the washbowl.

"Who's a little girl now?" Tuscus smirked. Celsus lifted his head before quietly lying back down. Cato got dressed and lay down.

"I'm not sick," he said. "It's gone now."

I looked over at him with his crooked nose and great chin. His mouth twitched like the small shivers of a hurt animal. He shut his eyes, then opened them again. Closed them and opened them.

"Those were our orders," he whispered. "It wasn't our fault, they were orders."

That very moment we heard a strange sound of weak laughter. We stared at each other. There was the laughter again, louder this time. There was somebody in here with us. Tuscus was already on his feet. Cato signaled at him to stay calm.

"Oh, you can hear me, can you?" said a voice. It was a sharp voice, yet deep at the same time, like a knife grating through black sand.

"It wasn't nice of me to laugh at you," the voice continued, "but you're like little children, trapped in those beastly bodies of yours."

A man was sitting there, hidden in the shadows by the door. How had he got in? How long had he been sitting there? Cato got up and walked over to the stranger. Tuscus followed him. They'd both taken out the knives they always kept on them when they slept.

"Stop," said the stranger. "What good will it do you to cut holes in me? You've cut so many holes tonight that the town can't hold all the blood pouring out."

The stranger's eyes were a grayish white. He was older than any of us. A walking stick was leaning next to him where he sat.

"Who are you?" asked Cato.

The stranger breathed in, then let out a slight sigh of sorts before he spoke: "I'm blind, and yet I see many things. I'm what stays in the shadows while the light falls elsewhere. I'm here as an envoy of King

Herod, but my knowledge extends all the way to Emperor Augustus and his generals."

We were all taken aback. I felt myself stand up straight.

"Everything changes," said the stranger, "but you men here may endure forever. The ancestors of those who belong in this land were kings. What about their descendants now? They're under your heel. And what about your descendants, where will they be many hundreds of years from now? Under the heel of others. Even with all that's happened before, all that's happening now, and all that is yet to come over the hundred or thousand years of night ahead of us, know this: there's a place for you in this story. What you do now may be remembered. Children will sit and listen to their mothers and fathers telling the story. There's no yesterday or tomorrow in tales like these; there's no thousand years ago or thousand hence. Everything is now. Everything. Even the creatures that walked over this land before we existed. Even the things they'll build in worlds yet to come. Roads, walls, palaces, and castles. The air will be filled with all of creation, and the birds will no longer fly alone."

The stranger stopped, leaning down toward the ground and shaking his head, before turning back to us, his eyes open.

"But now it's nighttime, and day will soon be upon us, so I'll be brief," he continued. "I've got a few little stories for you, if that's what I may call them. I want to tell you that you mustn't worry about what you've done tonight."

"We're not worried," I said. Cato turned toward me and told me to be quiet.

"Capito," said the stranger, suddenly seeming old. "You'll become a great warrior in this army. Maybe there's an officer in you too."

"How do you know who I am?" I asked. "I've never seen you before."

"I know who all of you are," said the stranger. "Otherwise I wouldn't be doing what I'm doing now."

Then Cato spoke, asking the man to tell us who he was and what he was doing here, but I wished Cato would shut up. I just wanted to hear more. The stranger smiled, and his teeth were white, as if he had shining stones in his mouth. He held up his hands, and even though he wasn't near us, it felt as if he were touching our faces, stroking us on the cheek.

"You're skilled soldiers," he said. "Better than any Herod has ever had in this wretched realm of his. The best the rulers in Rome can send to a backwater like this. And you know that. You know what you are. Nobody can guard you like Celsus can, keeping an eye on everything that's going on in the evening darkness or at the market."

Celsus was still lying on his side, turned away from us. Nothing of what was being said appeared to stir him.

The stranger continued: "Nobody can walk like shadow better than Tuscus can, striking with the force of a lion, coming at an enemy like a leviathan from the ocean depths, dark, heavy, precise, and without mercy. You're a warrior melted down and reshaped into a new kind of soldier, a kind that generals dream of, and that the weak fear."

Tuscus looked down at himself. His giant hands hung down along his sides, and there was a strange motion in his fingers. It was as if Tuscus's whole body began to glow, and I was about to say how ridiculous he looked when the stranger said my name again. And now he seemed younger, his hair soft, his skin taut, and his eyes as clear as the coldest water.

"Capito, Capito," he said. "Maybe you're wondering what I'm about to say now. There's nothing to wonder about: you already know it. Everyone in this room knows it."

Then he said the words that have followed me ever since. I can still hear those words. They're like honey, like sweet wine. They make me feel warm, they sharpen my senses and make me drowsy at the same time. I dream of those words moving me through valleys, over desert sands, along walls, and over city squares with my sword in my hand. I am indestructible. I do things I can't explain, and so quickly, so accurately that I struggle to remember them. The world beneath my feet, a soft breeze brushing over my brow, the weight of iron in my hands, the sound of leather on my shoulders.

The stranger went quiet and straightened up. He turned his eyes to Cato.

"Cato," he said, but Cato gestured at the man to stop.

"Stay away from me," said Cato.

"I see you, Cato," the stranger continued. "Here you stand before us, handsome and ruthless. The generals in Rome know about you, I've seen it for myself, the people in the streets of Rome whisper about you: 'Cato, Cato, a future general, a man you can depend on to lead his soldiers through the deepest valleys and into the hardest battles, his men always trusting him like their own brother.' Don't worry about the people we've defeated, those miserable subjects, don't listen to what they think is right or what they think is wrong. Look at this light," he said. Suddenly, the stranger was holding a burning stick in his hands. "Look at how the light falls. One moment one of my feet is in shadow, and the next it's in the light. It keeps changing," he said, moving the burning stick back and forth in front of him. "What's in the light, what's in the shadows, what's right, what's wrong. We'll go on living, we'll survive, from one day to another, from one ruler to the next."

"I don't know who you are," said Cato, interrupting him, "but you're talking crap. I don't believe you."

The stranger got up. He was tall, much taller than I'd thought. His head almost touched the low ceiling.

"Don't argue with me, little soldier," he said. He reached out to Cato, palms open. "You're carrying this load for us," he whispered. "You, Cato, and your soldiers. Nobody can rule an inch of the Empire without you and your men."

"I've been cutting up children," said Cato.

"No," said the stranger. "You're fighting a war to rid this world of chaos, to defend everything that's been built." Cato's face was twisted, almost as if he were trying to smile. I wanted to back him up, but there was something inside me, and I couldn't get the words out. It was as if they were stuck in my mouth. I looked away.

"Get away before I strike you down, old man," said Cato.

"I'm bigger than you," said the stranger, still with his hands held out toward Cato.

"I've taken on bigger men than you before, and I'd do it again," said Cato, but his voice was quieter now.

"Little soldier," said the stranger. "Look at me, listen to me: are you that bad a man that you'd kill me?"

"I don't want to listen to you. I'm not a bad man," said Cato, having started to quiver. "I can still save myself and all the others here," he went on. "I'm waiting for a chance to do some good. I won't do anything else bad."

"What's that?" the stranger said. His voice seemed like thunder, filling the entire room. "Is that some of his light coming in here? What, didn't you get rid of the poor little creature? Take hold of my hands, little soldier." Cato stared at the palms of the stranger's hands. We all stared. The stranger held his hands in front of Cato, and a weak light emanated from them.

"Take hold of my hands," the stranger said again, and this time Cato lifted his arms.

Cato looked at his own hands. "No, no," he said. "Stay away from me."

My eyes met his, and I thought I saw something crawling inside. I'd never seen Cato like that. He started begging, pleading. He wasn't being a leader; he was being pathetic. His hands rose up and were heading toward the stranger's long fingers. Cato called out to me, to Tuscus. He called to Celsus. But it was as if we were all in a peaceful sleep. What was Cato fighting against? We were tough, we were made for this life. We were the chosen ones.

The stranger wrapped his fingers around Cato's hands and nodded. "Cato, Cato, you are mine," he said. Suddenly Cato twitched and froze where he stood. His head was thrown back, his chest rose up, and his mouth opened, with not a sound coming out. The stranger let go of Cato's hands, and Cato fell to the floor. I ran forward, grabbed hold of him, and Cato gazed up at me. His eyes were burning, his lips forged into a smile. There were dark hollows around his hairline, and his hair was damp.

"He's gone," I said, looking around. Tuscus asked what had happened.

"Nothing," said Cato suddenly. I let go of him and got up.

"Our mission is complete," he went on. "You did a good job, we need to sleep." His voice sounded so clear: "Help me up."

Tuscus took hold of him.

"Come on, Capito, help me up too," said Cato. I put his arm around my shoulder and pulled him up. He staggered as he balanced on his feet. "I want to sleep," he said. I nodded and said yes, looking over at the door. There was nobody there. Tuscus, who was standing with me, followed my gaze.

"I can't remember," said Tuscus. "All I can remember is a voice. What happened?"

"Nothing," I said. We put Cato down and rolled a blanket around him. His eyes were closed and he was breathing normally. He had a handsome face. So young, but battle worn. With those big hands and those broad shoulders. The way the blanket had been wrapped around him, it was as if a future emperor were lying there.

I was woken by a cock crowing. Everything was wrapped in a blanket of darkness. "Go back to bed," I muttered, but the bird was right, as the next time I opened my eyes, it was light. The world emerged. The small opening in the wall, the crack beneath the door, the bodies of the others in the room. Celsus was stirring next to me.

"How many were there last night?" he asked. I didn't answer; I was trying to remember.

"Sixteen," Tuscus said from the other side of the room. "We'll have to sharpen our swords now."

"Sixteen? Wasn't it fourteen?" said Celsus. "You don't need to sharpen anything, those creatures were like soft little animals."

"I always sharpen my sword," said Cato, clearing his throat and spitting. "It can never be too sharp. We've always got to keep our weapons in good order. They're the tools of our trade."

"But they were little children," said Celsus. "They don't count as much as a fully grown Jew."

"Divide it by two," barked Cato. "That makes eight, or seven."

"Eight," said Tuscus.

"Seven," said Celsus.

"It was more than that," I said. "At least ten."

"You mean divided by two or not?" asked Celsus.

Tuscus started sniggering, and Celsus followed him. Then Cato started laughing too, and I immediately joined in. We were filled with such power that it was as if nothing could stand in our way. We laughed, we got up, we found our way to each other. Cato put his arm around me, I put my arm around Tuscus, and Tuscus put his arm around Celsus. We were one, and the sound of our power must have reached out right across Bethlehem.

2 ||| THE FIRSTBORN

I

Jacob's coming up on forty now, and it looks like it'll be an auspicious age for him. I see him less and less, but if you see your grown-up children too much, it means they've still got a long way to go. I think Jacob is searching for everything that was hidden from him, and is finding it. It could've been the opposite; he could've tried to hide everything that had found its way to him.

The last time he was here, I noticed that his hair had lost its grip on top of his head. He didn't try to conceal it, and I tried not to stare. My own hair is long, with locks falling down from my head and over my shoulders. Sarah, Jacob's mother, had such hair that I couldn't get to sleep at night. I stayed awake, my fingers entwined in a weave I never thought would let me go. But she died, and I smoothed oil into her hair, packed it in cloth, and lowered Sarah's whole body down into the ground. When I saw Jacob's bald scalp that last time, I felt it was a sign: now Sarah's body has rotted away. The very weave that was to cling to me forever is no more.

"Father?" says Jacob.

"Yes?" I reply. I've always listened to my firstborn. His difficulties with words and how they stuck in his throat; I know of other parents who beat or mock their children for less. I heard tell of a father in Samaria who killed his two daughters and his son because they didn't speak clearly or properly. But I noticed that Jacob's words came more freely when I stopped and turned toward him. Jacob always needed me to stay quiet and listen. Now he expects nothing else of me, even though he no longer finds himself tongue-tied.

"We're lucky, Father," says Jacob. He tells me about high taxes, about what some farmers he met on his last trade journey told him, and about some problems with a merchant from Jaffa. I ask him short, quick questions. Jacob passes his hand over his head and says that far too many people have to give up too much. He doesn't like traveling around without stopping to care about other things than just his trading. I raise my voice to say that, even if it is our duty to help others in need, this land is full of needy people.

"My father, your grandfather, came from poverty too," I tell him. "We've worked our way up to where we are now. What you're doing for your family now, all the traveling, all the bargaining, will be the foundation for you and your brothers' children to build a living."

"Father," says Jacob, "you're getting worked up."

"I'm not getting worked up," I reply. Jacob smiles, and when he does, I can see Sarah in his eyes.

"Father," he says, "listen to this." He tells me a story he heard when he was last in Judea, in Jerusalem. It's a funny story and it makes me laugh. We laugh together. I put my hand on his knee, and Jacob puts his hand on my shoulder. Then he suggests we should pray together. We kneel down next to each other. He starts with God, the Father, our Lord, but ends with Jesus. The Son of God is in our hearts. I am glad neither of us bore witness to how they killed him. Jacob doesn't tell me much about what the two of them saw in each other, or what they talked about, but he still gives thanks, every day. I try to remember too, but there are days when I forget, and there are days when I don't dare. Even when I hear Jacob speak, the words trundling out of his mouth like little ripe berries.

My son, what was it that Jesus did? How did he get you to speak without stuttering or stammering or clenching your hands? What was it of God's love that he put in you to rid you of that trace of evil?

If only I knew.

What I do know is that there is evil in all of us, and there is evil in the Roman power ruling over us. Jacob speaks of the powers of darkness. I've seen what they can do, and I've given up trying to understand what God can do. After Herod's death and the fighting that followed, I saw with my own eyes how Publius Quinctilius Varus came to Jerusalem with three legions and crucified two thousand of our people outside the city walls. My family and I were spared, but was that because we'd kept evil at bay, or because evil had stayed close to us? Are we possessed by those dark forces? Are we the ones shattering our people's hope?

There was a time when I thought that my own child was possessed. Sarah was taken away. She gave me a child and was taken away. Our child was named Jacob, and I passed Jacob on to other women. I raised him up in their hands. I lifted him out of my life.

As he grew older and gained brothers and sisters from other mothers, I began to hear how his voice struggled. I could see his whole body struggle: his little face writhing, his fingers twisted, even his toes crooked. Sometimes he would close his eyes, squeezing them until they became two wrinkled slits. Other times his eyes were wide open, as if the evil were pressing on them from behind, as if the words stuck there were about to tear his whole body to pieces. At first I thought he was consumed by the memories of his birth, when Sarah's screams for mercy filled the whole world up to the vault of heaven. Then I thought evil had left its mark on Jacob, branded him when he came out of his mother. I thought this evil was waiting for him to rot and end up in the soil so it could consume him.

Jacob bears no external signs of all those years of evil. He can talk about anything at all and with whomever he wants, even with the people he holds responsible for the occupation and all the killing. I've seen him talk with high council priests, and he seemed so at ease. I've seen him talking with Roman officers, Thracian and

Gaulish soldiers red with rage, but Jacob made them laugh. What they were laughing about I never asked.

I've seen him standing together with a poor farmer, holding each other's hands, crowning each other with wreaths of flowing, barely audible words.

But I've also seen my grown son walking alone in the pale morning light, muttering, gray and ashen-faced. I've seen how he can close up, even in good company, like a flower blooming in reverse.

Jacob is not just one person. But there are no others like him. He's my son, my firstborn.

He's my son, and God knows how alone he was during his first few years. I was never there. Sarah had gone. Judith was there, Leah was there, Mary, Deborah, Elizabeth. I remember all the women's names, but I can't remember who they were anymore. All those hands holding Jacob, all those kisses he was given, all the times he cried, wanting to be picked up.

I didn't know my own child. I didn't want to touch him. If I went over to where he lay, or watched him crawl, I saw the shadows approaching me. And out of those shadows reached Sarah, her body decayed, with hands like claws, and gray, sullen eyes. She didn't come to me in my sleep; she came in my waking hours, every time I laid eyes on Jacob.

He grew up, little by little. He grew on me too. And Sarah had gone. Slowly, like twilit clouds, she was no longer to be seen, vanishing a second time. It slowly dawned on me that Jacob was mine. I was his.

Jacob's seven brothers and sisters have not always been good siblings. There were times, as I remember it, that they were horrible to him. The other boys made rhythmic noises and laughed at him. They repeated everything he said or tried to say. One time, they were so awful to him that Jacob went silent. He would no longer open his mouth or say anything. I had to beat him to get him to talk again. I beat the words back into him. I subdued the stain of evil that had been left on him.

Now his brothers and sisters are all grown up. I see them all the time. His brothers' wives, and their children. They are occupied with their own thoughts and families. They make offerings to the Temple and to the priests. They're what I used to be. Now, when Jacob comes, his brothers drop whatever they're doing. They no longer remember how Jacob used to be, and Jacob lets them forget, even though I know he remembers.

One night, last autumn, it was cold and we both wore dark, heavy clothes wrapped around our bodies. Jacob had been home for several days and had let his brothers take part in an important deal, but there had been problems and arguments. His brothers thought they hadn't gotten a big enough share of the transaction; they thought that Jacob was pocketing more than he deserved. They came to me and said they feared Jacob was planning to cut them all out of their inheritance when I passed away one day. I said that was nonsense and told them to put things straight between themselves. Jacob took care of it, but afterward he stared out into the night and asked me if I remembered the child killings in Bethlehem. I told him I couldn't remember anything of that sort from those days, but that I'd heard stories about it.

"Have you heard how he was saved?" Jacob asked.

I nodded, but I no longer knew which stories were true and which were just intended to make Jesus, the Son of God, seem like Moses.

"It was a spider," said Jacob. "A spider spun its web in front of the cave where Jesus and his parents were hiding. Because of that web, the soldiers didn't think there was anybody inside. I once asked Jesus," Jacob continued, "like the fool that I was, if it was true, if there really was a spider in the cave."

Jacob fell silent and bowed his head. "Jesus seemed so, I don't know what else to call it, but he seemed tired," he said. "His shining eyes, they were surrounded by shadows, and his hands were shaking. I could see it, even if he tried to hide them."

"What did he say?" I asked.

"He said he was scared of spiders," said Jacob. I remember that conversation; I even remember the night and those dark clothes we were wearing. The wind was silent like waves can be out on the water. The stars were faint, almost flickering, and there was Jacob's raspy voice. "He was scared of spiders." That's how he said it.

"A savior afraid of the smallest creatures: it's laughable. But I've thought about it," he continued, "and I think that Jesus was showing me how small and simple we humans can be, how we can all be afraid of the smallest things. We're small and simple when we let ourselves be driven by what we fear instead of what we love. Today, my brothers have shown me how small and simple they are."

Jacob is my firstborn. I am his. He has no children; I don't know why, and I don't want to ask. I have no right to demand any such thing or to grieve about it. I gave him so little when he was small, and as my first, he is entitled to more from me. I will admit there are nights, dark and cold and empty nights, when I think about how I've never seen him with a woman. He's my eldest, and Sarah, together with the man I once was, young and different, will both die with him.

Jacob will be with the Lord, while I will wander in the darkness, looking for Sarah.

Thoughts like these weighed heavily on me for several years, but now they're small and light, and eventually they'll fade away and vanish. I see a child, I see a grown person, I see people who have destroyed themselves, and I think of how Jacob will take everything I've built up on into the future. If it were to stop with him, what can I do? I've done my part. I had Jacob, I was his father. I led him to Jesus.

I was broken. Jacob was struggling with his words, they were tearing him apart. He bore his mark of evil. He was trying to say "I'm going for a walk, Father," but what came out of his mouth was: "I'm g-g-g-going for a wa-wa-wa forawa-wa-walk." He started to tear out his nails, his fingertips became all red, and I had to check them every morning and evening to see if there was any swelling or inflammation. I made sure that he always had someone with him, or that he was near me.

Some people said I should do the right thing and let him go. Others said I'd done all I could.

I made offerings at the Temple. Priests and officials gave me their advice.

"The Lord God has given you a sign," said one of my family. "It's up to you now."

One night, when I couldn't sleep, I got up before cockcrow and washed my hands and face in the light of the oil lamp. I scrubbed my fingers and palms and used my nails on my cheeks, nose, and forehead; it was as if I had oil stuck to my skin and hair. I knelt down, lowered my head, and immersed it in the water. I breathed through my ears and listened with my mouth. Everything was upside down and back to front. The water was alive; it ran inside me, whispered to me as it flowed and gave me resolve: I would have to fight. The water spoke to me.

I would have to take up the battle against the evil power in Jacob, against what was tearing his speech apart. I would do anything to save him, to cleanse him.

But I was no savior. I had no power over this evil. I would have to search.

Some men who worked for me, and who came from the city of Samaria, had spoken of an old woman who lived in Bethel. I summoned the men and asked them to tell me about this woman. They apologized and said they couldn't vouch for her. It was just a rumor, a story heard by the daughter of a sister of the husband of a sister.

"What kind of story?" I asked. The man who'd dragged his whole family tree into the equation stared at the ground and fell silent.

"I'm not going to punish you," I said. "Nobody will hear of this, you have my word. This is between us." The man nodded but still kept his eyes on the ground. He told me that a young girl in his extended family, a niece of his brother-in-law, had a neighbor, and the father of this neighbor had told her about his sore toe. His foot had been caught while he was working to clear a patch of land, and within a few days the foot had already turned a nasty color, so he traveled up to Bethel, since these people lived in the area around Jericho, not far from the river Jordan. In Bethel, there was an old woman who mixed some herbs in a bowl, poured boiling water on top, forced him to drink it, and then placed her hands over the poor man's sore toe. While he sat there, watching with his own eyes, all the agony and swelling, bruising and pain vanished. His skin regained its normal glow, and the happy man walked all the way back to where he came from without feeling anything other than the Promised Land beneath him.

I took Jacob with me and left for Bethel that same day. The men described the route to me and did their best to explain what the old woman looked like and where I might find her, but since neither of them had seen her themselves, I set no great store by their eyewitness accounts.

When we arrived in Bethel and began to ask around, it soon became clear that the people in those parts knew the old woman. She lived with a man I understood to be her son, and his family.

The old woman was blind, her hands shook, and when she spoke, she began shouting. I asked her son if she often had visitors, to which he shook his head and said that it had been a long time since people last came to her.

"People step aside if they see her now," he said. "Even my children keep away from her. She pulled out the hair of one of my sons. Since then she hasn't been allowed to stay in the house with them. She sleeps in the stable, with the animals."

"She pulled his hair out?" said Jacob, in his own way. The man looked at him, and then looked at the ground and asked me what Jacob had said.

"He was asking if she really pulled out your son's hair," I said. The man nodded and called out a name, and a boy with his head covered came running over to us. The boy went up to his father, and the father pulled the rags off his head. His hair had been shorn, but the skin on one side of his head was bright red.

"It'll grow back," said his father.

I gave them some coins, wished them God's peace and future happiness, and we went back the same way we'd come.

I didn't give up. On another journey, we crossed the Jordan and followed the river Jabbok up a valley, where we were greeted by a ragtag mob of men. We were far away from everything, but I'd been told that these people were peaceful and that they were led by a prophet with God-given talents. I wanted him to set Jacob free.

"Are you here to meet the Master?" asked a man with one eye and one deep, black hole. I told him we were and held on tightly to Jacob.

"This is my son," I said. "We wish to meet Hananiah and seek his counsel."

"The Master will see you," said the one-eyed man. "And remember, in the kingdom of the blind, the one-eyed man is king." We stared at him, and he began to laugh. "Come on," he said. "Follow me."

The one-eyed man took us to a tattered tent that had been pitched beneath a tree next to a mound of rocks. The crowd of men stood behind us now, whispering, and some of them came up to me asking for gifts and offerings. The one-eyed man batted them away with a stick.

"Keep yourselves pure," he shouted. "Remember the words of our Master and allow our kind guests to meet him before you speak to them."

"Wait here," he said, disappearing into the tent. He came straight back out again and signaled us to remain standing, before he turned back to the tent and knelt down. The chatter behind us turned to whispering, and then to silence when their prophet stepped out through the tent door.

He was covered with dark hair, even his beard appearing to grow up to his eyes, and his clothes were wrapped around him as if he were freezing and had no wish to be standing outside there with us.

"May God's peace be with you," he said, before coughing and spitting. He motioned to the one-eyed man. "Tell them to come to me, and then leave us in peace."

"Yes, Master," said the one-eyed man, waving us forward.

I'd heard Hananiah's name spoken by some of the workers of one of my tenant farmers. They said he could heal the sick and release us all, and they told me where I could find him. I thanked the workers and asked my tenant to turn a blind eye to what they'd told me. From what I understood, it was safe to seek out Hananiah's followers as long as they hadn't crossed the Jordan to approach Jerusalem. If the rulers saw him as a madman, they would have him flogged in public and let him go, but if he really was what he claimed to be, they would crucify him and his followers.

"You have come to meet me," Hananiah said once we were standing in front of him. I told him that was right and began to introduce myself, but he interrupted me.

"I don't want to know what you call yourself or who you are in this world," he said. He looked across at Jacob. "Is that your son?"

I nodded and introduced Jacob.

"What do you want?" Hananiah asked.

"I have been told that you are a prophet, and that God speaks and works through you," I said. "My son has something evil within him that prevents him from speaking. I want to do whatever I can to heal him so that he can speak freely."

Hananiah stood there looking at me, before turning to Jacob. "Why do people like you come to me?" he said. Before answering, he waved his hand again to quiet me. "Let me hear you speak, boy." Jacob looked at me, but Hananiah spoke to him. "Don't listen to him, you've come here to me, to my kingdom. Listen to what I've got to say. Speak to me, let me hear what's bothering you and your wealthy family."

Jacob introduced himself, saying his name and where we came from. He told him about our journey there and that it was the first time he'd crossed the Jordan. When he fell silent, I was filled with hope, as here was a man who had listened to my son, who let him speak, stuttering and faltering. Only when Jacob had finished did Hananiah turn toward me.

"Have you seen my people?" Hananiah asked.

"Yes, they greeted us," I said.

"My people," said Hananiah, "are those and many others, and you've seen what they look like, but you haven't heard them speak yet, or where they come from and the tales they have to tell. Don't come to me with your wealth and your son, asking if God can save him. You have already been saved here on earth; you are living in salvation. You don't know what suffering is. God doesn't care about how you speak or how you look. When God's kingdom comes, you will know suffering. He will turn everything upside down."

And on he went. He snarled and spat, and then turned his back on us, went into his tent, came back out and told us to go, before disappearing back inside. Jacob was scared and moved closer to me.

"It's all right," I said. "This was a waste of time, it's my fault. Let's go home."

I almost gave up after this. Word got about as to what I'd done, and all sorts of people came to me with advice, but I'd lost all faith. I'd heard about prophets before and seen what the Romans did with them, but it was no new Isaiah who'd stood there with us. God did not work through these preachers from the wilderness. They were new kinds of insurgents, imitations of dreams of old legends. Hananiah couldn't heal my son any more than he could save himself and his followers from the fate that awaited them.

I promised myself never to subject Jacob to anything like that again. I just wanted to carry on living, but I wished that Sarah were with us to give me an answer. If Sarah were by my side, I could have threaded my fingers through her hair, and maybe I would have found the answer there.

But then Jacob fell ill with a cough and a fever. I had some women look after him and gave them all they needed to make him fit and well again. One evening, a few nights before he would reawaken from his fever, pale but healthy, I went to see him. He was talking in his sleep, mumbling, sometimes audibly, and his head was moving from side to side, but there, in the land of dreams, his words were flowing like water down the Jordan. There was nothing chopping or grating the words as they came out, and even if they were only fragments that he wouldn't even remember or understand when he woke, they were complete. They were whole words. The evil power had no effect on Jacob as he slept.

I was filled with a strange new hope. If my son was able to speak fluently in his sleep, then he was also capable of speaking when awake. There was good and evil within him, and the evil had to be wrenched out into the daylight.

I asked the women who sat there by Jacob if any of them had heard him talking in his sleep. They said he'd been doing it every night while the illness was at its worst.

"He talks like people talk in their sleep," one of them said. I told them about Jacob and about what he was suffering with, and I asked their advice.

"I've heard about you," said one of the women. "You crossed the Jordan to help him."

"You've heard him yourself," I said. "He speaks like a healthy man at night."

"Why haven't you sought out Jesus?" said another of the women.

"Jesus?" I asked, and she told me about an unclean man, a leper who had been cleansed after being delivered by a man called Jesus of Nazareth. I asked her to take me to the man who had been saved as soon as morning came.

In spite of what the woman had told me, the newly saved man was still unclean. There were open sores and boils on his face, down his arms, and on his feet. I kept my distance and put up a scarf in front of my face. I took hold of the woman and asked her what was going on: Was she trying to make a fool of me?

"He's clean," she said. "He can't pass anything on to you. Jesus touched him with his hand."

"He's unclean," I said. "Can't you see?" The woman just smiled.

"You won't catch anything," she said. "What does it matter if he's unclean?"

"Can you speak to him?" I asked.

"Yes," she replied. "You can speak to him too. He's right in front of you; he can hear what you're saying."

I raised my eyes to the man. He looked at me.

"What can I do for the master?" he asked. I took hold of the woman again and asked her to speak to him.

"Ask him where I can find Jesus," I said. "If he really thinks he's been healed, he must be spreading some powerful words. Ask him how I can find Jesus."

"He's in Galilee," said the man, still staring at me. Underneath his strands of blond hair, I could see chapped and loose skin, as well as something glutinous and sticky. "The Lord saved me outside Cana," he continued. "You can go to Nazareth and ask them about the Lord."

I turned to the woman.

"Thank him from me," I said, giving her a few coins. "These are for both of you. May God be with you."

We dressed for the journey. I took food and servants I could rely on. I kept Jacob close by. All sorts of thoughts preyed on me. I feared that soldiers would storm out and arrest all of us for being rebels. I feared attacks by thieves. At one point, on the first morning, I even thought that there was nothing wrong with Jacob anymore, nothing breaking up his speech or making him stutter. Maybe the whole thing was over. Maybe faith was all that was needed, not a father who doubted so deeply whether his son really belonged to God. But when the first evening of the journey came, I asked Jacob if he was tired or if he was hungry, and again I saw his face writhe and squirm as he tried to answer, his hands clenching and opening, and his words grinding to a halt.

We traveled toward Galilee. We followed the road through Samaria, up to Scythopolis, and then northwest toward Nazareth. It was a small town, poor, as I'd been told, but we were shown the way to Jesus's family. We were met by two of his brothers, who told us that Jesus had gone back up toward Cana.

"You've traveled far," they said. "Stay with us tonight before you travel on."

The next day, on the way to Cana, we came across other people who were on the same mission. Some had young children with them, while others were carrying elderly relatives. A number of them were unclean or infected, but they kept their distance and were not rude. I got talking with some men who turned out to be rebels. I made my excuses and moved away from them. They shouted to us that they were neither Romans nor traitors.

"We're going to the same place," they called. "Do you think we're going to steal your riches and your son?" I told Jacob not to listen to them.

"This country has been torn apart," I said. "Everybody's fighting against everybody else."

When we arrived, I stood there, staring at the strange sight. I am used to large crowds, but I've never seen so many people all gathered together off the beaten path. There must have been three hundred, maybe four hundred people. Jacob speaks of a thousand. I don't know what I remember. My memories of that day are such that the fantastical seems just as naturally placed as everything else.

We stood at the edge of the crowd. Ahead of us, in the middle of all the people standing there, a small circle had formed. In the circle stood a man, and he reached out his hands and touched another man, but nothing changed. The light stayed the same, the sky still stretched out firmly above us, and the smell of sweat rose up as if we were part of a herd of animals.

"That must be Jesus," said Jacob. I nodded. Jacob had been quiet for the whole journey, but now, as we had this miraculous figure and his followers in sight, Jacob began to speak. The people near us turned around to see what was wrong with Jacob, as if their own sicknesses, curses, and misfortunes weren't enough. I laid my hands on Jacob's shoulders and told him to save his strength.

"We may have to wait all day," I said, "and even then there's no guarantee he'll have time for us."

"He has time for everybody," we heard somebody say ahead of us.

It was a young man with a full head of curly, dark hair. He smiled. Sitting crouched next to him was a girl with her face wrapped in a piece of cloth. She couldn't have been any older than Jacob.

"Her husband made her like this," the young man said. "Now all she's got is me, and Jesus. I'm her brother."

I was about to ask what her husband had done, but I wanted to fill Jacob with hope.

"H-h-h-ha-ha-how l-l-l-ooong . . ." Jacob began to say.

I finished for him: "How long do you think it'll take us to get to him?" The man said he didn't know. "How do you know that he has time for all of us?" I asked, immediately regretting the question. I tried not to look at his disfigured sister.

"I think he's the savior we've been waiting for," the smiling young man continued. "He saves everybody who wants to be saved."

I nodded to the servants that they could sit down. Jacob brushed the sand with his hands before sitting down next to the young man and his sister. Then the sound of shouts reached us, and from where I stood, I could see people getting up and holding each other.

When I asked the servants to bring out our food, Jacob invited the brother and sister to join us for our meal. The young man smiled and kept his eyes on Jacob's for as long as it took the boy to draw out his words. I sensed kindness in the way this man sat there with his sister, kindness in the way he listened and let Jacob finish before gratefully accepting the offer of food. When other people heard Jacob speak in my presence, they always turned away from him and toward me before saying something themselves. It was as if they all needed some confirmation to let me speak in his stead. Even women who had been mine turned away from him in the hope that I could take over the words that were stuck in his mouth.

"My name is Obed," said the young man, "and my sister's called Naomi. She has difficulty speaking," he continued, as he helped his sister to sit down. "Her husband assaulted her," he said. "He left her lying on the floor, battered and broken, in their own home."

Jacob told them our names and reached out his hand. Obed took it, lifted Naomi's hand, and laid it in Jacob's. Naomi said something, but it wasn't possible to hear what. Jacob leaned forward, tilted his head, and listened again to Naomi's soft, barely audible voice. I wanted to say something, but Jacob sat back up and said those words I can never forget: "Maybe God is a voice that only those who cannot hear can hear. Maybe God is the way you, or I, speak now. Or maybe God is your face."

People around us turned to see who was speaking in such a way. I think few people would have been able to join the broken words together into sentences, but Naomi heard Jacob's words. She lifted the cloth from her face.

The things we do to each other.

Her nose seemed to have been crushed, appearing as small broken pieces under her skin. Her mouth was swollen, with her lips covered in scabs. Her eyes were red and white where their light crept out through two narrow slits. Her hair was missing on parts of her head, and her forehead was like sheepskin, pale and flayed.

Obed covered her up, and Naomi let him. I saw tears run out from the slits where her eyes were.

"Don't cry," I said, sensing Jacob staring at me. "If he's what everybody here believes he is," I continued, "then he'll heal you."

My own voice left a bad taste in my mouth, as if I'd dipped my words in stagnant water.

Neither Obed, nor Naomi, nor Jacob said anything for a while. The sound of other voices drifted over to us. I tried to listen, trying to hear what everybody around us was talking about, what everybody had brought to show him, what everybody was asking to have cured.

I don't know how long we sat there. Naomi fell asleep and slumped over into her brother's lap, but she moaned when her head came into contact, and Obed helped her to crouch back up again. Jacob drew numbers in the sand. I yawned, bowed my head, and closed my eyes.

"My dear," I heard somebody whisper. The voice was familiar, so familiar, and I opened my eyes to see Sarah. She crept toward me between the people around us. I closed my eyes, then opened them again, and Sarah had gone. Jacob laid his hand on mine and asked if I was all right. I turned toward him and asked if I'd fallen asleep. Jacob said no, that I'd been awake. I got up and felt that I was shaking. My feet were hurting, my back was aching, and there was a faint buzzing drone that reminded me of flies. Then I noticed that the sound was coming from the crowd I was standing in. The voices rose like the buzzing rises from a flowering shrub when the sun reaches it. And then I realized that Jesus must be on his way. Everybody around me was facing the same direction, all their eyes following a towering, young, bearded man with large eyes, a slight underbite, and hair hanging down loosely over his shoulders.

"They're going," I said to Obed, who was standing next to me. He seemed anxious. With his hands, he shaded his eyes.

"Is he going to see us?" I said.

Jesus and his followers were dressed in shabby clothing. What was supposed to be white was dark, and what was supposed to be dark was stained. Faithless women walked among them, and around the women I saw children. People were pushing, shouting, and begging, but Jesus walked past all of them with a soft smile on his lips. He looked tired; his eyes were flickering back and forth. For a moment I thought he winced, which reminded me of Jacob, but then there was nothing there, just that flickering gaze and aquiline nose. As he came closer, I could see the pores in his skin, small, dark scars over his nose and cheeks.

Jesus came, and walked past us.

A sigh went through Obed, Naomi, me, Jacob, indeed through every one of us standing there. Obed's hands fell down by his sides. Naomi crouched back down again. Jacob stood there with his mouth open, his gaze resting on me. I turned toward Jesus and his followers and called after them: "I'll give you a talent to heal my son."

Jesus stopped.

"Come here," I called, "and you might get even more than that."

Obed had put his hands on me now, his voice low and nervous, but I pushed him aside. I was about to shout out again and promise even more, but then I saw Jesus walking back toward us. Naomi was still kneeling down, but she was chanting something or other. A soft, wheezing sound rose up from her. Jacob stood next to me.

"Father," he said, but I hushed him. "Be quiet, boy, he's coming."

The crowd parted in front of us, and into this opening stepped

Jesus. He looked at me, at Jacob, at my people, who were keeping close to me.

"Who are you?" he asked. Before I could answer, he went on: "What are people like you and your servants doing out here with us?" When he spoke, it was as if he were singing on his own. There was a soft rhythm in the way his words came out. It's hard to explain, but when I hear Jacob talk now, there's something similar in his manner of speaking.

"There are always people seeking to test us," Jesus said. "Are you one of them?" His voice sank with each word, and a short pause crept in before the last word. It was almost as if he were murmuring now.

"I want my son to be healed," I said. "I have no other wish here today than that, and I was told that you were somebody who could help him. But now you're leaving too without having done anything. You won't speak to my son either. I came here in good faith, I've been sitting here all day, I've been strong in my faith in God, in the Lord, but all I've seen is you walking past us when you're done for the day."

Some of the others in his retinue began to speak; they scolded me and moaned at me about everything I owned and all that I was asking for, but Jesus raised his hand at them.

"Lord," said the tallest one, with fiery eyes, "let me speak to this stranger."

"Not now, Peter," said Jesus. "We'll stay here tonight. Maybe we can carry on this discussion later in the evening or tomorrow when day breaks. But now I must rest, I'm tired."

I wasn't happy about sleeping out there in the wilds with all those people. I didn't wish for Jacob and me, or all our group, to be seen together with rebels, with the unclean and others of their sort who were present there. I put my servants on the lookout to guard the food we'd taken with us, and to keep an extra eye open for anybody who came too close.

Darkness had fallen. I wrapped Jacob and myself in a few blankets and asked him to follow me. Our servants followed at a distance.

The stars twinkled above us, and I asked Jacob if he could name the ones I pointed at, but he stared at the ground and didn't say a word.

Through the light of the bonfires around us, I found the way to where Jesus and his retinue were camped out. It seemed as if people had left them in peace for the night. The women and the men sat together, talking quietly with each other. The one they called Peter was sitting with Jesus. It looked as if they were brothers, they were so close and spoke with such familiarity. I couldn't hear a word of what they were saying, but there was something about the way they looked at each other, the way they each listened when the other spoke. But there was also the other side of brotherhood: competition, fighting, brotherly love under a cover of jealousy.

I don't know why I think I saw all this. It might be that there was something making me look for rifts and fractures. Jesus was sitting there, only a few yards from us, but he wasn't doing anything.

Still, the strangest things can happen.

Once, when I was younger, I was digging for water when I found the bones of a gigantic creature. It couldn't have been anything from this earth. Those huge bones, dirty and white in the soil, frightened me, so I put them all back and covered up the hole in the ground.

Another time, I saw something large, flashing, and bright move across the night sky. It looked like a leviathan with wings, and I fell down on the ground in amazement.

And now, on that strange and fantastical day, I saw my eldest son walk up to Jesus, without saying a word. I didn't move but let my son go. His feet were so strong, I could see it then. His hips, straight back, and long arms.

Some of the men got up to stop Jacob, but Jesus raised his hand at them and kept his gaze fixed on Jacob. Peter and Jesus spoke, and Peter got up, walked past Jacob, and went to sit with the others.

Jacob stopped in front of Jesus, and I saw his face begin to squirm and wince. His hands clenched and opened again in convulsions. His whole body was twitching and shaking, and I could hear the brief sounds all the way from where I was standing.

I thought then that it was all empty. I thought that Jesus was just another Hananiah, yet another person who could see how afflicted Jacob was but who wasn't going to lift a finger. It felt as if I was about to collapse. Come night, come darkness, I give up.

But it wasn't over yet.

Jesus got up. He stood there quietly, listening to Jacob. When Jacob had finished, Jesus laid one of his hands on his chest and the other on top of his head. Instead of speaking, Jesus closed his eyes, and for a brief moment, they both stood there facing each other, motionless. It was a sight that might have made me laugh, or perhaps shake my head, but there and then I almost stopped to hold my breath. That stranger had his hands on my son. Jesus was touching another person, one who was at his weakest, and the way he laid his hands on Jacob, it looked as if he were crowning my son. I have no other words for it: he put a crown on my son's head. Ever since then, Jacob has never lost his strength or his faith.

Jesus let go of Jacob. He lifted away his hands, and Jacob was left standing alone. He opened his mouth, and even though I still couldn't hear what was being said, I could see that words were coming out of him. Words that were no longer stuck fast. My son wasn't wincing or writhing. He stood there calmly, only his mouth moving, and I think I saw him smile.

We left the next morning. I can't remember much of the trip home. I know that when Jacob had become a man and was independent, he later went back up to Galilee to meet some of the followers who lived in Nazareth. He's spoken to me of Obed and Naomi, and others I don't wish to mention here. Once he told me about Sarah, who came to him in a dream.

"There was a lady," he said. "She called me her son and said she'd sent the light of goodness to shine on me."

I told him to treasure that dream and to keep it safe. It's all he has left of his mother.

I still don't know what it was that Jesus did to Jacob. Perhaps it was just a small piece of salvation Jesus put into my son. Perhaps he took away the evil like other people might brush a fly out of their hair. I've tried to come to terms with the fact that I'll never know. His brothers don't want to know. They saw a healthy Jacob return and didn't ask any other questions. Jacob never talks about that meeting out in the wilds either, as far as I know. But I'm old, and I don't have enough time left on this world to let myself be fooled by everything that people keep hidden. We live in a world that's evil, and when my time's over, I'm letting Jacob take over everything. He'll maintain our wealth and salvation and will take care of the family.

This is the story of my son. It's the only story I wish to leave behind. My son, my firstborn, is the last leaf on the last branch of the great, tall tree that is our family. But I believe in the small things, and I believe in the great things, and who knows whether or not another branch will shoot out. Maybe my first son will lead our family to new heights, so I say that, when I leave and make my way to the Lord, this is all I'll ask of Jacob: to carry on working on the great monument we've been building so far. May the Lord keep you.

II

After my father died, I gave my half brothers everything they wanted. I bade them farewell, took the clothes I was wearing, a donkey, some food, and my name: Jacob. Even though I miss what I grew up with and shared with my father, it's over now. None of it will return. Only new memories will grow, and I don't want them to destroy the good things I still remember. In the same way I've treasured in my heart what little I have of my mother, I wish to treasure all the memories I have of my father.

Naomi was waiting for me in Nazareth, and we were united. Obed was there too, and he gave his consent. Many had departed, but others had joined the fold. We were scattered. The rain was rolling in from the vast sea, and it had become cold. We remembered Jesus, his deeds and words. We prayed for freedom from the occupying powers and those who collaborated with them; we prayed that the forces of darkness would give way to the light of goodness. And finally we sang and danced to celebrate that I had come. All I saw were Naomi's eyes. They were what kept me sure and steady. If I should ever lose my way, I'll look for those eyes.

The sound of the rain on the ground, the smell of our bodies, it all swayed softly and tasted sharp and sweet on the tongue.

I kissed Naomi that evening. I slipped inside her and held her beautiful, battered face between my hands while she moved on top of me. I was free in this world.

It was a new beginning, and we knew what was coming. Some of us had been persecuted and beaten, and a couple, John the Younger and Mary of Sepphoris, had been taken by the Romans, and nobody had seen them since. I was one of the eldest now, and my bald head and Naomi's disfigured face made us stand out. We left Galilee and traveled down through Samaria, remembering Jesus's words about the Samaritans. When we'd gone as far as Bethel, we both longed for the fertile area around the Jordan. I told Naomi about the trips on which my father took me.

"My father did everything for me," I said.

Later on, I told her about my mother and how I remembered her from a dream. Naomi put her arms around me, and in the shade of a tree, by a spring where nobody else could be seen, she kissed me.

In Bethel, people welcomed us. I wasn't able to find the family with the old woman whom my father and I had visited, but the people who opened their doors and invited us in were kind and friendly. Some of the children were frightened by Naomi's face, but once we'd explained that she wasn't ill, that there weren't any open wounds or infections, none of them were afraid to touch her.

"I had problems breathing and speaking," Naomi told them. "My previous husband tried to kill me. But the Lord Jesus healed me. You can hear me now, and you can see me."

I spoke to the men. They listened to my story, and I heard what they had to say. Their taxes were high and were difficult to pay, and they were afraid of what would happen if the occupying forces found rebels among them. But they all straightened up to listen when one of them told the extraordinary and mysterious things he'd heard about Jesus. They wondered if it was true, and who he was. I tried to answer, I tried to sketch a picture of the Master and of everything that had happened.

We left Bethel after a few days, heading for Jerusalem, but it was full of soldiers in the area, so we went on to Jericho and crossed the river Jordan. We spoke with people we met, and set up camp for the night with another group of travelers. I got speaking with an elderly man who spent the whole time sitting there with his eyes closed and a walking stick in his hand. He seemed odd, and Naomi kept away from us. The old man told me that he'd been looking for followers of Jesus, and that he'd once spoken with somebody who'd been close to the Master.

"But he was strong," the old man said. "Stronger than anybody I've ever met. He beat my doubting ways hands down, can you believe it? I've lost control of it now, it's growing bigger and bigger. The story your master created will be everywhere sooner or later. But I'll always be there by his side, like I am here. Faith and doubt, me and him."

I noticed a black creature sitting on the ground next to him. The animal's claws tapped against the man's stick, and the sound kept making me look back and forth between the old man and the animal.

"Is he making you nervous?" the old man asked. I apologized, but the old man just smiled and whispered something to the animal, which then crept off.

"Was Jacob your name?" the old man asked.

I nodded.

"It's taken its time," he said, "but here you are."

I told him I didn't understand.

"I promised to free you," he said.

The old man had now placed his hand over mine and was staring right at me. His eyes were a grayish white.

"I'm blind," he said, "and yet I see many things."

He lifted up his other hand and ran it over my face. I felt cold, freezing, and I wanted to pull away.

"I'm what stays in the shadows while the light falls elsewhere," he said. "Let me smell you, he's taken it away from you. You no longer carry the mark, you're like your mother wished now."

I tried to snatch my hand back, tried to get up. What did he know about my mother?

"No, relax," he said. "Your master has touched you, he's taken it away, but it'll never vanish altogether. You're part of his story, maybe you're my way into it. You're one of his followers, and you could do with something to doubt, couldn't you? Listen to this. Did you believe yourself when you believed your master? I say that doubting or giving up is natural. I'd like to have a word with you. Could we be alone for a minute? I'm hardly ever alone, I'm doubting even now. Can you believe that? I give you my word."

That was when Naomi came over to us. She must have noticed that something was wrong, as she took hold of me.

"Jacob," she said, "what's happening?"

"Go away," the old man said. "Get lost."

"Let go of him," she said.

"Get away, woman-creature," he said. "This has nothing to do with you."

Naomi hit his face, her nails scratching him. The old man began to hiss and spit, but he didn't seem old anymore; he seemed younger.

"In Jesus's name, get away," said Naomi. The man began to laugh as he backed away from us, away from the firelight and into the darkness.

"Have a pleasant journey," he said. "You won't remember me, but everything's stored away in your heart, Jacob."

And then he vanished.

We asked the others who that creature was, but nobody could answer us. They said they didn't know who we were talking about. Eventually we stopped thinking about it. Naomi never mentioned him. Everything he said, how he looked: sometimes I think it was just a dream.

That night we slept in shifts, and as soon as day broke, we headed north and crossed the river Jordan. We were careful about whom we talked with. I felt tired; I slept badly and had terrible dreams. We prayed together, but something had taken hold of me and wouldn't let go.

Early one morning, we went along with a family that was on its way up the valley where the river Jabbok ran. I recognized it from when I'd met Hananiah there, and I wondered if the false prophet and his followers were still in the area. How had they been doing? I asked the family we were walking with if they knew anything, but when I mentioned Hananiah's name, they asked me not to mention such things. Naomi apologized and told them that it didn't matter. Still, something had stirred in me, and I asked the eldest in the group if he could help us to find those lost people. He stared at me.

"I think there are still some there," he said, "but if you go there, may the Lord God be with you."

We followed the directions the eldest man had given us, and some distance up the valley, we found a path leading into a cleft in the terrain. The cleft was narrow, and a foul stench met us that grew ever stronger the farther we entered. There was nobody to be seen, just rocks, dry, yellow plants, and the foul smell.

I was about to turn when somebody called to us. A person was standing outside a cave farther up the mountainside, dressed only in rags. His head was covered with hair and a grimy and uneven beard. His whole body was dirty. As he gradually climbed down to us, it dawned on me that he had excrement smeared all over him, and both Naomi and I began to move back the way we'd come.

"Have you come because of Hananiah?" the man shouted. "He's still here, he's among us."

He was thinner than when I'd last seen him, smaller, and there were red and black sores underneath all his hair. I recognized the man, but I struggled to understand how it could be possible. It was the one-eyed man my father and I had met all those years ago. He didn't seem to realize who I was. His gaze was constantly fixed on the air between us and the surrounding rock faces.

"Can we meet Hananiah?" I asked.

"Oh yes," he said. "The Master is here, let the poor and the weak come to him, and he will give them salvation."

Naomi stared openmouthed, and it seemed as if she were having trouble breathing. I lifted up a scarf and held it in front of my face before handing one to Naomi.

"He'll be pleased to receive you," the one-eyed man continued. "Come, come, follow me to greet the Lord."

"Where is he?" I asked. "What's happened here?"

"Everything's happened here," the one-eyed man replied, waving his arms about. "The world has ended, it has risen again, and it will end again, just as our Master has told us. Everything happens according to his will, death and life, life and death, darkness and light, mountain and flood, skin and hair, and the rocks, have you seen the rocks? They can speak, I've heard them, down in the water, if you lift them up. Oh God, dear God, he speaks through the rocks, through water." The man waved his arms even more wildly and bowed to us, before he turned around and began walking back to the cave, climbing back up where he'd come from. I told Naomi to wait.

"Don't go in there with him," she said.

"I'll come back," I said. "Just wait here."

"There's sickness there," she said. "Watch out, be careful what you touch." I nodded, held the scarf around my mouth and nose, and followed the one-eyed man up and into the cave.

It was a large cave, and the walls glistened with moisture. There was water running somewhere, and the smell was even worse in there, like clods of earth sticking to the skin. It was dark, and I had trouble seeing. The one-eyed man had gone, and I called after him. I took a few steps and trod on something soft and wet. I bent down to see what it was and felt the cold seize hold of me.

"God," I said. "Good God." There were bones and corpses across the ground and along the sides of the cave. I began to step back out of there, but there stood the one-eyed man. He came toward me, and I could feel the sickening warmth emanating from his mouth.

"You shall meet the Lord," he said. "Hananiah is ready to receive you."

I stepped backward.

"Greet the Lord," said the man, lifting up a head in his hands. I recognized the features from some years ago, even though the eyes and mouth were just black holes. The one-eyed man began shouting now, his voice echoing in the cave.

"Come to the Lord, let him taste you, let your body become his," he shouted.

I turned and began to climb back down. The light outside blinded me, but I didn't stop. I called out to Naomi, telling her to get away.

We didn't stop to rest until we made it back to the river Jordan, by which time it was dark. I wanted to wash. Naomi asked what it was I'd seen in the cave, but I told her I couldn't talk about it.

"It was just death and sickness," I said. "They've been consumed by darkness."

"What's happened to them?" she asked.

"They are no more," I said.

We traveled up to Galilee to seek out our brothers and sisters in Nazareth. We said little about what we'd experienced. One evening around that time, while I sat there alone, staring into the starry heavens, I felt everything stopping up again. I got up and started walking about in the dark. I picked up stones and tried to chew them, I scratched the inside of my mouth with my nails, I retched.

When Naomi eventually found me, and I had to speak to her, I couldn't look at her. I shook my head, my fingers twisted up. Naomi started crying, but she held on to me tightly and kissed me on the forehead, kissed my hair and whispered in my ear.

"Relax," she said. "Try to take deep breaths. Talk to me, Jacob."

I tried, but everything was broken, it was stuck.

Naomi wasn't giving up. She begged me to speak and held me closely.

"It, it's, d-d-diiifficult," I said. "It d-d-doesn't m-m-make sense."

"Jesus touched you," she said. "He made you conquer this. You must fight against it, Jacob, it won't go away. Don't let it grow, Jacob."

"D-d-don't l-l-let it g-g-grooow," I said.

"Don't let it grow," she said.

III

Sarah opened her eyes and got out of bed. She fetched water for herself and her beloved. Her husband woke up with a start when she got over to him.

"A dream," he said. "A bad dream."

"It's morning," she said. He nodded, looked at her, smiled, and reached out his hands to her.

"Come here," he said, pulling Sarah toward him. He put his hands around her pregnant form. "When he comes out," he said, "he'll be the first of many boys. He'll be called Jacob. He'll be big and strong."

Her hair flowed down over his. He smelled her, all the scents of her long curls, her neck, her stomach, and below.

"It's a good world he's being born into," said Sarah.

Her pains began later that day. He'd already summoned women to be ready to help. They would tend to Sarah, and he promised them whatever they asked if this first child made it into the world fit and well.

3 ||| I SMELL OF THE EARTH

I know there are others. They smell like it too. Just a faint hint, but I'm fresh. I'm almost warm. There are some who don't have that smell, who can't be seen with your eyes. There are some who taste of the cold wind.

I can see stars, but can't fly up to them. I hover, like a fly, before crashing back down like a small child. Oh, it hurts. My name's Sarah. I don't need the ground, and the ground doesn't need me. I'm in the air, I'm under the earth. I tried to dig my way out, but not a single grain of sand moved. I tried to find my beloved, but I have a lover here. He bites at my toes, at my fingers. Black teeth, as hard and cold as rocks in water. I don't know his name. My name's Sarah, but he calls me Sahah, Sahah. His eyes are hollow. His fingers are spread out along the ground, like roots. "Sahah, Sahah."

My beloved, where is he?

And my boy. Jacob. I say his name, and I hear somebody laugh. Others repeat it: "Jacob, Jacob." Somebody brushes past me and asks me to tell them, tell them.

"My name's Sarah," I say.

"You smell of the earth," they say. "Fresh and warm, but still earth." I tell them I don't. They say I do. There are so many of them. One moment they're here, the next they're gone.

I'll never find my way out. The way's gone. The light always stops just in front of me. The darkness is honey, sticky and soft. It clings to everything.

My boy, Jacob, has grown now. My beloved misses me, he's counting the days. Like small, dry twigs lying in rows, that's what time's like for him. But Jacob's different. He doesn't know who I am. I don't know who he is. But I listen to Jacob. He stutters and falters. He can't speak properly. The words won't come out, only sounds. My lover says there's something inside my son. Something that will consume him, my lover says. Something he's put in so my son will rot away. And when Jacob rots, my lover will take him.

"You and me and Jacopp, Sahah, you and me and Jacopp, Jaaacooopp."

I kick at him, but my lover's teeth are still there. He laughs, and his mouth is just a wider opening than his eyes. He says he's going to have a son. My son. A son by his side. A son to join him hunting in the darkness.

My lover.

My beloved.

My son.

My lover is in two places.

Missing me is my beloved.

My son will be destroyed. My son will become evil.

I try to stay in the cold light. But it moves, like a fly. I walk back and forth, forth and back, and every time I stop, I wonder: Is that light all I have?

Time passes so slowly here, but time is rushing by for my son and my beloved. They change, they grow and mature, they travel farther and farther away, and when they've gone so far away that I can no longer see them, then they're here. Then my lover's waiting for them.

Sometimes I'm torn. My lover takes hold of me with all his body and tears me apart. Like I was when I came here. Like I was when he took me. My first son and my first tear. Jacob's warm shrieks and my lover's cold grip. My beloved standing next to me, saying, "Sarah, Sarah," and then I was gone, and then I was here. Torn apart.

"Thhat'ss how I like you, Sahah."

I slip into the darkness.

My name's Sarah. My beloved was calling for me. By the sound, by the sound, I followed his voice. "Sarah," he called. Sarah. My name.

I was right by him. I could hear him breathing. I lifted my hands. But he wasn't there. Did he see me? Did he see his Sarah torn apart? Did he see his Sarah rotting? My skin is no longer smooth. My eyes are no longer brown. My hair is just a few shreds, my mouth just a hole.

My lover laughs.

"I'mm yourss, Sahah, and you'rre minne.

"Minne, Sahah."

I screamed, he laughed. He bit at my feet, and down I went.

"You'rre minne, Sahah.

"Sahah, Sahah."

My name's Sarah, I try to stay in the cold light. In the darkness, it's not quiet, but something else. There's something scratching away. Small feet through the sand. Beetles, maggots. Scratching, scratching, and Sahah, Sahah.

My name's Sarah. I have ten fingers. I have two feet, two arms. I have a son, I have a husband. My son and my beloved. The cold wind says my beloved has remarried and remarried and remarried. The ones who smell of earth tell me to listen, listen. They don't laugh anymore, not even when I say, "I'm warm."

I must find my beloved. I know about my son. I know what's inside him.

Light, I need more light, warm light. I have cold light and darkness. Insects and honey. I'm my beloved's queen.

But how can I get out of here? My lover comes up through a gap. His fingers are roots reaching forth everywhere, searching, searching, for me, for me.

"Sahah, Sahah.

"You wantt to be withh themm so muchh, Sahah, but I'mm nott letting you go. I'mm yourss, you're minne, Sahah, Sahah."

He took me down here. He tore me away as I gave my son to the world.

He put something evil in my son and became my lover.

I must find my beloved and tell him how to set Jacob free. From his stuttering and from the rot and from my lover's teeth. I know my lover's waiting for mother and son, son and mother. He doesn't care about my beloved. I don't know why. Maybe he knows that my beloved will come. Maybe there's hope yet for Jacob.

My name's Sarah. I've got to get out of here.

Out into the darkness, I now see. I mustn't follow the cold light. Just open my ears and follow the sound.

My lover searches through the cold light. He's waiting for me. I'm in the honey. Stuck, stuck.

The darkness has a color. Not black, not blue, not gray. The darkness has a color, like a starry sky that's been beaten, beaten, beaten.

There are sounds everywhere. Women washing clothes, boys calling to other boys, girls giggling, skipping, and crying, husbands talking to sheep and to donkeys. The heartbeats are short and soft. They go *thump, thump, thump, thump.*

I walk and walk, but where's my beloved, where's my son?

"Hey, you," I hear a voice say. I stop. There's a man there in the darkness, I can see him. A man, and he can see me. I hear him sniffing, breathing through his nose.

"I'm blind, and yet I see many things," he says. "I'm what stays in the shadows while the light falls elsewhere. And you smell of earth, but you were so warm, I almost thought . . ."

"Thought what?" I ask.

"I thought you belonged to the living," he said, "but the way you are now, I have no use for you. You're earth, you're soil, you can't rot anymore. You're nothing to me, the dead are useless."

"How can you say such things?" I ask.

He stops sniffing. I can't hear him anymore. Where is he?

"Hey, where are you?" I call out, but there's no answer. I shout out.

"I need help," I cry.

I hear a soft whisper, asking what the matter is.

"I've got to find the way," I say. "The way to my beloved. I need to find my son."

At that same moment, something pierces my side.

"There you go," says his voice. "Be still."

"What did you stab me with?" I ask, and he smirks.

"You're so fresh," he says. "You could've been mine, but somebody else has taken you. You've got a lover, haven't you? He took you down here. I can smell him on you."

"Let go," I say.

"Your son," he says. "What's wrong with him?"

"Let go," I say. "It hurts."

"Listen to me," he says. "I can help your son."

"My lover's put something inside him," I tell him. "He's going to rot, and my lover will consume my son."

"You must tell me his name, so I can find him," he says.

"What are you going to do?" I ask.

"If you give me his name, I'll help him," he says.

"Let go, it hurts," I tell him. "You're evil."

"Evil?" he says, and I sense something in front of my face. A hand, I see a hand, and out of the hand comes a light, so strong. It shines on the ground beneath us, on a beetle, then on a spider, then on the beetle.

"Evil, good," he says. "It depends where the light falls, and on whom. The whole world up there, the one you can barely hear, lives for stories. Some of them are mine. I tell the stories they want. They need my doubting ways. Faith and doubt. Good and evil. People always need to correct the balance. I'm not like your lover. I don't collect dead things. But maybe your son, maybe he needs help from me."

"You must promise not to hurt him," I reply.

"I'll give him a story. I can free your son from the mark your lover has put on him," he says.

"A story?" I ask.

"A place where he can belong, who knows what I can give him?" he says.

"Do you promise to free him?" I ask.

"His name," he says.

And I tell him: "Jacob, Jacob." He lets me go and whatever was stabbing my side vanishes.

"Do you know my lover?" I ask, trying to stand up, but it still hurts, even though the sharp object has gone. Whoever the man is, he sniffles again and wanders off.

"Your lover needs dry land. Go to the sea," his voice says softly. "Give him water." Then I hear laughter drifting away.

"Hello?" I say. "Are you there? It hurts. What do you mean dry land? Go to the sea, give him water?"

There's nobody there.

"My name's Sarah," I say, and at that same moment I hear my beloved. It's not my name he's saying. He seems tired. Rows of small, dry twigs have formed. I close my eyes. The darkness is honey but, with my eyes closed, it turns into water. I float toward my beloved. Not there, but not here either.

"My beloved," I say softly. "My dear, it's me, Sarah." And then I hear him say my name. I'm so close to him.

"Sarah," he says. "What should I do? I'm alone with him. If only you were here, Sarah. You would have known."

"My beloved," I say. "My dearest, I'm here. I'm back."

"I have nobody," he says. "I don't even have Jacob. I can't stand him. The sound of him, at night and during the day. I give him away. Can you believe it, my dear? I give him away to others all the time. If you'd seen the women here now, Sarah, you would have scratched off my face. None of them are like you, but they take care of Jacob."

"My dear," I say. "My darling. I'm here, reach out your arms! Feel me! It's me, Sarah!"

"Every time I see Jacob, I see you," he says. "You're there, right next to him. You're crawling around there in the darkness, all black and decayed. I can hardly recognize you."

"My dear," I say. "Don't talk like that. I'm yours. I'm here. It's me, Sarah."

"You've gone," he says, his voice becoming weak, cracking like dry flower stalks. "You are no more. What should I do? Should I go to your grave and dig you up? Should I lie down there myself? Should I take Jacob with me?"

"No," I scream, and I see my beloved. He's there, right in front of me, with his back turned. Oh, how he's changed and how he's shrunk. Time has taken its toll on him. I've been with my lover.

"Sarah," he says.

He kneels down. I try to walk across to him. Words feel like gravel in my mouth.

"My dear," I say, and he gets up, turning toward me.

"Sarah," he says, staring at me.

"My dear," I say.

He takes several steps toward me and then walks right through me. Something warm and cold at the same time, and then my beloved is gone. I turn around. There he is, holding an oil lamp.

"I thought you were there," he says, blowing out the light.

The darkness is honey.

"My dear," I say.

Now he's gone.

But there's something else. Scratching. And teeth, hard and cold.

"Sahah, Sahah."

I shout, I scream, and I see the cold light.

Into the cold light I'm dragged.

I lift up one of my feet. The other foot is tied down. My lover's roots.

If I lie down, I'll hear the scratching. My lover's gone. He was angry. He bit and tore at me and was ash and charcoal.

Darkness and sounds are out there.

I close my eyes, but I can still see. My lover has fixed my eyelids. He cut them off, and they were gone. I lift up soil and sand and rub it in, but I can still see. My vision is stained and speckled.

I can see something crawling. It comes into the cold light. Here it comes.

"Hello," I say.

It's a spider. Legs upon legs, see how it crawls.

"Hello," I say.

But it's no spider. It's a maggot.

"Hello," I say. "Maggot." It starts digging. I reach out to it, but then it's gone. I shout out.

"Hello," I shout. And something scratches at my hair.

"Hello," I shout, pulling at my hair, and there's the maggot in my hand. Small bugs have been taking strands of my hair. There it lies in my hand, twisting about. Twist and wind, in the light to find. Come here, come here, into the dark disappear.

"You will fly," I say.

The maggot gets up. It has wings now. I gave my hair, it grew wings. And it flies away. I hear it, I hear it, such a beautiful buzzing.

"Farewell," I say.

Twist and wind, in the light to find.

Come here, come here, into the dark disappear.

My lover approaches. I can hear scratching. I hear his voice there in the darkness. "Sahah, Sahah." He's coming. Teeth so black. Teeth as hard and cold as rocks in water.

"Sahah, I'mm backk, I'mm yourss, Sahah, you're minne."

"Sahah, Sahah."

I pull at my foot, but my foot is stuck, I'm stuck.

And then there's a hum, buzzing. His voice, the scratching, and a long, deep sound. My lover's getting faster. He doesn't speak to me anymore. My lover's words are something else now, like scratching in his mouth.

Something moves in the darkness. My lover's coming. But into the cold light comes a great, dark cloud. Part of the darkness has been torn away.

They're flies.

They come to me. They swarm around the roots, their wings beating and cutting, cutting, cutting. My foot's free, and then the flies are all around, everywhere. The cold light becomes gray, and the sounds of my lover are far, far away. I lift up my hands and wave them in the swarm, and then I'm stuck. My hands are stretched up and out to the sides.

Twist and wind, in the light to find.

They lift me up.

Come here, come here, into the dark disappear.

My lover's voice is an animal, growling and snarling. But I'm in the air. The flies take me with them. They fly into the thick, thick darkness, to the sound of voices and soft, short thumps. Everything has its own sound, but oh, what a beautiful sound the living make. I can make such sounds too. Sometimes, when I'm alone, I try. I talk and beat my hands on my chest. Come, come to me, I'm waiting, waiting. And the flies came. The flies took me back.

But then there's nothing there anymore, just the darkness and me falling. When I hit the ground, there's a snapping noise. I don't feel anything, but my foot is loose.

I get up, close my eyes, try to walk. There's the voice of a child, whispering a prayer. I follow. But then it's gone. Another voice, a lady's. She speaks softly at first, but then louder and louder. Oh, she's furious! But she vanishes too. My foot is loose. I'm not fast, I'm no fly. I'm a beetle, I scratch away. My foot, my foot.

I crawl around in the darkness, turning toward the voices. Some whisper, some shout. Some are hushed, some scream. They all disappear before I can find them.

Everything is darkness. Darkness clings. Everything clings.

A voice rises louder and louder, and I try to get up.

It vanishes, and another appears. I can't get up. I open my mouth and spit out words. They fall into the sand and black earth.

My beloved, where are you now?

My son, don't let yourself be consumed.

I try to sing, but I have dust in my throat.

I try to walk, but I walk so slowly.

Darkness is everywhere. Black and blacker. The humming drone and voices. If I close my eyes, I can still see. The darkness runs through me.

One voice won't leave me. I stay still, and the voice is there, right next to me. A woman, so young, she speaks between short pauses, and then she starts screaming. She screams and screams until she falls silent and is standing next to me. There are cuts and deep holes in her head.

"Hello," I say.

"Hello," she says, looking at me, before looking at herself. And when she looks back at me, there are tears running from her. Tears running from her whole body. Out of her fingers and ears, out through the clothes she's wearing.

"My name's Sarah," I say, and then: "You smell of earth."

My words feel cold once they're out of me. She smells of earth, moist, warm earth, but me, what am I? Am I cold wind?

Back I must go into the honey-like darkness.

But I stop when she says, "I'm Ruth."

"Ruth?" I say. She nods, and her head is strange.

"He hit me so suddenly," she says, lifting her hand up to her forehead.

"The man who hit you has gone," I tell her. "You're here."

"He hit me, suddenly, with all his strength, he beat me and beat me, and then I was here," she says.

"We must go," I say.

Ruth stares at me. "I can't go," she says. "I must help my sister."

"She's not here," I tell her.

Ruth looks around her. I lift up my hand and close it around hers. I tell her we have to go and pull her along behind me. I think about my lover. He'll be looking, wanting to find us. He'll snatch her, he'll snatch me. I've got to get her away. Not into any light, just into the darkness. Ruth tries to pull her hand back, but I hold on, hold on, hold on, and Ruth follows me.

"Who are you?" Ruth asks.

"I'm Sarah," I reply.

"Who's Sarah?" Ruth asks.

"I'm like you," I say.

Come here, come here, into the dark disappear.

"How did you die?" Ruth asks.

"I was giving birth to my child and was torn in two," I tell her.

Twist and wind, in the light to find.

"Oh," says Ruth, who then falls silent. Her hand loosens, I let go of it, and she walks by my side. She smells of earth. The remains of what we were. I'm the remains of what we become.

We walk and walk, and I see, and Ruth says, "Look," and the darkness around us is no longer darkness. Black has become gray, and something large and tall rises up in the grayness. It's a mountain, and Ruth says we'll have to cross it. Pitch darkness is behind us, but here it's gray darkness, and I agree with her, we'll have to cross it.

My foot can't climb over rocks, so Ruth has to drag me. She holds my hand, but once we get farther up, her head starts to drip away. She needs both hands to stop everything from running out of her. We stop by a well, and the mountain's above us, and I hear my lover whispering softly far behind us there.

"What's that?" Ruth asks.

"It's the wind," I reply.

"That's not wind," says Ruth.

"It's flies," I tell her.

"Is it him?" Ruth asks.

I nod, and Ruth takes my hand again. We kneel down by the well.

"Is that water?" says Ruth, putting her hand down into the well, and the water creeps up her hand. It splashes and flows. It trickles over to me. Cold water, and it makes my mouth twitch. Ruth's mouth twitches too.

"What is it?" I say.

"You're smiling," says Ruth.

"No," I tell her.

"We're smiling," says Ruth.

Then something touches my foot. I turn around.

"Feel," says Ruth. "It's alive."

But I turn around, and they're roots. They're around my foot.

"Sahah, Sahah."

"No," I shout. "Ruth," I cry. And the mountain changes. Ruth begins to scream. The mountain cracks open, and out come the roots.

"You're minne, Sahah, I'mm yourss."

"He's everywhere. He's everywhere."

"Thhat'ss how I like you."

My eyes are open, they're always open. I hear a buzzing and lift my hand to stroke their wings. But it's Ruth's hair I'm stroking.

"Sarah," she says. "He's here."

I feel the roots binding my foot. My lover's here to take me.

I'm in several pieces. Ruth gathers me together. She has a needle, she has thread, she stitches me together.

"Hush," she says. "I'm going to free us."

"Hush," she says. "We're going to the sea."

The roots tighten around my foot. I belong to my lover. Wherever I go, whatever I am. The cold light, his grip. I'm his.

"Sarah," says Ruth. "Sarah, you're Sarah again, you're in one piece."

He's my lover. I'm his.

"I'm going to free us," says Ruth.

"The water," I tell her. "You have to give him your water, Ruth."

My eyes are open, they're always open. I hear a buzzing and lift my hand to stroke their wings. But it's my lover's mouth.

"Sahah, you tasste of salt and earthh."

"Ruth," I say, and he pulls at me.

"You're bothh minne, everything here iss minne."

"Ruth," I say, and my lover tears himself out and away. He goes into the cold light and says that this mountain isn't his, he's going back to the sand and the black darkness.

"I tasste wetnesss here, Sahah. You should be dryy."

My lover vanishes into the cold light. Through the darkness out, I must seek the drought.

My eyes are open, they're always open. I hear a buzzing and lift my hand to stroke their wings. It's the flies. It's Ruth. She's covered by the winged creatures, the water's dripping from her to me.

"Sarah," she says. "I'm going to free us." And I hear my lover. I see him coming in the cold light.

"You're bothh minne."

"Sahah and Ruthh, small and dryy and finished."

"Come," says Ruth, taking my hand. The flies' wings beat and cut, and cut and cut and my foot's free. But my lover's here now. The cold light and his howls.

"Ruth," I say, and my lover begins to grab at me. He takes hold of me and pulls. Then I hear Ruth, she's dripping and dripping. She's water, screaming and flailing and flapping, and the gray light blinks, or is it me? My lover snatches Ruth, he tears her skull apart. Ruth is left in pieces, but out of Ruth comes gushing water, and my lover stops everything. He's in the water, burning up, and I blink and crawl toward what was Ruth.

"Ruth," I say. My lover burns and growls.

"Ruth," I say, and the pieces of Ruth are wet. The gray light blinks, or it flashes, or is it me? Everything blinks, everything flashes, gray and black, and Ruth and water and the buzzing and the wings and my beloved and my son and I blink.

"You're here," says Ruth.

She's back in one piece; her skull has mended again.

"Sarah," she says. "I've found light, we're there, listen."

There's no buzzing, but it's not silent. There's something else.

"Listen," says Ruth. "We freed ourselves, your lover's no more. The light will come to you soon."

"Where is he?" I ask.

"He's gone," says Ruth. "He burned up in the water. The light will come soon."

"The cold light," I say.

"No," says Ruth. "More light, warm light."

There's no buzzing, but it's not silent. There's water, so much water. It's the deep and the rulers of the deep. And then comes the light, it's there ahead of us. Not cold light like my lover, not light like the hand of evil. Another light, a light that is great and warm and good, and it comes down over me like a soft, light carpet.

No voices, something else. Not my lover, not my beloved. Not even little Ruth. Something else, and it shows me the sea. That's where I'm going. I'm free from the evil that bound me. There is a great light in the world, and it will give light and life where I want. Ruth, me, everybody who smells of the earth, the ones who are cold wind, everything will be lit by a great light. The ones who have been in the clutches of evil, who have been torn apart, smashed to pieces, broken. They'll all be lit by a great light.

"Say it," says Ruth. "Say your beloved's name."

I look into the light, and I can feel my beloved in my hand.

But I open my hand and let go of it all.

"Jacob," I say. "Set him free, take away the evil, set him free."

And the light lifts up, rushing over my stomach, my chest, shoulder, hand, then it vanishes.

My beloved's gone, my son's gone. But I've sent out a light. I've sent a light of goodness.

Ruth places her hand in mine. I put my hand around hers. The sea is there ahead of us, blacker, deeper. As if the darkness we came from were merely twilight. This is the night.

"I smell of earth," says Ruth. "I'm still warm."

"I'm Sarah," I say.

"Sarah?" says Ruth.

"Yes?" I reply.

"Everything's gone, hasn't it," says Ruth. "No light, nothing growing. Everything just dies and dies, even after everything's dead."

"Yes," I say.

"I've spent my last night on earth," says Ruth. "The light's been sent, my sister will be saved. Now I'll come to an end. I won't be here any longer."

"Yes," I say. And we go forth. Down to the sea, where dark waves carry us away, foot by foot. I hold Ruth, Ruth holds me. I'm going now, my beloved. I'm leaving now, Jacob. You'll be set free. One day we'll be together, on the other side of the blackness.

4 ||| CHILDREN OF GOD

My brother, Jehoram, held his hands out to me and asked if they weren't a wonderful color, and I nodded and agreed. His fingers glistened, and he asked me all kinds of questions. Reuben was panting, stabbing and kicking the men we'd just killed. I turned to Nadab. He just stood there, watching. Jehoram, his arms red, his face red, fell silent.

"Nadab?" I said, but Nadab didn't answer, still staring at the bodies on the ground.

"Nadab?" I said again, and this time Nadab looked at me. He blinked. In the failing daylight, his pale, white skin seemed to shine softly. His red hair and beard almost made him glow. Jehoram started to speak again, while sweat and the dead men's blood ran down his forehead and cheeks. I asked him to be quiet.

"Nadab?" I said. "Why aren't you joining in?"

"It's not right," he mumbled. "I said I didn't want to do any more killing."

"Right?" said Reuben, who'd also stopped and was standing still now. "Not right? What are you talking about?"

"I shouldn't have done this. We shouldn't have done this," said Nadab. "We promised to go with them all the way to Jerusalem."

"Nobody tells us what to do," said Reuben. "I'm sick and tired of being a mercenary for the rich." He spat and tried to dry himself off.

He was so tall that he looked like some strange, giant animal that didn't know how to clean itself.

"It's like Reuben says," I said. "We're not in anybody's service, we take what we can get. Have you seen the money they've got with them?"

I went over to the two slain bodies, lifted up their clothes, and showed them the purses that were now red with blood.

"I didn't want to get involved in what they were planning to do in Jerusalem," I continued. "They would've got themselves killed anyway, and maybe dragged us into it too."

"I didn't do this," said Nadab. "It's putting out the light inside me."

Reuben took a step toward him, but I raised my hand to tell him to take it easy.

"Nadab," I said, "what we do, you do. You're us. There's nothing you didn't do. We do what we do, we are what we are. Now, shut up and give us a hand."

I stopped to see if he would say something, but he said nothing.

"We've got to hide them," I went on. "If the bodies are found, their people will come looking for us. If nobody finds them, they'll wait before coming to look for us. Sooner or later, they'll forget about us."

Nadab stared at me and then nodded weakly. Reuben nodded too, went over to Nadab, smacked him on the head, and told him to help. They started to drag away one of the lacerated bodies. Jehoram grinned at me. I pointed at what was left and asked him to get to work.

I snapped a few twigs off a bush to rake the blood-stained ground. The remains of the dead were absorbed down and into the sand. This world consumes us all. Some time ago, I decided that we should try out another life. I sold our services to rich families who needed protection. I transformed us from thieves to mercenaries. It wasn't right; I could feel it in my hands, in my stomach, in my chest. Even at night, when I slept, it came to me. I can't change us. We are what we've always been, and we'll remain like that until there's no breath or thought or anything beating within us.

These two young men we'd killed had paid us to offer them safe passage to Jerusalem. They'd been sent by a group that was fighting an armed struggle against the authorities. They had a plan to go up to the Temple and kill priests. I'd heard about others like them, hiding in the mountains and moving from village to village so as not to be captured. They said they were fighting for the ideals of our people, but who isn't? Nadab had spoken of Jesus and his followers, and how they were something different. They were peaceful, according to Nadab, and they weren't fighting a battle against the Roman forces or the authorities. They were leading a struggle for the Kingdom of God and for justice, and whenever Nadab said this, I always found myself wondering whether or not Nadab was still one of us. Reuben was annoyed and had asked me several times what we'd become, and how much longer he'd have to listen to that prattle. Still, there was something about Nadab, something that could make us believe in what we no longer dared to believe. Maybe that was why I'd transformed us into mercenaries, until I finally realized what we were.

Both Reuben and I had seen that the two men we were accompanying to Jerusalem were hiding money in small leather pouches beneath their tunics. I told myself that I didn't want to be dragged into their plans, but neither that nor the money was the reason why we killed them. When all's said and done, I agreed with Reuben. There was a time for everything, and the time when we served other people had come to an end. Nobody would buy or hire us anymore.

Maybe Nadab thought we would end up doing something else. I'd taken him in, made him into one of us. I liked to see him and Jehoram together; he was good to my little brother. And as I've already explained, there was something about Nadab, as if a fire that had been extinguished in us was still burning in him.

Sometimes we do things I don't even try to understand. Reuben says it's something inside us. When I gave the others the signal, it was over for those two very quickly. We are what we are, we do what we do.

"I thought they'd be tough," said Reuben, "but they were as soft as overripe fruit." He was standing behind me. "What are you doing?" he asked. "There's nothing left."

I looked down at the sand and the stones I was raking up with the sticks in my hands.

"There are four of us," I said, "and two of them."

"They were soft," Reuben insisted. "I could feel it. They were believers, the sort who kill for their beliefs. But they can't believe in killing like we do."

"I don't believe in anything," I said, "and you're talking crap."

"We're craftsmen," said Reuben. "They were soldiers without an army."

"Where's Jehoram?" I asked, throwing away the sticks. It would soon be dark.

"He's over there finishing off with Nadab." Reuben stared at the trees, the bushes, and the heights off to the west. "I don't like Nadab's talk," he said.

"We'll make a bonfire over there," I said.

"He didn't join in," Reuben went on. "When one of us doesn't join in, it breaks us apart. He's been different lately."

"Leave him alone," I said.

"I don't like any of them," said Reuben. "Lesser knifemen, rebels, that Jesus Nadab talks about, or all the other prophets popping up like weeds after the rain. They cause chaos. None of them can be trusted."

"Like weeds after the rain? You're talking as if you were one of them," I said, walking over to a small thicket nearby. "We need wood for the fire. Come and lend me a hand."

Reuben spat, muttered something about prophets and animal dung, and headed back over to where Nadab and Jehoram were digging.

"We do what we can," I said to him as he left. "We take what we can get."

The two men who were being buried and covered with stones had been younger than us. Both seemed ready for their mission, and both seemed surprised at how quickly it could all end. One of them was missing a finger on each hand, and the other had no facial hair, and there they were talking about killing priests at the Temple in Jerusalem. "No one who collaborates with the foreign occupiers, no one who's a Roman puppet is safe," they said. "God is with us," they said. "Whether we fail or whether we're triumphant, God is with us." They spoke about traitors against the people; they were going to surprise them, create chaos, spread fear, and get away. I'd heard similar talk from other people. There were several organized groups rebelling against the authorities. Some were suppressed and persecuted, their leaders nailed to crosses. Other groups dissolved, probably having become disillusioned, and went back home again. There were also several unarmed groups, and the followers of Jesus of Nazareth, whom they call a prophet, were among these. Nadab had told us several times about this carpenter's son.

But the two men whose lives we'd taken now, there was something about them that made me feel uneasy. They were willing to sacrifice their lives for their cause without getting anything out of it for themselves. They were so full of everything they believed in, but at the same time they seemed cold and distant. They'd discussed with Reuben how they were going to make a kill with their first blow.

When I gave the signal that we could do it, they didn't understand what was going on. One of them tried to say something, but I didn't catch what. The other flew into a rage, all to no end: he was cut into pieces before he hit the ground.

There was a golden light in the firmament above, as if a king's cloak had been draped over us. Along came Jehoram with Reuben and Nadab. They'd finished digging. My brother, Jehoram, was covered with red marks, but only a few of them were open sores. He'd been like that for as long as I could remember. I covered him up and put oil and ointment on his skin if it began to chap or split. Nobody wanted to look at him, nobody wanted to speak to him, nobody wanted to touch him. He was already an outcast, so he was made for the life we led. One time we came across a leper colony. Jehoram killed two of the victims before I could pull him away. Another time, outside the Temple in Jerusalem, a man of riches thought that Jehoram was one of the unclean, a leper begging for help, so he gave him some silver coins. Jehoram followed the man, and when night came, he broke into where the man was sleeping and took his life. Jehoram didn't take any money. He told me it was unclean, with a grin. Always grinning. His gums shining out from behind his ragged lips and his chapped face. Nadab once said that Jehoram was no different from us. When I asked him what he meant, he said something about how Jehoram might be falling apart on the outside, while the rest of us we were falling apart on the inside.

"Let's go and get washed," said Reuben, but Jehoram sat down by the fire.

"Jehoram," I said. "You too." Jehoram shook his head.

"Go and get washed," I said, but he didn't move an inch. I went over to him and slapped him on the head.

"Go and get washed, you're dirty," I said again. He stayed there, sitting still. I raised my hand again, but Nadab bent down and helped Jehoram get up.

"Come on, Jehoram," he said. "We're all going to get washed, it's for our own good. If anybody comes past here this evening, we want to be clean." Just as he said that last word, Jehoram twitched. "No," said Nadab, "not like that, we've got to wash off the blood, that's all." He put his arms around Jehoram, around all his wounds, all the cracks in his skin.

When they came back, I noticed that Jehoram's hands and face were bleeding. It looked as if his skin had burst from the inside out.

"He was scratching himself," Nadab said.

I took out the blanket and the small pot. Jehoram sat down, and I put ointment on his hands before wrapping them up. I tried to grease the wounds on his face. His tall forehead and crooked nose. When we were small, he looked like me, but we each grew up differently. He became bigger, and his skin split. We'd always stuck together, even when he didn't understand, and even when I couldn't stand the sight.

"Are you bleeding anywhere else?" I asked, but Jehoram said he wasn't.

"When we get to Jerusalem, we've got to try and get some oil and some more ointment, maybe some more blankets too," I said. Jehoram nodded weakly. His eyes were dark and red in the firelight. He mumbled something, but all the saliva in his mouth made it sound like noises made by a reptile.

"We should go somewhere where nobody will look for us, take the road to Sychar, go into hiding," said Reuben, poking the fire with his knife.

"I don't know," I said. "Maybe something will turn up in Jerusalem." Reuben put down his knife.

"We can't stay there long," he said. "It's full of soldiers and guards."

"Nobody knows anything," I said. "Nobody's looking for us. And I need some decent food and pussy. I'll need at least one night, maybe two."

Reuben muttered something about the girl he'd had in Sychar, but then Nadab cut in. His voice was hoarse, and he cleared his throat before trying again.

"I want to go there," he said. "I have to do it."

Jehoram lifted his head and stared at Nadab. "Do what?" he asked.

"He's here, in me," said Nadab. "I can feel it, he's working through me. I have to go there tomorrow, I must do what's right. I have to speak out."

"What are you talking about?" I asked.

"What little light I'm carrying," said Nadab, "it mustn't go out." I got up and told him to shut up.

"He won't let anybody be put out," said Nadab. "I've seen the lights flashing in the sky, we were in the storm. I've been waiting to do some good."

His voice was low, as if he were speaking to somebody in the shadows and the darkness around us.

"Shut up, Nadab," said Jehoram.

"Jesus is working through me," said Nadab. "Look, we're going to Jerusalem, and if it's the only thing I do, I have to speak out, I have to tell them about the savior."

I was on top of him at once. I struck him on the cheekbone, and his head jerked backward. I punched him once again and struck him near the hairline. My knuckles cracked, and it looked as if his head detached from his body. Reuben took hold of me. I tried to shake him off, but he held me tightly. Jehoram joined him now, and together they pushed me down. Jehoram let go of me, got up, and stared down at me.

"Get away," I said. "Go and help him, I hit his head."

Jehoram took a few steps, crouched over Nadab, and knelt down.

"He's all right," he said.

Reuben spat. I looked over at him.

"I'll have none of it," I said. "We stick together. He's out of his mind."

I got up, and Reuben laid a hand on my shoulder.

"If you want, I'll keep an eye on him," he said.

I nodded, and Reuben turned, walking out into the darkness. Jehoram looked at me with wonder in his eyes. Night had fallen around us. Jehoram had rolled Nadab over onto his back and had Nadab's head between his feet.

"It'll be all right, he's awake, he's fine," Jehoram said.

I stood there. We were lit by the dying embers of the fire. Soon we'd be enveloped in the blackness that reached across the world and up to the great space above us where everything comes from.

Two days later, we were near Jerusalem. After passing Bethany, we stopped by the great gardens to rest. Nadab's face was discolored. The morning after I'd knocked him to the ground, he'd woken up with a smile and asked me if my hand hurt as much as his head. Jehoram grinned and jostled him.

"You're in perfect health," Jehoram said to him. "What the hell were you drinking yesterday?"

Reuben had gone ahead to Jerusalem to see if anything had changed and if anybody was expecting the two men we'd killed. I knew that he thought we should keep going when night fell, not stopping there any longer. He wanted to head north to Sychar, lie low, and rest for a while. He wanted to be sure that nobody was out looking for us after what we'd done.

"I've got Anna in Sychar, I want to meet her again," he said over and over again. "I promised her, she's waiting for me."

But I wanted to head to the coast, to Jaffa. The sea air would do Jehoram good, even though Jehoram always said he didn't like the sea. He said it smelled like a woman's piss.

Reuben came back, and he'd brought some food, bread and oil, grapes and olives. The sun was a piercing white glare. We sat in the shade of a tree.

"Everything looks normal," Reuben said.

"That sounds good," I said.

"Not necessarily," he said.

"Don't be so sure," I said. "Remember that we're special, we're God's chosen thieves, isn't that right?"

"Go to hell, Jehoash," said Reuben.

We smiled, ate, and prepared to enter the city. I helped Jehoram to cover himself up and wrapped his face so that only his eyes were visible. Nadab went over to Jehoram and took one of his hands.

"What is it?" Jehoram grumbled.

"I'll go alone," Nadab murmured, "but when I see you again . . ."

Jehoram pushed Nadab away before he could say any more.

"Stand still," I said. "I can't tie this up."

"I can go alone too," Jehoram said behind all the rags. "I don't need you to look after me."

"The two of us will go together, Jehoram," I said. "If anything should happen, we'll deal with it together."

Jehoram said something unintelligible from beneath his dressings.

"What?" I asked.

"I don't want to stay too long in the sun," he said. "It itches like hell."

Jerusalem was a hive. Whatever could walk or crawl or buzz or hiss was moving about. We split up: Jehoram and I went to look for oil and ointment, cloth and blankets, while Nadab went off with Reuben. We were to meet again in the evening.

Jehoram cursed the heat and all the people walking around him.

We went into a dark tavern, got something to drink, and came back out into the light and the heat. Animals roamed about, bleating and letting off smells that wafted about, mixing with everything else there. Some of the soldiers and the guards pushed anybody who came too close, shouted at them, grabbed young men and took knives from them that could barely shear the wool off a lamb. Some children came running up asking for money, and I waved them off before Jehoram could start tormenting them. An elderly lady with gray hair and gray eyes, and a mouth with nothing but a tongue inside, grabbed on to me and said she could pray for us. All possible worldly things were squeezed into this city: we even saw a cage of snakes, in the most peculiar colors.

As we stood in the shade by the colonnades in the temple square, Jehoram asked how they'd managed to get everything so straight, and who'd taken the trouble to build it all.

"What are we doing here anyway?" he asked.

"Be quiet, Jehoram," I said. "Look around you, this is something you can take with you in your dreams when we leave here."

Jehoram smirked. "I can't see any girls," he said. "All I can see is a damn big building."

I wanted to see what it all looked like. I'd been there before, but it was some time ago, and I couldn't remember much. It wasn't the Temple itself I was interested in, a house of God, as if anybody was listening, as if anybody with such power would bother with such insignificant beings as us. Still, those two men we'd left back there, I couldn't understand what they were thinking. How would they have got away? There were walls, stairs, guards. They were prepared to die, just to take the lives of a priest or two. I couldn't understand what they were fighting for, or what they were fighting against. Killing a few people wouldn't make any difference, spreading fear like that. This land is ruled by those who hold sway, so let them get on with it, let them hold sway. What else can we do but hold on to what little freedom we're given?

"What are we doing here?" Jehoram asked.

"Nothing," I said. "We're just having a look around."

Some children in rags sat there begging, and one of them stared at Jehoram and me. Jehoram asked him what he was looking at, and the boy barked at us. Before we could say anything, the boy was up on his feet, running away from us. Jehoram started to follow him, but I got a hold of him and told him to calm down.

"There are guards everywhere," I said, pointing. "The soldiers are based not far from here, in the fortress."

We walked toward the gate at the end of the open square. I started going up the steps, and Jehoram followed me, mumbling about us not going to be let in. When we'd made it through the gate, I heard someone speaking loudly. Around us, a number of people were starting to gather. Jehoram grinned and said that maybe it was a gladiatorial contest, but he cut off and his face took on a strange expression. The sound of the speaker reached us, a voice that was loud and clear. It was Nadab.

We followed the others going toward the Holy Temple. Everything had become strange and quiet. The only sound was of Nadab speaking. His words grated, tumbled between the walls, and reverberated back and forth. Jehoram tried to force his way through all the people standing there, but he gave up. Some guards pushed him away, as they were trying to get there themselves. I stretched up and stared at Nadab. He couldn't see me, and his eyes were full of tears. In his hands he held a sword and a dagger. How he'd got hold of a sword I had no idea. He threatened the guards with the weapons, telling them to stay back.

"I'm not here to fight," he shouted to them, before turning back to the crowd. His voice struck us like iron. He spoke of how the Temple was no longer a place for prayer, no longer a place for stories about good. It had become a den of thieves for the rich and powerful, a haven for those collaborating with foreign powers.

"Do not concern yourselves with priests and men of riches," Nadab shouted. "Do not concern yourselves with those who've run and hidden. They know everything that's been written down but nothing about the Word of God. They work for the infidels."

Two of the guards tried to seize Nadab from each side, but Nadab saw them both. He struck out at one of them with the sword, then turned quickly and raised the dagger at the other one.

"Don't," he said. "Keep back, don't try your luck. If the Lord will stand by me, I'm here to tell everybody that the light hasn't been extinguished, it's still lit, the Lord is here with us. Listen to the prophet Jesus. Don't listen to the ones with all the power. Don't listen either to the young ones who thirst for justice, but who would lead us all into war. It's Jesus, Jesus of Nazareth, you should follow, that's who."

And then he was cut off. Several of the guards went for him at the same time. But when one of them was in range of Nadab's sword, Nadab hesitated. He didn't stab him with the dagger. I heard Jehoram groan as Nadab lowered both his weapons and lifted up his face.

The guards were on top of him at once. One of them struck Nadab on the head with a club, and when he fell to the ground, they kicked him in the face and chest and arms and stomach. The crowd began to shout: "Hang him, hang him." More guards arrived and told people to stay back. Jehoram was on his way up to where Nadab lay, bloody and curled up. I took hold of him, pulled him away, pushed him out and down the stairs.

"They're going to kill him," Jehoram said.

"Shut up," I said. "Shut up, Jehoram, just go, don't look back." But Jehoram didn't want to listen and tried to stop me. I got hold of one of his hands and pulled him close to me.

"Do you want to die?" I snarled at him. "There's nothing we can do now. We've got to find Reuben."

Jehoram nodded in agreement.

"Yes," he said. "Yes, it's true, there's nothing we can do, nothing."

He started to tear off the fabric he had wrapped around him. He scratched at his sores and spoke to himself, and I knew I had to get him out of there. I dragged him across the square toward the colonnades. There were some children gathered in the shadows. They looked like a gang, and I recognized the boy who'd barked at us.

Before I could say anything, Jehoram ran at the children, the loose fabric from his bandages flapping around him. It was a while since I'd last seen him like this. He was about to fall apart. Jehoram bellowed at the children, striking those who couldn't get away, knocking them over, and grabbing the boy, lifting him up, and shaking him.

"Do I look like a dog?" Jehoram said.

Some of the children stood there, staring at him, while others screamed and fled. The boy hanging in the air punched and kicked. Jehoram just grinned and asked him again if he looked like a dog. I told him to stop.

"Stop," I said. "Let go of that boy and pull yourself together."

Jehoram looked at me. His eyes were red, and he was drooling. He let go of the boy, and the boy fell to the ground. The other children, those who were still there, stared at us. One of them, a tall lad, asked who we were to lay hands on one of his people.

"One of your people?" said Jehoram, starting to snigger.

I grabbed him. "Let it go, Jehoram, calm down." Jehoram shook off my hand, spat, and snarled.

"You have no business here," said the tall boy. "He's possessed, isn't he?"

"No," I said. "He's not possessed, he's my brother. Keep your distance from him if you still want to see the light of day."

Jehoram smiled at my threat and nodded. "Yeah, Jehoash, that's right. Come on, tell them who I am."

"Who are you?" I asked the tall one while I looked around. Nobody seemed to care about what was happening here. There were no guards or soldiers heading in our direction.

"I'm the new Saul, King of the Temple Dogs," said the boy.

I nodded and tried to understand what he was talking about.

"So," I said, "you and those kids, your gang, you have control of everything that goes on here, do you?"

Saul nodded.

"All right, Saul," I said. "Listen here. I need some help. There's money to be had if you help me."

Saul stood there looking at me. He was quiet and the children around him were standing still.

"What'll happen to the man they caught in the Temple just now?" I asked.

"There'll be a crucifixion," Saul said.

I asked him when and where. Saul moved and pointed at some of the other children, who came over and whispered to him.

"It's happening now, right away," he said. "They're taking him to Golgotha."

"Can you show us the way?" I asked.

Saul said we'd have to pay, and once we'd paid, he'd let two of the children take us there. I took out some coins. Jehoram said it would be cheaper just to make them do it.

The two children walked down from the Temple Mount and into the city. We followed them through the crowds, through the streets and around corners.

I didn't think we'd be able to stop it. I wasn't planning to step forward and declare that Nadab was insane, or that there was a raging fever inside him. I just wanted to see what they'd do with him. And if he'd stay alive until nightfall.

After walking a short way, the two children stopped, pointed ahead, and started running back. We stared at where they'd pointed and saw a procession heading out through an opening in the city walls. The soldiers went out in front, and in between them was Nadab. He was carrying a wooden cross. People were shouting, and some young men threw stones and spat at Nadab. The soldiers didn't seem to care as they dragged Nadab and pushed him forward.

We followed behind, right at the back of the procession, out of the city and up toward a hill. There were a number of crosses still bearing the remains of the dead. I felt empty as my legs climbed up, my hands cold. The soldiers chased away the children and told people to stay back. They held Nadab down while they nailed him to the cross. He screamed and wailed, and they had trouble keeping him still. One of the soldiers, the one holding his feet, yelled to the others, and another one went up with a staff and hit Nadab on the head to keep him still.

They finished their task, and Nadab was raised up. His clothes were torn off, his whole body broken. I'd never seen any of my men in this way before. If one of us was injured, we tended to him. If one of us was killed, we put him where wild animals couldn't reach. I'd taken Nadab in, and he'd seemed ready for this life. But seeing him like this . . .

"We shouldn't have come here," I said.

Jehoram didn't move. He stood there, facing Nadab.

"We've got to find Reuben," I said. "We've got to get out of here."

Jehoram said something, but I wasn't listening.

"Come on," I said. "We've finished here."

"No," said Jehoram. "He's not dead yet."

I turned to my brother. Blood ran from some of the sores on his forehead.

"Jehoram, we've got to go."

"No," said Jehoram. "Listen, he's still alive."

I turned to where Nadab was hanging. He was making a sound, a weak, whining lament.

We met up with Reuben when it had grown dark. The stars were hidden behind black clouds. A chill wind was blowing in, and Jehoram had undressed. He'd begun to scratch and claw at all his sores. He shouted to Reuben and told him to hurry up. Reuben asked what was wrong, staring at Jehoram, who was sitting there, almost naked, and bleeding.

"Why weren't you with Nadab?" Jehoram asked him.

"Nadab?" said Reuben. "It's not my damn job to look after him."

"Nadab's been caught," I said.

"Caught?" said Reuben. "What do you mean caught?"

"I thought he was with you," I said.

"He wanted to be on his own," said Reuben. "Was I supposed to follow him around the whole damn city?"

I called over to Jehoram and told him to get dressed. "Follow me," I said, leading them through the streets to a row of stables at the back of a worn-down house. There was a boy guarding the stables, so I gave him a coin and asked him to leave us alone.

"Just don't disturb the animals," he said. I nodded and told him not to worry about us.

"Nobody will look for us here," I said to the others.

"We haven't got time for this," Jehoram said. "We've got to go and take him down now, straightaway."

My hands were cold. I held them up to my mouth to warm them. Reuben asked what had happened. I told them to sit down, and in the dim light of a torch burning outside, I explained what had been done, and what we were going to do.

Over the following years, when Jehoram forgot himself and started talking about that day and that night, I would close my eyes, and it was still difficult to remember everything the way it had happened.

When Reuben lay dying, and Jehoram and I sat there with him, he carried on about Anna from Sychar. He'd promised to take care of her, and everything he'd done had been to save Anna. Jehoram and I took turns sitting there and listening to him, neither of us trying to understand what he was talking about. But then, after a while, Reuben wanted to talk about Nadab.

"I'll meet Nadab now," he said. "He died fighting for something he believed in, there's honor in that. I've been proud of him ever since that day, and I'm going to tell him. He's waiting for me; I've been waiting for him."

Jehoram tried to get him to drink some more water, but Reuben didn't want any. He just lay there, on the ground, with his hands by his sides. He lay there, talking and talking, about what Nadab did that time in Jerusalem and how it was right, about how Nadab truly was a child of God. Jehoram became impatient and excused himself while he went to find some more wood for the fire. I stayed sitting there with Reuben. He asked for Anna, and I told him that she wasn't there.

"Maybe she's waiting for me too," said Reuben. "I'll have several people to meet. I've got so many to meet. Nadab and Anna."

I got up and could hear Jehoram walking about out in the night air.

"Jehoash," said Reuben. His voice was so weak.

"Yes?" I said, still facing the sound of Jehoram.

"Jehoash," said Reuben again. I turned to him and knelt down.

"What?" I asked.

"I shouldn't have done it," he said. "Should I?"

"No," I said. "Maybe not."

"I shouldn't have done what the old man told me," he said.

I had no idea what he was talking about.

"What was it he said? I'm blind, and yet I see many things, something like that. I can picture him now. He had pale, gray eyes, he talked about light and shadow, he touched me."

I told him to hush now, to relax, but he wasn't listening to me anymore.

"You're going to bury me," he went on. "You must bury me here. Don't leave me lying here so the old man can find me, bury me. Don't let him find me."

I nodded and told him we would.

The next morning he was dead, and Jehoram and I dragged him over to a small cave that Jehoram had found. We had to break his bones to fit him in, and we covered the opening with rocks and with sticks. There was glaring sunlight, and a chafing wind.

"When it's my turn, just leave me," I said. Jehoram nodded. I didn't know then that Jehoram would also die by my side, while I would be dragged away, alive and tied up. A new and final chapter would begin. I didn't know then, I couldn't see it.

Neither did we know what was coming as we sat there, in the stable, that evening in Jerusalem. The city lay in darkness, while Nadab was hanging there alone, nailed fast.

"They did it so quickly," Jehoram said. "They just took him and nailed him up there sooner than you can count to three."

"He was still alive when we left," I said.

"I've never heard him like that," Jehoram said. "He was screaming."

"Do they know about us?" Reuben asked.

"We've got nothing to do with it," I said. "He was talking about Jesus."

"I told you," said Reuben. "He's not one of us."

"Shut your mouth," Jehoram said. "Don't talk about him like that. Why are we sitting here talking anyway? He's still alive."

"I warned you," said Reuben. "I didn't like his talk."

"He was still alive when we left," Jehoram said.

"We can't leave him hanging there like that," I said. "I won't let one of us be strung up like that. If it were you, Reuben, I'd take you down. If it were Jehoram, I'd do the same. Nadab's one of us. If he's going to die, he should die with us, not in front of those people who want us to serve them."

Reuben fell silent. He glanced down at his hands; he turned them and stroked them across his beard.

"If they get hold of us, we'll be strung up there with him," he said. "He's no more now. Nobody can stand being nailed up like that."

"That may be so," I said, "but Nadab's one of ours, he's tough."

"What do you want us to do?" Reuben asked. "Take him down? Are you going to climb up there and bring him down?"

"Yes," I said. "We're taking him down, and we'll leave into the night when it's all over, toward Jaffa. We're going to get Nadab, we'll fix him up. If it doesn't work, then we'll bury him. None of us should hang like that."

Reuben was about to say something, but I cut him off: "I know you're surprised, Reuben. I don't know how to say this, but Nadab's given us something. Since he's been one of us, it's as if something new has opened up. I've been fighting against it, I've been holding on to what we are. But when I saw them taking him, when I saw them putting him up there . . ."

"It's all right, Jehoash," said Reuben. "I'm joining you. You would've done the same for me."

"We took him in," I said. "We stick together. What we do, he does. What he does, we do."

"Yes," said Reuben, "but they're going to come looking for us."

"They'll go hunting for insurgents," I said. "They'll search the city, the mountains, they won't find us."

Reuben nodded. I saw that he was ready. If not for the sake of Nadab, then he was ready to do what we were made for.

The guards were positioned by the city walls. They stood facing away from us, staring into the darkness where Nadab was hanging. I could hear dogs and soft, hoarse cries. One of the guards sneered and yelled out into the night.

"Whose cries are those?" Jehoram said. "Is it Nadab?"

"The animals feed on the ones who stop moving," said Reuben. "Were there any others hanging there?"

"The others were dead," Jehoram said.

"How are we going to do this?" Reuben wondered.

I nodded at the guards.

"There are only two of them," I said. "We'll go through from the other side of the wall. They won't see us. If they hear anything and come to see, we'll kill them. Nobody will look for us, nobody knows who we are, and we'll be on our way to Jaffa before daylight anyway."

"They're soldiers," said Reuben.

"Good," I said. "Maybe they're not so soft."

We walked through the darkness, disguising ourselves in the night. A faint, dancing light came from the torches on the city walls and where the soldiers were standing, but otherwise nothing. Jehoram later told me how he'd held on to my right hand and let himself be pulled along. He said I had such powers that night, as if something were guiding me, and he could taste, more than smell, the saltiness and stickiness in the air. Reuben walked behind us.

"Jehoram," I said, stopping dead. In front of us, a body was hanging from a cross. We fell silent. I touched the foot of what was hanging there, but it didn't say anything. An animal, maybe several, growled around us. I lashed around with a stick and hit something that whimpered and moved away. We walked on, and I heard a soft whispering.

"Nadab?" I said, but the whispering stopped. Then I heard Reuben.

"He's here," said Reuben. "It'll take several of us to get him down."

"Where?" I asked.

Reuben came over to us; he took hold of me and led me with him.

"Here," he said.

The cross was made of rough wood. I lifted my hand and touched Nadab's feet. I could hear him speaking softly. There was an awful stench, and his feet were covered in something sticky. Reuben stood close to me.

"We can't get him down," he said. "It's impossible." We heard the animals, some barking, some snarling. The guards moved. They stood in the torchlight, staring out into the night.

I pulled Jehoram close, put my arms around Reuben and him, and whispered to them: "Lift me up."

I climbed up, with their help, and took hold of the cross. Nadab was still mumbling. I put my hand on him and asked if he could hear me.

"Jehoash," he said. Or did he say something else? I don't know.

I raised myself up until I had my ear to his mouth.

"Nadab," I said. "We're going to get you down."

"No," he whispered. "I'm here."

"Nadab," I whispered back. "Can you hear me? It's me, Jehoash."

"The little light," he mumbled.

"What?" I whispered.

"The little light," he mumbled. "It flashed. I saw the light, high up there, it was searching for me."

"Nadab," I whispered. "Nadab, it's Jehoash."

"Jehoash," he murmured. "She told me about him, Jehoash, it's cold. She told me everything, the little light, it flashed down at me."

"Nadab," I whispered. "We've got to get you down."

"I could see it, Jehoash," he mumbled. "The flame wasn't out, she was keeping it alive."

"Be still," I whispered. "Listen to me."

He kept on mumbling, but I could no longer understand what. I tried to reach out for his hand, but I lost my grip. My hands slipped over his shoulders and ribcage. And then there was nothing until I hit Jehoram and we fell down together to the ground. Reuben was on top of us, pulling at us and hissing.

"They're coming," he whispered. "The soldiers are coming."

We stood up in the dark. The soldiers were heading straight for us. There were two of them, both carrying torches. I grabbed onto Jehoram and whispered in his ear what we were going to do. I gave Reuben the signal, and we walked out to the sides. Jehoram walked between us, toward the torches and the soldiers.

One of the soldiers yelled at Jehoram when he saw him. Jehoram stopped and stood there, smiling at them. Then we rushed into the light. Reuben went up to the one who'd yelled and stuck a knife in his side, sending the torch falling to the ground. Reuben put his hand over the soldier's mouth, pulled out the knife, brought it down again between the soldier's shoulders and neck, and twisted it around inside him. I was on the other soldier, but my knife bounced off a leather strap around his chest. The blow was still so hard that the soldier took a step backward, and there was Reuben, who grabbed his head, tilted it back, and cut his throat.

I told them both to be quiet. There was nothing to be heard, apart from some faint sounds coming from within the city and the gurgling of one of the soldiers.

"Come on," I said. "We've got to get back to Nadab." Reuben found the torches and hit them against the ground until they were extinguished. Jehoram smirked in the darkness and asked if the soldiers were tougher, but Reuben told him to be quiet.

"Nadab?" said Reuben when we got back to the cross. We couldn't hear anything from up there.

"Lift me up," I said. "I'll try once more. If it doesn't work, we'll end it for him."

Reuben took hold of Jehoram. "Come on," he said. I clambered up on top of them, grabbed the cross, and put my feet around the wood.

"Nadab?" I said, but he didn't answer. I reached out one of my hands to find Nadab's. I could feel the nail going through it. It was impossible to pull it out.

"Nadab," I said, "I can't get you free."

He was still silent. His warm breath rippled out through his nose.

"Nadab," I said again, carefully taking out my knife. "You're one of us, you shouldn't have to hang here like this." I got the knife ready.

At that very moment came a strong gust of wind. It snatched me, I dropped the knife, I lost my grip. I fell again, and when I hit the ground, I saw the first bolt of lightning rip open the whole world. Jehoram screamed, Reuben cried out, thunder reverberated in the sky, and when the lightning struck again, I saw Nadab fall down.

I lay struggling on the ground. I had trouble seeing; my eyes hurt. Reuben took hold of me.

"Come on," he said. "We've got to get away from here."

I got up. Jehoram was holding something in his hands.

"Jehoash," said Reuben. "Are you hurt?"

"No," I said, and we started walking. They carried Nadab. The night was torn open, again and again. We walked through the flashing darkness and kept walking until we found something to crawl into. It was a cave, not big enough to stand up in. Reuben and Jehoram put Nadab down between us.

"I can't see him," said Reuben. "Is he alive? Jehoash, is Nadab alive?"

I leaned forward and looked until I could see his face. There was nothing coming out of his nose or mouth. I felt for a heartbeat, but even his warmth had gone.

"No," I said.

"It's so cramped in here, I need to get out," Jehoram said. "I need to get out of here."

The storm abated. We left Nadab lying there, crept out of the cave, and headed westward toward Jaffa. The moon rose. The road was like a deep, dark rift through the cold light. Jehoram walked in front, talking to himself. Reuben and I walked on either side. At one point, Jehoram called out and asked where we were going. I didn't know what to answer, but Reuben broke the silence.

"Jaffa, we're going to the sea," he said. "I can't show myself to Anna, not yet."

Jehoram made a sound, and we stared at him. He was standing with his hands raised in the air. "The sea, Nadab," he shouted. "We're going to the sea."

Reuben told him to shut up. "They'll be looking for us," he said.

"Nobody knows us," I said. "Besides, there are so many people for them to keep track of. Maybe we'll go to Antioch eventually."

"Nadab," Jehoram cried. "Can you hear me? You have the skies in your hand, I'll soon have the sea at my feet." Reuben started off toward him, but I grabbed hold of him.

"Let him be," I said.

"Maybe we should go to Sychar instead," Reuben said. "Nobody will bother us there."

"No," I said. "We're going to the sea. We need to go back to what we were." I tried to see his face, to see if anything had changed. But even if the moon was above us, our faces were in shadow.

"I don't know how you got him down," Reuben said.

Jehoram was just a shadow in front of us now. It seemed as if he were still talking to himself, but we couldn't make out his words anymore.

"I must keep an eye on Jehoram," I said.

When daylight came, through a long, narrow gap at the end of the world, we stopped by a small grove of trees. People had been there before us. The grass had been trampled; there were the blackened remains of a fire. I treated Jehoram's hands with ointment and wound them up in a blanket. Jehoram smiled at me, and a sound came from his mouth, as if he had something stuck in there. Reuben lay down next to us. Jehoram wrapped his face in a thin, dark strip of cloth, and I helped him down to the ground. I said I could keep watch, and Reuben muttered that I should wake him when I needed some sleep too.

"If I dream about Nadab, please wake me up," Jehoram said. His words were muffled behind his dressings. I folded up my own blanket and put it under his head.

"What should I tell him?" Jehoram asked. I looked across at Reuben, but his eyes were closed. Birds were singing up in the trees, sunlight shining softly through the twigs and leaves.

"What should I tell him?" Jehoram asked again.

"Don't tell him anything," I said. "Don't ask him to come back." Jehoram lay still, his face hidden behind the dressings.

"Yes," he said.

We made it to Jaffa, but we stayed there for only a few days before starting the journey to Antioch. On the way there, we met a group of several children, who started to scream when they saw Jehoram. He tried to catch some of them, but Reuben and I held him back. In Antioch, we knocked a man to the ground and robbed him, then we filled his clothes with rocks and threw him in the Orontes River. Another man we took had Roman coins carved out of wood stuffed in a purse. Jehoram kicked the man in the face so hard and so many times that he started gurgling before he died. Reuben took the small wooden coins and burned them on the fire that same night. He said there was no beauty left in the world and wondered who the hell made coins out of wood. One evening we were stopped by some soldiers, but they let us go once we'd given them all the stolen money we had on us.

And there are also many other things that we did. If I told all of them, I suppose that the world could not contain a faith like the one for which Nadab died.

5 ⦀ THE BLACK BIRD

I

On her way to the well, Anna noticed a bird with feathers so black, but with a gaze so empty and distant, that it reminded her of Andrew. Of all the men she'd had, Andrew, her fourth, was the only one who stroked her on the cheek, who kissed her neck softly, who let her lie on top. Andrew, oh, Andrew! What was wrong with her? Why did the mere sight of a bird remind her so much of him? One morning, he'd leaned down to her, whispered a few words in her ear, "I'll return," and left. He was seen around the sixth hour, wandering out of Sychar in the direction of Judea, and then he vanished. She missed him. His smell, his gentle fingers, the way he sometimes slept with his eyes open, with a gaze so empty and distant. So she asked around, and a man thought that Andrew was there, in Sychar, in a small stone house on the edge of the city. But when she sought out the place, there were only two young shepherd boys living there, who both stared at her as if driven by an enormous hunger. Another man, a traveler from Nazareth heading to the Temple in Jerusalem, thought he'd seen Andrew in Samaria. But who knew if it was Andrew or somebody else? Anna tried to verify what the man had observed. Was his hair long and black, were his eyes dark, was his nose long and bent at the bridge, did he hold the fingers of his right hand up to his mouth, like he always did when he felt nervous? The man smiled at her and said he didn't know.

Andrew had gone.

She thought of Ruth, her elder sister. Ruth always said that the men who came to them were men who'd lost their way. "All we need to do," her sister said, "is to let them think they've found the way home."

The bird was sitting in the thin top branches. Those black feathers and those black eyes. Anna looked down at the stones, the tufts of grass. A chill wind blew, taking hold of the trees, and when Anna looked up again, the bird had gone.

Voices were coming from the well. A group came walking toward her, heading down toward the city. Anna moved between the trees, put down her pitcher and stood there, watching the people pass. They were dressed in rags, filthy, men and children and a few women, holding each other's hands. Anna picked up the pitcher and set off on the last short stretch to the well, but she stumbled on her sore leg and let out a slight whimper. A swollen red mark went from her calf down toward her ankle: Reuben's mark. Andrew used to rub oil on her leg and foot. He'd never once asked her what had happened.

Reuben, her third man, and later her fifth too, had left that scar. She screamed so loudly when it happened, so loudly that he knelt down, started stroking her hair, and tried to make her quiet down. The white bone sticking out of her skin made her scream as if she were possessed. Looking back now, she can't remember feeling pain, just a thud and a ringing in her ears. She fainted, came around, and fainted again.

Reuben carried her to an old man with pale eyes, who reset her bone.

"I'm blind, and yet I see many things," the old man whispered. "I'm what stays in the shadows while the light falls elsewhere."

She tried to stay awake, but her eyes slipped shut. The only details she remembered were that the old man smelled of earth and sour goat's milk, and that there were small jars on the shelves along one wall. Anna can only just remember Ruth coming to find her.

"I'm going to heal your sister," the old man said. "She'll be able to start all over again."

"I'll look after her," said Ruth. "She has nobody else but me. I have nobody else but her."

"You don't have each other anymore now," the old man said. "She was given to me."

"She hasn't been given away to anybody," said Ruth.

Everything was in fragments, and Anna floated between sleep as the voices buzzed around her.

"Let go of her," said Ruth. "Let go of me, let us go."

"She's free," said the old man. "Reuben's made sure of that."

And then Ruth disappeared, and the old man was left sitting by Anna. In a whisper, he told her to rest, close her eyes, take deep breaths.

Anna lay there for a long time before she came around, and for a few more days until she was able to get up. She kept asking for Ruth. Reuben came to collect her and carried her back home. He gave her something to eat and something to drink. His tough, broad face was unchanged. She asked where Ruth was. He kissed her, said that Ruth was fine, and carried on clumsily stroking her hair. One evening, when Anna's throbbing pain wouldn't let her sleep, he sang to her. His voice was so strangely soft and faint.

When Reuben left her the first time, it wasn't the memories of when he broke her leg, beat her, or threatened her with a knife that made her hobble along the sides of the houses, asking if people had seen him. What made her hobble about were those times when he just sat there next to her. But she couldn't find him, nobody knew anything. Then she asked about Ruth: "Where's my big sister, have you seen her?" The answer was the same. Nobody knew. Not being able to speak to Ruth, not being able to hear Ruth's voice or countless attempts to comfort her, made Anna keep looking. She walked around the outskirts of Sychar, staring at everything that seemed unusual, everything that seemed new. She walked through Shechem and came back in the evenings, alone and exhausted. She collapsed on the floor and prayed, talked to herself, tried to remember everything Ruth used to say to her. And when she couldn't remember any more, when sleep descended on her like a heavy, warm blanket, she could hear Reuben singing faintly.

Those memories of Ruth's words and the times when Reuben sat next to her led her, blind with longing, into Andrew's hands. And Andrew, Andrew, what was it about him? How did he find his way so close to her? Why did he never hurt her? Sometimes, when he was sleeping next to her with his eyes open, she sat up and talked to him. She whispered about why she was there, in Sychar, she whispered about her mother and father and what little she could remember. She told him about Ruth, who'd taken care of her and taught her everything she needed to know, but who'd gone. She asked if he'd stay there, with her, forever, at which Andrew moved and blinked before lying still again. She lay down close to his warm body. His hair-covered arms were like great wings.

The next morning, Andrew leaned over Anna and kissed her on the breasts, on the neck, on her closed eyes. His hand lingered on her torn ear.

"It looks like a shell washed ashore by the waves," he said.

One day, when Andrew had gone too, Reuben came back, and she just stood there in her small room, trembling. She tried to pull herself together. She made him food and lay down next to him, but her trembling wouldn't stop. She trembled all through the night, in the pitch darkness, with Reuben's warm breath on her head. Only when he held her tightly in the soft morning light and pushed his way inside did her fingers, hands, and feet become still.

Those last days Anna and Reuben had together did her good. She didn't scurry back and forth, dripping with sweat, cold, muttering, moaning. When Reuben came back, he found what she'd forgotten. He made her see that the world in which he sang, in which he caressed her, the world in which Andrew's fingers, his mouth, soft hair, and gentle voice could be found, was a false world, and it had made her lose her mind. Underneath Reuben, she was pushed back inside herself and back into the real world.

When Reuben left her the second time, he took out a small purse of silver coins.

"This is for you and your foot," he said. "I see you've still got a limp."

Three men stood waiting outside. One of them had his face bound up in rags, while the second, tall and thin, stood facing the back alley that led to where she lived.

"Reuben," the third man said, "it's time to get going." The man's eyes looked gray and glowing, his hair cut close to the scalp.

"I'm coming," said Reuben. He turned, but then Anna reached out to touch him.

"Have you seen Ruth anywhere?" she asked.

"She's gone," said Reuben, but Anna started to describe her big sister and what she looked like. He cut her off. "I know who Ruth is, I haven't seen her. I've got to go now."

"Will you come back?" Anna asked. Reuben looked down at her before putting his hands up to hold her face. He looked surprised, as if what he held were something he hadn't seen before.

"I'll return," he said. "I promise you."

She never saw Reuben again. Ruth's words had been true. All the ones who came to them had lost their way. Anna made them feel found. But none of them stayed. Even Ruth had gone. A rumor went around that her elder sister had left with a man from Judea and his children. She'd dropped everything and left, but Anna wouldn't blame her for it.

Anna would dream of Ruth, talking to her in her sleep. In the soft, blue world of dreams, Ruth told her about the children who called her their mother, about her husband who gave her gifts, and how they were truly blessed by the Lord God. She told Anna to visit them, that they had space for one more in their house. Her dear husband had a brother too, and maybe this handsome, gentle brother would ask Anna to marry him?

But everything dissolves in the light of day. Like the man Anna had now, Baasha, who came to her in the evening and vanished by morning. He didn't beat her, but he pulled her hair and would only enter her from behind. He smelled of nothing, and sometimes when she woke up and he'd gone, she wondered whether he was human or just something evil that came alive in the dark of night.

This morning, while the world was still only lit by a faint light, and before Anna went up to the well and saw the black bird, she'd woken to Baasha standing there, staring at her.

"You're dirty in the light," he said, leaving her.

She got up immediately and shouted after him. Anna screamed and shouted, and Baasha ran away. She didn't know what was wrong with her. She grabbed one of the jugs she had standing there and smashed it on the ground. The jug was a present from her second man, Aaron. He'd found it among the possessions of his late mother and wanted to give it to Anna as a gift. That was only a short time after Anna's first man, Philip, had broken all his promises and left her.

Aaron kept on bringing her presents, and when she started to say no to the things he brought her, he stammered and told her she couldn't say no. He told her he didn't have any money of his own; this was all he could pay her with. Those words made her lunge at him and scratch his face. He ran off but came back that same evening and forced himself on her. He beat and kicked her so hard that she couldn't walk for several days.

Ruth had found her, nursed her, and told her that wasn't the way to act.

"You mustn't let them see you like that," her elder sister told her. "They get scared of how powerful you can be, how big you are. They'll try to destroy you, make you small again."

One of her ears had been battered. Anna always made sure to cover it up.

Like Aaron had come back at the end of the day, Anna knew that Baasha would come back that evening too. There was nothing to do but wait. First she was paralyzed with fear. The mark Reuben had left began to hurt. A soft rushing sound beat at her wounded ear. Darkness crept in and descended over Anna. She blinked, but it wouldn't go away. It was like sand in her eyes. She opened her mouth, but her tongue was dry. There was something cold and raw inside her; a soft voice began to speak, a faint whisper about empires rising, empires falling, about the lowly ones in the dust, about people and grains of sand and the wind blowing it all away. Anna gasped for air; she couldn't breathe. It was all over. Never again the morning, never again the day. No moon, no stars, only a haze that would drive her out of her mind if Baasha didn't kill her first. It came to her that the few things she'd been able to call good had all gone. The people to whom she offered herself left her. And the people who left her kept her awake at night.

She knelt down to gather up the remains of the broken jug. The shards lying there were sharp and black. She held one in her hand and pressed it against the other hand, where her warm pulse was beating.

"God," she said, "take me."

But a great roar came up the alleyway, she could hear it, as if the ocean were coming, roaring up from the alleyway into her house. The door opened, and a force hit her chest with such power she was almost knocked over. She got up, staggered backward, dropped what she had in her hands, and slammed into the wall. She squeezed her eyes shut, and when she opened them again, the shards were lying on the ground, and the door was wide open. Everything was quiet.

Years later, Anna would speak about that peculiar incident, which at that very moment had something familiar about it, yet at the same time something impossible to comprehend: the morning light, Baasha running off, the dark haze, the broken jug, the roar, her trip to the well. Anna would recall how she'd been filled with a power so strong that nothing could threaten her or keep her down. A light, flashing in the dark, the flapping of a wing, who knows. The truth was that, right there and then, on the way to the well, carrying the tall, round, flat-bottomed jug, Anna had become somebody else. Her new life had begun with that roaring sound and the black bird. But in the years to follow, there was no bird, there were no men, there was no Baasha or Reuben or Andrew in her story. Even dear Ruth had gone. Anna's story began with Anna's own words about the roar she'd heard. And Anna's words tell of when she met Jesus at the well.

Other women told her that Jesus had such hair and a beard as if he were a lion from the banks of the river Jordan. Jesus had limbs so brown and tender that they could taste salt on their lips. Jesus had eyes that were as bright and dark as day and night. And his voice was honey, sweet and thick and golden.

But Anna didn't want to speak about him in those terms. There was something else about Jesus. Something that linked him to the last kiss from Andrew, to Reuben's soft singing. It was the strange pattern in which his fingers moved. It was the way he smiled when he was with her, as if she made him shy. It was the way her fingers became so warm when he was near her. It was more, more than that, it was the way he might sit next to her while they ate. The way he asked her questions and listened, waiting while she answered, and then asked more questions. What were their first words by the well, other than hesitant, childlike tentative efforts, like the first time a young bird beats its wings.

"Where have you come from?" Anna asked him, putting down her pitcher.

"Nazareth," he said. "Galilee."

"What are you doing here?" she asked.

"We're traveling about. We stopped here to rest."

"Were you with the people who just left here?" she asked. "All those women?"

Jesus opened his mouth to say something, but Anna continued, saying that he reminded her of Andrew.

"The way you speak," she said. "Or, I don't know, maybe there's more of a Reuben in you, the way he was on good days."

Jesus stared at her.

"Who are these men?" he asked.

"Oh, they're no one," said Anna.

"One of us is called Andrew," he said. "Might he be the one you're talking about?"

Anna shook her head. "No, no," she said. "My Andrew's gone. I'd have seen him if he was with you."

"There are more of us," said Jesus. "Andrew's in Nazareth, he's waiting for us there."

Anna stood there, completely still.

"What does he look like?" she asked.

"What does he look like?" Jesus replied. "He's the brother of Simon Peter, one who's close to me."

"Is his hair long and black?" Anna asked. "Are his eyes dark? Is his nose long and bent at the bridge? Does he hold the fingers of his right hand up to his mouth when he's nervous?"

"That sounds like Andrew," said Jesus, "but I'm not sure. You can ask Simon Peter."

"I want to come with you," said Anna.

Anna didn't know what else to say, or what she could do. Had she found Andrew? She tried to stay calm, brushed her hands on her clothes, touched her ear and heard fluttering: there was something in the air, wings beating. It was the black bird. It flew past, over the well, and Anna thought it must be a sign from Andrew.

"I want to come with you," she said.

"If you want to, you can come," said Jesus. "We travel about spreading the Word of God. We move about as free people. Nobody owns us. You can ask Simon Peter about Andrew, as I think he can give you a better answer than I can. We're heading back to Galilee now. I come from Nazareth. My brothers live there, the ones I grew up with. Andrew is with them. I'd like you to come with us, if there's nothing here, nothing binding you to stay."

"But you do realize what I am?" Anna asked.

Jesus looked at her. "Yes," he said. "You're like me." Then other voices could be heard. Anna turned around. It was some of the women she'd seen while she was standing between the trees. They'd come back and were carrying small baskets, talking softly, smiling to each other, but when they saw Anna and Jesus, they stopped and fell silent. Anna stood there, one hand on the pitcher, the other over her chest.

"Who are you?" one of them asked.

"Are you from here?" another asked.

"This is Anna," said Jesus. "She's coming with us to Nazareth."

"I want to meet Andrew," said Anna.

One of them came over, took Anna's hand, and held it in her own. "Hello, Anna," she said. "My name's Orpah, and I know Andrew."

"Can you take me to him?" Anna asked.

Orpah nodded, smiled, and said she would.

Then the other women joined them. One of them raised her hands toward Anna's head, and Anna flinched.

"I'm not going to hurt you," the woman said. Anna let her stroke her hand over her forehead, over her cheekbone and her torn ear.

"It's been damaged," the woman said. "It's like sand in a little leather pouch." One of the other women, who was younger than all the others and who wouldn't stop smiling, lifted up her hands and touched Anna's ear.

"It's like dough," she said.

"It was crushed," Anna said, moving their hands away. "It was my second man." The women were standing around her now, they were so close. Jesus said something, and Anna turned toward him.

"Anna, if you drink this water," he said, touching the water in Anna's jug with his hand, "then you'll thirst again. You've chosen to join us, and I'll tell you that the water we drink turns into something else, it's alive. Here, take my hand."

Anna took Jesus's hand, and his fingers came between hers. They were cool to the touch, they were warm, she held on to him, he pulled her toward him, and a haze fell over them.

It was in the middle of the day, as Anna remembers it, even though she sometimes said, in her latter years, that it happened beneath the morning sun. When she thought back to it, everything was surrounded by his glow. Her hands, her ear sticking out, the way she whispered Andrew's name, Jesus's eyes, bright, dark. The sultry but cold smell of the well, the women's soft humming, a faint murmur between the bushes and trees, from the tiny insects. In the middle of the day, a new day was beginning.

Anna didn't go back to Sychar. She waited until Simon Peter came, together with the other men. Orpah introduced him to her and explained that Anna was looking for Andrew. Simon Peter seemed surprised and said that his brother hadn't said anything to him about it.

"But he doesn't talk to me about things like this," he said. "I'm his big brother, you know what it's like. When was it you met him?"

Anna tried to explain when Andrew was with her, for how long, and when he'd left. While she spoke, Simon Peter scraped at the sand with a small stick.

"That might add up," he said when she'd finished. "There was one spring when Andrew was away from me, which might have been about that time. That was before the Lord found us. I thought I'd never see him again, but then he came back."

Anna nodded, wanting Simon Peter to tell her more, but he fell silent. He was taller than Andrew, with paler and thinner hair, but they had the same nose. He got up, threw away the stick, and told her that she'd meet him if she came along to Nazareth. Anna thanked him, but he told her she didn't need to thank him, as he hadn't done anything.

"You came to the Lord, just as Andrew came back to me," he said. "Maybe Andrew's been waiting for you to find him."

Anna stayed by the well all night, together with the women, the men, and the children. She lay there in the open air, thinking of Andrew and staring at the stars. What if everything that glimmers were connected, what if all you had to do was to move your finger from one twinkling star to another? Would that create a pattern, a plan that could reveal everything? One that would show where to press, where to touch to make it all open up, so that she could be with him and find out why he left.

"It was the same for me too," a voice said close to her. It was Orpah. "I couldn't sleep for the first few nights. I thought the people I was escaping would come to get me."

"Who were you escaping?" Anna asked.

"I belonged to a man who kept me locked up and hidden away at night," said Orpah. "He said I was his, he said he would brand me like an animal if I ever tried to flee."

Orpah's breath was warm against her cheek.

"But I'm with the Master now," she said. "I'm not alone anymore. We're not alone anymore."

Her hand found Anna's.

"Do you know Andrew?" Anna asked her.

"Yes," Orpah answered.

"What's he like?" Anna asked.

"He's nice," said Orpah. "He doesn't say much. Who is he to you?"

"He was my everything," said Anna. "I've been searching for him. But I can't sleep."

"You'll get used to it," said Orpah. "Here, hold my hand. I'll stay here until you fall asleep."

Anna stuck with Orpah and didn't ask any more about Andrew. She would wait to see if he was still her Andrew. Orpah taught her the names of the others, first the women and then the men. A woman called Mary, who was close to Jesus, welcomed her.

"You're one of us," said Mary. "We're with you, just as you're with us. If you have any questions, you can come to me. I've asked Orpah to stay with you for the first few days."

Anna asked Orpah who the children were. Some had names, while others were just boy or girl, little one or child. A girl with a bright red wound along her neck and face, a mark of the beast, came to Anna the next evening and sat in her lap. At first, she didn't know what to do, so Orpah told her to sing. Anna sang and tried to speak to the girl, asking her what her name was, where she came from, and if she was hungry.

"I'm Esther," was all she said. She said nothing else and just sat there with her cheek against Anna's bosom.

"Esther," Anna said to the girl.

Anna was no longer alone. Orpah was always by her side, and Esther ran around, tugging at her hands and clutching her legs. She started to talk now and told Anna that she'd run away from Jerusalem, where she'd been living with some other children. She didn't have any family apart from Jesus and Anna. She was ten years old, maybe eleven, she wasn't sure. Anna nodded and stroked Esther's hair.

Anna saw little of Jesus over the following days. All the way from Jacob's Well at Sychar up to Nazareth she was looking for a reason to approach him. There was a special circle around Jesus made up of the people closest to him, with Mary and Simon Peter among them. Anna couldn't bring herself to go up to them and ask to speak with Jesus.

One morning, she found him by some rocks alone in the pale sunlight. Jesus seemed tired, with bags under his eyes and his hair tangled. Anna asked if everything was all right. He said everything was fine, got up, and asked if she was all right.

"Yes," she said. "They're taking care of me."

"We'll soon be there now," he said. "Then you'll find Andrew."

Anna wanted to ask how he'd come to be with them, but the words that came were: "There are others like me here."

Jesus nodded, but then said, "No, there are no others like you." And again, Anna sensed him coming toward her; she felt her hands lift up to meet him. But Simon Peter was heading toward them. He called at her, telling her to come with him.

"Leave the Master in peace," he said.

"Peter, it's all right," said Jesus.

"You need rest, Lord," Simon Peter said.

"It's all right," said Jesus.

"No," said Anna. "He's right, you look tired. I'm just thinking so much about Andrew. I'm looking forward to seeing Nazareth, I've never been outside of Samaria."

Simon Peter nodded. "There's not so much to be seen," he said, "but Andrew will be there."

They arrived in Nazareth the next day. The sky stretched out over the mountains like a gray blanket, and some goats ran ahead of them on the narrow road up to the city. The first ones to see the group approaching were children. Boys and girls ran from house to house, shouting, and people came out to welcome the new arrivals. Anna tried to spot Andrew, but he was nowhere to be seen. He'd gone to Sepphoris on an errand and wouldn't be back until the evening. Anna stood there not knowing what to do.

"You'll just have to wait," said Orpah, who was by her side. "He'll be back."

She took Anna to show her around.

Everything was new, everybody welcomed her. One of Jesus's brothers lifted her up. "Look," he said, "you can fly up here, did you know that?" He laughed, and Orpah scolded him for always fooling around like that. Esther tugged at Anna, wanting to show her a secret place only she knew of. Mary came over and asked if Orpah was looking after her. Anna nodded. She stayed close to Orpah, as she felt tired. It dawned on her that she'd left everything in Sychar. Everything she owned, everything she was. Now that she was so close to Andrew, she felt as if it all might fall apart. She thought of Ruth, who'd disappeared. Anna tried to remember her voice, all the things she used to say, the way she would make her little sister feel safe and at home.

"Orpah?" said Anna.

Orpah turned to her, but Anna didn't know what to ask her. She would just have to wait, she thought, and all the answers would come in the evening. Everything would come with Andrew.

"What is it, Anna?" Orpah asked.

"Nothing," said Anna. "Nothing. Everything's just so new."

The strange thing was that, as the sun was setting and Andrew came walking up toward Nazareth, it was as if Anna had forgotten about everything for a moment. She sat there with Esther, telling her about kings and queens. Anna tried to remember the stories she'd heard, and Esther sat completely still, her eyes wide and dark. If Anna stopped to think, Esther told her to keep telling the story.

"Anna, Anna!" Orpah shouted, and Anna got up immediately, realizing straightaway what was happening.

She kissed Esther. "He's coming," she said, and began running toward Orpah.

A man came walking up the narrow path toward the city. He had the glowing sun behind him. His hair was shorter, and his clothes were ragged. He was staring at the ground, and it seemed as if he were talking to himself, before he stopped and looked up to where they were standing.

It was Andrew, Anna was in no doubt about it. He'd gone, but she'd found him.

Andrew walked up the last short distance toward them, staring at Anna. Orpah didn't say anything; she just held on to Esther and told her not to cling to Anna.

"Anna?" said Andrew as they stood opposite each other.

It was impossible to know what to say, or where to start. She thought about Ruth, who'd never seen him, how she wished to show him to her. She thought about how he'd gone away, how he'd left her there, in Reuben's clutches, at Baasha's mercy.

"Anna?" he said again, lifting up a hand and moving the hair away from her battered ear. But Anna swatted away his hand, only to grab it again and hold it in hers.

"Anna," said Andrew, "what are you doing here?"

Anna held his hand, not wanting to let go. She leaned toward him, lay her head on his chest, and heard his heart beating. He was warm and wet, he smelled like she remembered.

"Anna?" he said yet again.

But before he could say any more, Anna said, "I'm here, I found you."

Everything happened so quickly after that. Things were made ready for the night, fires were lit, and everybody was given somewhere to sleep. Anna and Andrew didn't talk much, just holding each other's hand, while Orpah and Esther walked behind them. Andrew said he had to talk to Jesus and promised to return before nightfall. Anna let him go, and Esther came over and put her arms around Anna's leg.

"Come," said Orpah. "He won't be going anywhere now, come with me."

Anna went with her, and they went to see Mary, who told them where they were to sleep.

They were given some space in a family home, up against a wall, on the floor where something had been laid down for them to lie on. Anna sat down with Esther, but she couldn't face telling any stories now, so she tried singing. Then Andrew came and asked if she wanted to come with him. Esther grabbed Anna's hands and held on to her tightly.

"Just go," said Orpah. "I'll sit here with her."

Anna bent down to Esther, kissed her forehead, and freed herself from her grip.

"I know this place well now," said Andrew, as they walked together along a narrow path of large, jagged rocks. He pointed at a gnarled thicket and said he sometimes played hide-and-seek in there with the youngest children. He waved his hands and said there were small paths everywhere, and that he knew almost every single shortcut that was worth using, and a few more. He told her how it rained more up here in the hills, about the smell of the fruit trees, and how some of the children gathered the resin that ran out of the trunks, thinking it would turn to myrrh. Anna walked next to him. She yearned for him to stop talking, she wanted to touch him, she just wanted him there, still and close to her.

Andrew stopped. A lone tree reached up from where they were standing. Anna hadn't spotted it in the twilight. She peered at the thick branches and the leaves hanging still. The sun had set, but the whole sky still shone above them, clear and black. Far away from Nazareth, down in the plain, a small bonfire was burning, like a single, glowing piece of coal in an oven. Anna stood there, staring at it, and Andrew said it was probably shepherds.

"You want to know why I left you that time," he said.

Anna turned to him and nodded.

"I'd been quarreling with Simon, my elder brother, Simon Peter," he said. "I went off on my own. I had nothing when I came to Sychar. I found you, but I had to keep going, I had to find a job to survive. I thought you didn't need me, I couldn't give you anything, there was nothing there for me. I went back to Capernaum, to Simon. That was where Jesus found us."

"You left me," said Anna. "You left me when I needed you most."

Andrew didn't say anything and just stared ahead.

"If you'd known that Jesus was going to Sychar," Anna asked, "would you have gone too? Would you have gone to find me?"

Andrew shook his head. "I don't know, Anna," he said. "I don't know if I'd have brought you here to this. Some of us say that the soldiers will come, that they're waiting for us. I've told myself that I must believe in the power of the Lord, in the Lord's mercy. But even Simon is worried about our safety. Still, I feel at home here. I was in Capernaum, with Simon Peter, when I met Jesus. I followed him here. I like it here."

"I waited for you," she said. "I thought that you were out there somewhere, waiting for me."

"I thought you'd forget me," he said.

Anna didn't know what to say. She started to go, but she turned around and went back to him.

"You've got to tell me, Andrew," she said. "You've got to tell me straight out. I've come all the way here, I've waited for so long. You've got to tell me."

Andrew took her hands and held them in his.

"I never thought I had this in me," Andrew said. "I don't what's happening. I don't know what this is, but I want to be with you. Not like with the others. I want to be with you like we are now. I've spoken with Jesus and asked him if it's right for me to be with you."

Anna fell silent. It had turned dark, and the sounds of the others rose up to reach them.

"He said he lights a beacon for everyone in love," Andrew went on, "for everyone who's walking around in circles, unable to find the way. He said he lights a beacon for all love that's lost, lighting a path through the night to the promised land."

Anna tried to pull back her hands, but Andrew wasn't letting go. His fingers were warm and soft, and she remembered the way he used to stroke her.

"He said that was all he could do," Andrew said.

Anna tried to hush him, asking him to be quiet.

"I didn't wait for you," Andrew said. "I didn't dare to wait for you. I thought I'd never see you again."

"Don't say another word," she said, pulling him close. "Just come here."

When she came back, confused and bewildered, Esther wasn't there. It was dark, and the children weren't supposed to be out alone at that time. Orpah was sitting outside by a bonfire.

"Where's Esther?" Anna asked, and Orpah gave a start when she realized that Esther was missing. She got up and ran in to check where Esther should have been lying.

"She fell asleep straightaway after you left," Orpah said.

Andrew told Orpah to stay there while they went to find her. "Maybe she'll come back while we're looking," he said.

Anna and Andrew went around asking those who were still awake. Nobody had seen Esther, nobody knew anything, so they began to knock on the doors of the houses where their group had been taken in. They called out into the night, but there was no answer. When Anna eventually gave up and Andrew took her back, Orpah was standing there waiting for them. She said that Esther had suddenly come back.

"She didn't want to talk to me," said Orpah. "She just went to bed."

They crept inside and found Esther on Anna's blanket, her legs up against her chest, her mouth open, and her hair spread out loosely in a circle around her head.

"Maybe somebody who lives here thought she was a leper," Andrew said, speaking softly so as not to wake anyone. "Maybe she was chased."

"But it's night," Anna whispered. "What was she doing out at night?"

"Maybe she was just sleepwalking," Orpah whispered. "I've seen others do it. She's got nobody else but us. What do we know about her dreams, her nightmares?"

Andrew knelt down and stroked his hand over Esther's hair.

"What happened to her?" he muttered. "I've never seen a wound like that, what do they call it, a mark of the beast?"

"I know what it is," Orpah whispered. "It's water that burns. I knew a girl who had it thrown on her by her brother. Her nose and her lips disappeared, and her eyes couldn't see anymore."

"But Esther must have been a child when it happened," Andrew said. "How old is she now, ten, twelve?"

"It's a mark of the beast," Orpah whispered. "It can be put on anybody, in the same way evil doesn't distinguish between adults and children, men and women."

"Don't say things like that," Anna whispered. "She might wake up, she needs to sleep now."

She kissed Orpah, kissed Andrew, wished them good night, and lay down next to Esther. Her tiny body was so warm. She gathered together Esther's hair, draped it over her neck, and patted her head gently.

"Esther," she whispered. "My little Esther."

Anna closed her eyes and thought about how everything had changed and was new now. It was a strange feeling. She had been blessed with a new life, but there was still a flicker, a quiver, a twitch. She'd learned that good was followed by bad. All that time with Ruth, and then she vanished. When Andrew had been closest to her, he left. Reuben had sung to her softly, and then he went away when she got better. Was there something bad waiting for her now? Would she be taken back one morning, one evening, one night, by a Reuben, or by a Baasha? Would they all be surrounded one day by troops and punished for following Jesus? Once, several years ago, just outside Sychar, Anna had come across six crucified men. Their broken bones, the nails, their crooked fingers, and the smell made her run home, crying and afraid.

She held on tightly to Esther. She thought about Andrew, about everything he'd told her, and how quiet he'd been when she held him tight. She'd caressed his face, and down over his neck. She'd laid her hand over his warm stomach; he'd closed his eyes and whispered her name. "Anna, Anna, Anna."

Morning came, darkness left, everything rose and shone. Esther didn't want to get up. She whimpered, laid her cheek against Anna's, and said, "Sing to me, can you sing to me?" Anna stroked her, sang softly, and told her it was morning. Esther eventually got up, but she didn't run off that day, she stayed close to Anna. All day there was a small hand with tiny fingers getting caught in Anna's clothes or around her leg.

When Andrew came, he lifted Esther and threw her up into the air, calling her a little rascal and asking where she'd been last night. But Esther began screaming and crying, so Andrew gave her back to Anna. He apologized and returned with some flowers he'd picked.

"These are for you," he said, crouching down and giving the flowers to Esther. "Please forgive me, I don't know what was wrong with me. It's a good thing you have Anna and Orpah to look after you."

Esther didn't say anything and just stood there with the flowers in one hand.

"I'm not going to take Anna away from you," Andrew said.

Esther glanced up at him and nodded.

"Andrew's nice," she said. "He can come and meet the King."

"The King?" asked Andrew. "Who's that?"

"He's my king," said Esther. "He sent me away, but now he's come back to fetch me."

"What are you talking about?" said Andrew.

But she said no more, in spite of Anna and Orpah both trying to get her to tell them who this king was. Andrew made her promise that the next time she met this king, she would take him or Orpah or Anna with her. Esther nodded and agreed.

"Maybe that's what the children call him," Orpah wondered. But Anna thought it was odd. 'There was something about the way Esther had said "the King."

"The children love Jesus," said Anna. "They don't talk about him like that."

That evening, a great meal was prepared for the whole group and for anybody else who wanted to join them. A family opened their house, others helped out, setting up tables outside, and gathering torches and vases. Mary got somebody to fetch food, and the children helped to collect firewood, build bonfires, and fill the vases with flowers. Anna stood there with Esther, watching Andrew whittle. He sat there with some of Jesus's brothers, cutting away at small, rough pieces of wood, turning them into horses, bears, birds, smooth sticks, and slingshots. Andrew gave Esther a small, round disk with tiny marks etched on it. Anna laughed and asked what it was.

"It's a sun, can't you see?" Andrew said. "It's a sun that'll never set. It'll always shine, even through the darkest of nights." Anna laughed again and shook her head. Andrew was the worst carver of them all, but the children appreciated him. Even Esther seemed to like him now. She hid the figurine under her clothes and smiled at Anna.

Anna went to help sort out the food and put it in bowls and on plates. She didn't notice, but Andrew followed her. He went up to her and put one of his hands in hers.

"Anna," he said, "can I speak with you again?"

"I don't know how to say this," he continued when they'd got away from the others and were walking alone at the edge of Nazareth. The sun was going down, darkness was creeping in on a chill wind.

"I don't know how long all this will last," he said, "how long we'll be together like this." Anna was about to say something, but Andrew spoke first: "No, no, just listen to me, Anna. I'm telling you I don't know when we'll be leaving again. I want to be by your side when the Master summons us. I want you to come too. It's so long since I was with you, Anna, I thought you'd forgotten me. I didn't think there would be a place for somebody like me with you. But now, I don't know. Let me put it like this. There's something about you, you change me into a different person. I don't know quite what it is, but it's all that I can be. I don't normally talk like this, Anna, I don't talk like this to other people. You're something else, when I think about you, when I see you, when I hear you speak. You know when it rains, when the whole sky comes falling down? The next time the rain comes, if you're without me, then I will be the gentle rain falling on you. If you're in the rain, I will be the lucky droplet running off your nose. I will be the water you catch in your hands. I will beat on the roof over where you sleep. I will be the gentle rain that nobody fears going out into. I will be the crowns of the trees, making puddles for the children. I will be the gentle rain that sends you to sleep. And then I will rise up through the dream, like a shaft of rising sunlight."

They stood there in the last remains of the day. Andrew and Anna held hands, they moved closer to each other, they kissed, strands of hair tickling their noses, their cheeks. Anna closed her eyes and thought of the rain, how it could come drifting over the land, drenching everything. She thought of Ruth, who said, "All we need to do is to let them think they've found the way home." She thought it was the other way around, it was Ruth and she who had lost their way. They'd lost their way again and again. And it was only now, in Andrew's hands, that she was really found.

II

Night had fallen over Nazareth. The meal had begun, somebody sang, and in the middle of the song, a very high-pitched voice, Judas's, carried the whole song before everybody else joined in. The song seemed to lift up the tables and the roofs of the houses, even the stones on the ground. After the song died down, Jesus spoke. He spoke of the small and the weak, of his father's kingdom, and justice and courage and the struggle of all those who followed him. He turned to Mary, and she began to sing. After one verse, Judas joined in, their voices intertwined, as they sang about the Lord and his holy kingdom, about everything that had been built, and everything that had been torn down. When their song ended, all that could be heard were the shouts of the children running around.

Anna stood there, watching everybody walking around her, everybody brushing past her, whispering and laughing and shouting. She heard Andrew's words, his soft voice. I will be the rain. The bowl of water you catch in your hands. Orpah was there; she came over and gave her a hug, carrying a candle, a small, burning candle. The rain that sends you to sleep. Men and women and children danced, their arms around each other, they sat on the ground, stood on stools and benches. I will rise up through the dream. Those who were bound in rags took them all off, and in the faint light, their cuts and wounds resembled dark hollows. Like a shaft of sunlight.

They were all there, together.

"Anna," said a soft voice.

"What?" said Anna, turning around, but there was nobody there. Something brushed by her foot; she bent down, and it was Esther. She held on tightly to Anna and said something.

"What's that, Esther?" Anna asked.

"The King," said Esther.

"What?" said Anna, putting her head close to Esther's mouth.

"I want to show you the King," said Esther.

Esther took Anna's hand and dragged her along. Andrew was there, and Anna waved at him. He waved back and said something she couldn't hear. She smiled and could still sense his fingers, his warmth, and his salt taste.

"Come," said Esther, and Anna followed her. They were heading away from the gathering around the meal, and Anna asked where they were going, but Esther didn't answer. It became dark, the torches and the bonfires fell behind them, and Anna suddenly felt afraid. Nobody could see them, where were they heading? She pulled away her hand.

"Esther," she said. "Stop."

"It's here," said Esther.

"I can't see anything," said Anna. "We're too far away from the others. Maybe this can wait until tomorrow, Esther, maybe you could show me this king when it's light?"

"It's here," said Esther. "Can't you see it?"

Anna stared into the darkness ahead of them, and there, she saw it now. There was a deep shadow in the darkness. Esther took her hand again and pulled her closer to it.

It was a cave, and they'd have to crawl inside. Esther let go and disappeared. Anna could hear her crawling into the cave. She followed her, kneeling down and feeling her way forward with her hands.

"Come back, Esther," said Anna. "We can't do this in the dark."

No answer. Everything had suddenly fallen silent. Esther had gone.

"Esther," Anna shouted.

It was too late to turn around, she couldn't leave Esther in there, so she'd have to follow. She crawled, her knees bashing into stones. Then she tried to stand up. "Esther, Esther," she said, first loudly, then more quietly, as she realized to her astonishment that she couldn't reach the ceiling of the cave with her hands. It was no longer a small, dark cave. She held her fingers out ahead of her in the faint glow, and they were covered by a strange color. "Where am I?" she whispered, and Esther answered, as the little girl suddenly appeared, standing by her side.

"We've arrived at the King," said Esther. "He's waiting for us."

"King?" said Anna, kneeling down in front of Esther. "Who is this king, Esther? Maybe we should go back. If something happens, nobody would find us."

"He's my king," said Esther. "He took care of me when I was younger, he protected me. I was his queen, but he sent me away."

Anna had never heard Esther speak like this. The words were streaming out of her mouth. Her hands moved in time with her words. She smiled and seemed happy, so Anna thought that it couldn't be anything threatening or dangerous in there.

"But why the cave, Esther?" Anna asked. "Can't you ask him to

come out? Can't you ask him to come and join the others outside?"
Esther didn't answer. Instead she knelt down and bowed her head.

"Meet the King," she said.

Anna gets up.

At first, she's frightened by the man approaching them. Then she
notices that there's something familiar about him.

"No," she says. "That's impossible."

The man stops and lifts up the lantern he's holding. He's old, his
eyes are a grayish white, and he strokes her face with his hand.

Anna wants to run out of there, but it's impossible to move.

The man smiles slightly, and lowers his lantern, shrouding his
face in darkness.

"I'm blind, and yet I see many things," he says. "What do you see?"

Then he raises his lantern, lighting up his body.

The man in front of Anna makes her quake. He's found her. He's
lured her in here, away from the others.

"What do you see?" he asks again.

"How did you find me?" she asks.

"I never lose anybody," he says. "Answer my question. What do
you see?"

"Reuben," says Anna.

"Good," he says. "Now, look again." Then he lowers his lantern to
the ground, leaving it there for a moment before lifting it back up again.
Again, he stares at Anna, and again he asks her, "What do you see?"

Anna gasps and holds up her hands.

"What do you see?" he asks.

"No," says Anna. "No, dear God, help me, go away, be gone."

"Silence," he says. "Silence and answer my question. What do you
see?"

She tries to stand up straight again while looking at him.

"Baasha," she says.

"Good," he says. "Now, don't be afraid." And again he lowers his
lantern, again he leaves it hanging down by the ground for a moment, before lifting it back up again.

"There," he says. "What do you see now?"

Anna struggles to stay standing. It feels as if something's holding her up, something inside there. She stares at the man in front of her.

"Aaron," she says.

And with those words, she falls down to her knees too. Esther remains silent.

"I'm none of them," says the man standing there. "I'm not that King David who your little girl thought had come back. I'm not your Reuben or Baasha or Aaron either. You'll always think that I'm the one you lie awake waiting for. The one you dream about returning."

"No," says Anna. "I'm not waiting for them, I don't want them back."

"You're not listening," he says. "This isn't about what you want. This is about what you know will happen, what you know will come. We've met each other before, Anna. Do you remember? I was there when Reuben broke your leg. I made that small mark on your leg. I straightened you out, I gave you to Reuben, and Ruth disappeared. Now I'm back. The one you're with now, your master, likes to tell stories. But they're not real. They're not of this world, like mine are."

"My master fights against all evil," says Anna, putting her hands together. She starts praying the way she has been shown, trying to remember the words she and Orpah say with Esther every evening.

"A prayer?" he says. "Not now, I don't want things like that here." Anna feels her hands disobey her, letting go of each other and falling down by her sides.

"You think that I'm evil," he goes on to say. "You think that I'm the ruler himself of flames and demons and all those things you come up with. But I'm not evil. I'm just what stays in the shadows while the light falls elsewhere. So don't come with your prayers, not here. You pray for good, but good and evil are nothing to pray about. You should pray for a story to belong to, one you can believe in, one you can doubt. We're filled with faith and doubt. Did you believe yourself when you believed your master? I say that doubting or giving up is natural. I'd like to have a word with you. Could we be alone for a minute? I'm hardly ever sure, I'm doubting even now. Can you believe that? I give you my word."

Anna tries to look at Esther, but the little girl is lying there prostrate, not making a sound.

"She can't hear us," he says. "She's somewhere else."

"Are you her king?" Anna asks.

"No, I'm nobody's king," he says. "Esther sees the man who looked after her. The man who gave her a place to belong. That was her king. She's nothing to me, she's just here to lure one of you to me."

"She's with us now," says Anna. "She's with Jesus."

The man turns away, the lantern swaying slightly in his hand. He rocks back and forth with his back turned to them, before turning around again and looking down at Anna.

"Your master," he says. "I want to speak with him, that's why you're here, Anna. I want to meet him, your master, your lord, your king. If not him, then somebody close to him. I've tried to meet Simon Peter, but he's difficult to turn. Maybe you could be a good place to start. Imagine what a story it would be if you all lost your faith, if you weren't up to following him. Imagine how such a story will cast shadows and light everywhere. Everything he's trying to say now will vanish. Something else will be created."

He stares at Anna. There's Reuben, there's Baasha, there's Aaron. His face changes.

"What do you want with me?" Anna whispers. "Why am I here? What do you want with us?"

"I'm not going to harm you," he says. "Neither you nor Esther. I won't touch you, but I have a story, and I think I will sow it in you. A tiny seed, he likes to talk about seeds, doesn't he? You'll be the first one to hear this story. I'm going to tell you how it will all end, what will happen."

He smiles, opens his mouth, and even the teeth are there, Baasha's teeth, or are they Reuben's? But then he falls silent.

"What's that?" he says.

Anna can feel it in her hands, getting warmer.

"What's that?" he says again.

Flapping. Anna hears it and looks up. A bird is flying in there, a black bird.

"Andrew," says Anna.

"Andrew?" says the man. "I didn't see any Andrew, where did you hide him, who is he?"

Before Anna can say any more, the bird swoops down toward Anna. Feathers so black. Say "I loved you." With a gaze so empty and distant. Then Anna gets up.

"I loved you," she says.

"What is this?" says the man. "Has some of his light reached in here?"

He comes over to Anna and grabs hold of the bird.

"Do you think you can come here with wings like that?" he says. He closes his hands around the black-winged creature. Anna hears a small snapping sound. Or is it something crackling, a fire catching dry twigs? The man opens his hands, and light comes spilling out of them. Light has come, and it cascades on down to Anna and Esther. It falls between them and the man, and the man steps back. He looks at his lantern, which has gone out. He looks at his hands.

"This means nothing," he says. "I'll return. You can play with your little light as much as you want."

Then he turns and starts walking back farther into the cave, while Anna and Esther sit there by the light. Esther falls right over, and Anna picks her up. She tries to find the way out. The light moves, it makes its presence known. The cave narrows. Anna has to carry Esther on her back, with her arms around her neck, while crawling for both of them. The light burns and vanishes, but she keeps on crawling. She thinks she hears soldiers speaking a foreign language and striking swords on shields. Everything's dark now. Some people shouting, and something rushing in the air, and then it all slams to a stop. Again and again, and it makes her think of animals being driven across a field. She hears banging, as if somebody were hammering nails into wood, and she hears something snap, and there's laughter and a faint voice begging. She hears animals snarling and tearing at something, and she still can't find the way out. Then she hears her name.

Somebody was calling out in the dark, and Anna tried to get up. She put Esther down on the ground, and everything around her vanished. The air seemed so sharp and clear, and high above, the stars sparkled through the night.

"Anna?" somebody shouted, and Anna answered.

"Here," she shouted. "We're here." A number of their group were coming, and Andrew was the first to find her. He put his arms around Anna, picked up Esther, and gave her to Orpah.

"Where have you been?" Andrew asked. "We've been looking for you. What were you doing out here at night?"

Anna was about to answer, but just as she opened her mouth, Orpah said that they should get some rest.

Andrew nodded. "That's right, we must get back to Nazareth." He stroked Anna's cheeks and forehead. Anna tried to speak to him, but he just hushed her. "It's all right," he said. "It's all right. We found you both."

"Where's Jesus?" Anna asked. Orpah was sitting with little Esther, who was asleep and stirring gently beside her.

"She's hot," said Orpah. "I'm going to stay awake and keep an eye on her."

"He's gone off on his own," said Andrew. "He does that now and then. Nobody knows when he'll be back."

"You should sleep," said Orpah. "You both need some rest."

"What were you doing out there?" Andrew asked. He stared at Anna, as if he were searching for a sign, or something that could tell him what had happened.

"It was nothing," said Anna. "She wanted to show me her king, but we got lost in the dark."

"You should have found your way back," said Andrew. "Why did you go so far?"

"Andrew," said Orpah, "let her get some rest, it's night. Get some more water, Esther's so hot."

Andrew got up, but he stood there, looking at Anna, then at Esther, and then back at Anna again. It was quiet; most people were sleeping. The meal had finished a long while ago, and the town was resting. An animal plodded past next to them, making Anna turn and stare out into the darkness. Something moved just beyond them, maybe a rat looking for scraps of food. Maybe a smaller animal digging in the sand.

Anna lay there throughout the night, listening to the world in darkness. Every time she closed her eyes, she heard the sounds from the cave, cold and raw, trying to piece together a story she didn't want to hear. She lay there awake until a glint of day returned, until the light spread imperceptibly across the sky.

Esther crept over to Anna and lay next to her. The girl wasn't too warm anymore; she smiled and laughed when Anna asked her about her king. Esther didn't know what she was talking about. When Anna took hold of her little body and shook it, Esther began to cry, and Orpah lifted her up. "It's all right, Anna's just tired, it's all right, my little girl."

Jesus returned. He was thinner, but he no longer seemed tired or exhausted. Anna thought there was something else too, something about him that had changed but that she couldn't put into words. He went over to Anna, kissed her on the head, and whispered to her, "I'll tell you, not here, but I'll tell you."

Later that day, in the shade of some trees, and with buzzing from the flowers around them, Jesus sat down with Anna. Andrew hadn't asked what was going on, he'd just said that he'd wait, that he'd be there when she came back.

"I know you're wondering," said Jesus, "why Esther doesn't remember anything, but you remember everything. Evil is reaching out for me. It'll tear some of you away from this world, but it won't be able to keep you."

"What was he?" asked Anna.

"He'll come to you in dreams, but he can't touch you. He'll try to tell you a story, but you'll believe in our story. You'll remember him, but you'll remember me too, Anna. Call for me if he comes to you again."

"It was Andrew," said Anna. "It was Andrew who came."

Jesus fell silent. He sat still, and his eyes were dark and warm.

"A beacon has been lit," he said, "for all love that's lost."

Anna closed her eyes and lowered her head. Everything that had gone, everything that was left. She saw Andrew, she saw Ruth. She saw Orpah, she saw Esther. She was back in her small house in Sychar, she was back by Jacob's Well. It was the bird it started with, the black bird.

"All I can remember is Jesus, all I can remember is opening my eyes, and there was Jesus by the well."

This is how Anna wishes to tell the story the morning she dies under the palms at Ashkelon surrounded by her nearest and dearest. Andrew has been gone for a long time. Anna's become old, older than many of the others from the group. She saw what they did to Andrew, and she's heard rumors and been told stories of how others have died. She held some of them in her own arms. She took Andrew down from the cross and buried him.

Now it's her turn. Orpah and Esther are there with her. Barely a year will pass before Orpah passes away too. Esther, no longer a child, will sit by both Anna's and Orpah's beds. She'll never mention the King again, she never speaks of the night when she and Anna disappeared. Esther's story begins when she finds Anna, and Esther's story ends when Orpah dies. A disciple says that once, a short time after this, he saw a woman with the same devil's mark as Anna's little Esther when he was in Jerusalem. She was going around asking for somebody called David, but he's not sure, he's so old now.

There are no other traces. Esther was with Anna, sitting under the palm trees in Ashkelon, listening to Anna telling her story, while Anna holds her hand and Orpah's hand, telling them that she misses Andrew.

"I miss him so much," she says.

Andrew was always there. Not as a mark on her body like Aaron or Reuben. He wasn't a name threatening her in the coming evening dark. Andrew stayed there, just like light doesn't go out and only goes on rumbling around the world, until one day it comes creeping back, beneath a door, through a curtain, stroking the skin with the touch of gentle fingers.

6 ║ WE ARE ALONE, YOU ARE HERE

I

"I know you're here," he says softly. "I'm hardly ever alone, am I?" His fingers answer him, stroking his cheeks, his chin, before wrapping themselves around his warm neck. "I've got a story for you," he says. "Do you want to hear it?" The fingers crawl up from his neck, up over his chin, and start pulling at his lips. "That's what I thought," says Peter. "That's what I thought." The fingers creep down, the hand wrapping itself around his neck again, and Peter tries to see through the dark. A hyena howls; it's the sound of the cold night. "Hush," says Peter. "We must be quiet, so quiet." He puts one hand on top of the other, and for a few seconds he doesn't know if he's standing up or if he's falling, if the night means he'll keep falling until he's surrounded by the light of day again.

"There was a man," he whispers, "whose whole body was on fire. Every day he woke with the flames burning, every night he went to bed with the flames. He wondered what he should use the flames for. What could this fire do? He became a fisherman, but he scared all the fish away. The other fishermen didn't want to sit in the boat with him. So he started building houses, but the houses collapsed, the flames having made them so fragile. He made one last attempt, trying to grow fruit and vegetables and sell them in the markets at Capernaum and Gennesaret, sometimes even as far away as Tiberias. But the food shriveled up; it was all dry and scorched. When the city guards saw what he was trying to sell, they beat him and chased him away. He came back the next day, and then they chopped off his right hand. But no blood came from the stump, only smoke. The smoke came pouring out of his arm, the soldiers' eyes filled with tears, and he got away. The man sought shelter in the mountains, where he joined other men who'd gone seeking shelter. They saw his flames, they saw the smoke coming out of him, and they asked him to join them in their struggle against the occupiers. They gave him a sword, they gave him a spear, and they took him with them into battle. The battle came, and the Romans cut them down, every single one of them. The man was left lying in the grass, and he saw the flames go out, everything turning to smoke. When the children found him later that day, the man was just a charred piece of coal, like wood burned away beneath the sun.

"What did you think of that story?" Peter whispered.

The fingers let go of his neck, hanging poised in the air in front of him.

"You change it every night," a voice says from behind him, and Peter turns around, but there's only night there too.

"Do you really remember what happened to Father?" the voice says.

"Be silent," says Peter. "You have no business following me."

Somebody reaches out a hand and hesitantly grabs Peter's clothing.

"I'm keeping an eye on you so you don't get lost," says Andrew, trying to hold on to his brother. Peter takes his hand and pushes it away.

"Are there others here? Has anybody come with you?" he asks. Andrew calls him a fool and tells him all the others are sleeping.

"It'll soon be morning," says Andrew. "Can you see it?" Peter turns around but can see only the same darkness everywhere. "I can feel it," says Andrew. "It's like a silent rumbling."

Peter's cold. "It's still night," he says. He hears Andrew breathing, a faint sound of something warm.

"Have you spoken with him about it?" Andrew asks. Peter crouches down. His hands pat the ground. His skin is dry, the grass is dry, the soil is hard and the stones cold. Once he believed that water could change everything.

"Look," says Andrew, and Peter looks around him. A faint glint far away, as if something were opening up, but it's still night where they are.

"Did you get some sleep?" Andrew asks, and Peter can hear him rubbing his hands together.

"Sleep?" says Peter. "Who gets any sleep?" Andrew stays quiet for a moment, and when he starts to say something about the Lord, Peter interrupts him. "It's only a matter of time," says Peter. "He can't stop them. They're going to hang him. They're going to hang us all, none of us will be buried, we'll be fed to the dogs."

"He's the Lord," says Andrew. "If anything like that were to happen, then the Lord will be there with us." Peter holds his head in his hands, feeling his sticky hair and his oily skin. His hands tremble.

"You saw what happened today," he says. "Even our own people are afraid, and they reject us."

"Simon," says Andrew, "we're all afraid, but we believe. We know what the faithless occupiers might do to us, but we can't judge those who have so little and would stand to lose everything."

"I'm not judging them," says Peter. He gets up and takes a step toward Andrew's silhouette.

"We must believe," says Andrew.

"I believe," says Peter, "but we know what's coming."

"We must believe, Simon," Andrew says again.

Peter tries to see Andrew's face in the dark, but there's something else there in front of him, and Peter remembers the stranger who came toward them earlier, in the daylight, out of the cave tombs, with the damp, rotten air stuck to his skin like soil. With no clothes, and with his body covered in a pattern of cuts, cracks, lesions, and swellings. His hands hanging by his sides, two eyes like something dragged up from the bottom of the sea. Their party stopped; Peter took a step toward Jesus and stood in front of him. The thing made a noise, like stones grinding against stones in a dark sack. They all stood there, staring at the monster. People in the village had told them that he was a good husband and a good father, until his wife and children died of an illness, and he was infected too. Then he became possessed and started living in the cave tombs where the remains of his family lay.

Jesus put his hand on Peter, pushed him aside, and stepped forward. The stranger stayed quiet, he smiled, his teeth black and yellow, and then out of his mouth came words, words none of them had heard before. Jesus took another step closer, and the man speaking changed his voice, starting to whisper, but Jesus didn't stop.

"You know who I am, don't you?" said Jesus. "You know that I'm not here to judge you." The creature fell silent.

"Come, step forward," said Jesus, turning to Peter and the others. He said the names of three of his followers who had open wounds that were covered up.

"Come and show yourselves," said Jesus. The three of them came up to him. Jesus asked them to take off their dressings and show their wounds.

"See," said Jesus. "These people are with us, they are us."

The thing stared at the three who had undressed, at their wounds, at the mouth of one of the women, whom Peter had never heard speak. Her lips had gone, and her teeth were darker than the gums around them.

Several of the people who lived in the area and had come to watch began to talk and shout. Jesus lay his hands on one of the people who had got undressed.

"They're not unclean, and we're not clean," said Jesus, still facing the stranger in front of them. "They're us, and I ask you: join us."

Jesus called out: "To all the things they've put on you, I say be gone." With his hands raised to the sky and his eyes rolled back, he said the last words: "Leave him."

And the creature fell to his knees, reaching out his arms and feeling his way along the ground. The crowd's talking subsided, and no shouting could be heard anymore.

Jesus turned toward Peter and Thomas. "Help him," he said, and they went up to the man, took him by the arms, and held him between them. His skin was cold, he stank of something rotten, a sickening, sweet smell. They could hear him whispering. A slight tremble shook his body, but everything that had seemed so great and evil was now minuscule and shattered.

Jesus turned to all the others gathered there. He raised up his hands and said, "Demons have occupied this land, they're the army of darkness. A legion of them is moving across the land, through the valleys, blowing across mountains, dragging us out of our homes, throwing us to the ground, and hanging us up with nails on wood. This army of darkness is hunting us down and spreading fear, we're pushing each other away. We're full of the evil of their sharp swords and spears. Their evil fills us until we can't take any more, until we carry out the most abominable acts. Their darkness makes its abode in us, their evil becomes our evil. But remember the words of Isaiah: my father, the Lord, will be a strength to the needy in distress, a refuge from the storm, a shadow from the heat. The breath of an aggressor is like a storm against a wall, like heat in a drought-stricken land. That was what the prophet Isaiah said, and I say to you, I will drive out those demons. I say to you, I will push them out, I will throw them into the abyss."

When Jesus had finished speaking, he stood in front of the man being carried between Peter and Thomas. He put his hands on him, leaned forward, and whispered in his ear.

"Master," said Peter, nodding his head toward a group of elder men approaching. Jesus turned around, held up his hand, and told the men to wait. He asked some other followers to come and help the man from the caves. They carried him away, gave him something to put around his body and something to drink. Jesus signaled that he was ready. The group of old men went over to him. They greeted Jesus and stared at him, before one of the eldest went closer and spoke to him quietly so that only Jesus could hear.

"What do you want from the Lord?" said Peter, interrupting. Jesus looked over at Peter.

"They're asking us to leave," he said. Peter turned to the man talking to Jesus. His head was like the bark of a withered tree; a tattered, white beard covered his face.

"We've lost so much," the man said. "We have nothing left. I beg you to leave. If the occupying forces were to come here, if they heard what had been said, they'd wipe us out."

Peter said nothing. He turned to Jesus. Jesus nodded and said yes. He put his hand over his mouth, nodded again, and said they'd leave as soon as possible.

The glimmer of light at the end of the world spreads out. Andrew looks at the golden tree trunks around them. Peter watches his brother emerge from the night. His short, black hair, his nose long and bent at the bridge, the shadow of his beard around his face, and his eyes glistening.

"The soldiers will be keeping watch over everything and every-body until Passover," says Peter. "There will be guards at the Temple." Andrew looks toward Peter. The light has returned, it's faint, so faint, but the night has passed, and now comes the day. The grass and the trees about them regain their shapes and their colors.

Andrew goes over to Peter. He's about to say something, but then he just shakes his head and puts his arms around his brother.

Several days later, while the group of followers are settling down at the edge of a few small houses outside Caesarea Philippi, Peter no-tices Judas heading off to sit alone on the ground by a group of trees. Mary's saying how she marvels at the fact all spiders have eight legs, and while Jesus remains quiet, John starts to praise the majestic web of those eight-legged creatures that can capture even the fastest of small insects. Peter excuses himself, takes the remnants of a loaf of bread, and goes over to Judas.

Judas stares up at him. His eyes are red, his face is wet, and he smells.

"I brought some bread," says Peter, sitting down on the grass next to him.

"I'm tired," Judas whispers. "I don't know if I have the strength anymore."

"It's all right," says Peter. "We can rest now."

"No, it's better when we're on the move," Judas whispers. "It's when we sit still, when we sleep, that it's worse."

"What are you talking about?" Peter asks him, trying to meet Judas's eyes.

"They're here," Judas whispers. "They're waiting for us." Peter opens his mouth to say something, but he closes it again and gives the bread to Judas.

"Here," he says. "Have something to eat."

Judas takes hold of the bread, and at that very moment, they hear Jesus speak: "How are you doing, Judas?"

"He's ill," says Peter. Jesus nods, having come over to them. He sits down on the grass, his feet together.

"I can see my father, I can see my brother, they're here," says Judas, his voice still like a whisper. "They're waiting for us."

"You've told me about your brother," says Jesus.

"Yes," says Judas.

"And about your father," says Jesus. Judas nods. "It was in a valley not far from where we're sitting now, wasn't it?" Jesus asks. "Your father pointed out your brother's body when ordered to do so by the soldiers, and then they hanged your father. You told me that you wanted to go out at night and take him down so you could bury them both, but your mother made you stay at home. You promised your mother to fight for your people, but not to die like your brother and father."

Judas cries. He dries his face, spits and coughs, and looks up at the sky.

"I can see them," he says. "They're here among us. They've rotted, and there are nails sticking out of my father."

"This is your story," says Jesus. "Everybody here has their own story, this whole country does. It's our story. But we're in the light of the Lord, our father now. We grow with new stories, we're not alone anymore."

"They're here," says Judas. "I can see them."

"It's not them," says Jesus, cutting him off. "It's not them you see."

But Judas carries on. "They want to cut us down, all of us," he says. Jesus leans forward to put his hands on Judas's hands.

"Listen," he says. "I'm here with you. Don't be afraid for your life. Who among us can add a cubit to his life? Your father in heaven knows all that you need. Seek out the Kingdom of God, and his justice, and you will have all you need." Then Jesus lifts up his hands and passes them over Judas's face. The sun above them is going down as they sit in the shade of the trees.

"Who do people say the Son of man is?" Jesus asks.

Judas coughs before he answers: "Some say John the Baptist, others say Elias, while still others say Jeremiah or one of the other prophets."

Jesus nods, his gaze still fixed on Judas. "And what about you?" Jesus asks. "Who do you say that I am?" The insects buzz in the trees, children shout from the houses some distance away, a woman calls to a man.

Peter lays his hands on Judas's shoulders, and together they say, "You are the Messiah, the Son of the living God."

Night falls, darkness envelops them. Peter walks between the trees, his hands brushing past the trunks, and after a while he stops. He hears somebody following him. He sits down in the dark. The fingers crawl up his chest, stopping at his collarbone.

"Not now," says Peter. "I don't have any stories for you now."

"Simon," a voice says from behind him.

"I'm here," says Peter. "Did I wake you?" Andrew's breath comes to him, a warm smell reminding him of when they slept together, side by side, as children.

"I was awake," says Andrew. "I was waiting."

Peter hears Andrew sit down. He raises his head, trying to see the sky between the tops of the trees.

"I heard you telling the stories about Father," says Andrew.

"I want to be alone," Peter tells him.

"You know, I can't remember Father anymore," says Andrew. "I can only remember what he looked like when we found him."

Peter gets up; he tries to walk to where he thinks Andrew's sitting, fumbling his way through the dark.

"Philip told me about two of his uncles and an aunt who were taken," says Andrew. "Mary's father was taken too, while he was looking for his neighbor. There are even more, there are so many who've been affected. We're not the only ones."

Peter walks through the darkness, waving his arms in front of him, hitting some twigs. "Be quiet," he says. "Go away, I don't want to hear these stories."

When he stops, Andrew's behind him, still talking: "You're not sleeping anymore, Simon, you look tired. I beg you, please put Father behind you and everything you remember about him."

Peter shakes his head, but they're in the dark, and Andrew can't see anything.

"Listen to me," says Andrew. "You need some rest, we need you, we're together, there are many of us, we're not the only ones here."

"We're not the only ones," says Peter, "but we're almost alone."

"We're never alone," says Andrew. "We're together, we always have been. We'll never give up, we'll never disappear."

"Leave me in peace," says Peter.

"It's no use, Simon," says Andrew. "You have to let go of Father, you have to let go of everything that happened."

When Andrew goes, Peter feels something move next to his feet. He bends down, catches it, and picks it up. It has several legs, it's hard, it's small, it seems fragile and unbreakable at the same time. He holds it up to his ear, and a faint sound comes from it. Is it the mouth or all the moving parts that are speaking to him? Is it a special language coming from inside the creature, or is it the faint clattering of its legs? Peter lets it go, and it vanishes at once. His fingers are warm, and he locks them together.

"Our Father in heaven," he whispers. "Your kingdom come, your will be done, on earth as it is in heaven." His fingers let go of each other and come up toward his face. They wrap around his neck, pressing warmly against his beard, against his skin and the pulse beneath.

"There was a man," Peter whispers, "whom nobody could understand when he spoke. The words he said were clear and plain, but when they came out, they were so delicate that they snapped. He worked with his hands, first as a fisherman, then as a builder. One day, he decided to sell the food he grew, and he went to the markets in the area. People bought what he sold, he waved his hands and made faces to show how good his wares were and how much they cost. One day, there was a person who'd stolen money from a merchant, and the guards in the marketplace suspected the man whom nobody could understand when he spoke. The guards tried to talk with him, but the words that came out were incomprehensible to them. They told him to speak clearly, but he went on the same way, so they held him still while they looked for the stolen money. The man began to shout, and people crowded around. The guards were now holding him so hard around the throat that something was crushed inside. They couldn't find the stolen money, and they let the man go, but now the man could no longer make a sound when he opened his mouth. His throat grated every time he swallowed, and the skin around it took on a dark yellow color. He went home to his house, and over the following days, everything he'd grown rotted. He left his house and went up into the mountains, where he met people who pretended to hear the words that wouldn't come out of him. They fed him, they armed him, and he joined them to fight against the occupying powers. When they were all cut down, one by one, the man whom nobody could understand when he spoke was left standing alone against the military power of their enemies. He dropped his weapons and opened his mouth, but nothing came out. The soldiers approached the man, and he knew what they'd do if he couldn't say the right words to them. So he picked up his weapons again and ran toward them.

"The children found all the bodies later. The man lay at the bottom of the heap, and when his mouth suddenly opened, words ran out that only those children could understand.

"Just one story," says Peter, with fingers in front of his mouth. "There's nothing else in there." The fingers descend, wrapping themselves around his neck again. Peter sits there on the ground. Eventually the fingers lose their grip, and he falls asleep against a tree.

He wakes up later in the same darkness and starts to crawl around on the ground, before sitting down to wait. When the first light comes, he tries to find his way back to the others again.

They wander about along the river Jordan, and one night, Peter falls asleep and dreams about singing fish, and about himself and his brother sailing in a boat across the water. They carry on through Judea until they eventually end up in mighty Jerusalem.

Judas has become thinner, his hair hanging down in front of his face, but he smiles when Peter talks to him.

Peter lies down next to Andrew every evening and stays there, lying awake throughout the night. He can hear Andrew lying awake too, falling asleep only in the early hours of the morning.

They spread out. Some fetch food, others gather information about the soldiers and the guards and the schedules at the Temple. Peter stays resting with Jesus. He tries to sleep, but his head is gently throbbing, and he tries to drink the water. Eventually, he falls asleep and dreams of birds talking and dogs wandering around a dead forest. When he wakes up, he's thirsty.

When evening comes, they gather together to eat. They don't invite any strangers to eat with them. They're cautious now, as they don't want to attract any attention. The city is under a strict watch, with soldiers and guards everywhere. While they eat, they talk quietly about what they've seen in Jerusalem, who they've met. Some of them who've been inside the Temple say that it's filled with merchants and Roman decorations. The chatter gradually picks up, with several people speaking at the same time. Some people sit on the floor, dipping pieces of bread in olive oil and sprinkling salt on top.

A boy begins to hum a lullaby softly, and two women sing along with him. Andrew leans back next to Peter and puts his arm behind his big brother's shoulders. Peter closes his eyes and pictures Andrew and himself on the beach, the water like a cold blanket around their ankles. Shells on their nails, on their skin, as if they'd come back from a magical world and these were the remains of a shining skin they'd now stripped off.

When he opens his eyes, he sees Thomas and John sitting on one side of Jesus, with Mary sitting on the other side. They all appear to be speaking at the same time, while Jesus sits there quietly, staring at Peter. Peter stares back. Thomas, John, and Mary are talking, but Jesus is sitting peacefully between them, and he's looking at Peter. Then Peter can feel something moving. He looks down in his lap, and it's his fingers. They lift up, one by one, first on one hand, and then on the other. Peter looks up at Jesus, and Jesus is still staring at him. Jesus opens his mouth, says something, and Thomas and John stop talking, Mary stops talking.

"I'm in you," he says. "I'll never leave you, I hear your story. Even if it's your own story, it's ours, it's the story of our land and our people."

"Master," says Mary, "I'm not sure I understand."

Jesus takes his eyes off Peter and looks up at Mary. "Sorry," he says. "I made a mistake, I was elsewhere." Then he starts speaking with them again, and Peter is left sitting there with his hands in his lap, feeling a strange warmth from his fingers.

"You're with us, you're with me," he whispers.

Andrew's left his side and is with Anna now. She gives his brother strength, he's sure of that; Andrew's changed since they found each other. Peter gets up and makes his way between the others until he comes to Judas, and Judas smiles. He takes one of Peter's hands, and Judas's fingers are warm too. Somebody claps their hands, everybody falls silent, and Judas suddenly starts singing. He has the most beautiful voice, as high as a bird's song, and then everybody joins in. Peter can hear his own voice, and Andrew's, the voices swimming together in the room. Judas's voice is so high, it's as if it soared above the others, as if it were the only voice that could still sing songs the way they all learned to sing them.

He doesn't know where he is. He was standing in the middle of all of them. He was singing, holding hands, and then he was out in the night, where everything is silent and full of noises at the same time. He must have walked out of the city, beyond the city walls, as there are trees and bushes, and a faint smell of flowers.

Peter sits down, his fingers still filled with a peculiar warmth. Once again he hears a hyena howling, he remembers the last few days, and his fingers twitch. They begin to move, crawling up his stomach, up his chest, his neck, pulling at his lips. He sits there in the dark, feeling the fingers open his mouth and crawl in. They enter his mouth, pushing their way down his throat, and he lifts them back out.

"It's you, Master," says Peter, but nobody answers. "I know it's you, Master, I'll tell you a story.

"There was a man who could see through everything," Peter whispers. "He found the fish in the sea because he could see through the water where they swam. But when he pulled the fish up, he could see through them too, and he said it wasn't right to take their lives. He began building houses, but when they were finished and other people were living in them, he could see through the houses and said it wasn't right that people like that should live in his houses. Then he started to grow fruit and vegetables to sell at the market in Bethsaida. He sold them to everybody, and everybody bought them from him, as he could see right through them and knew what kind of food people needed. But one day, some soldiers came who'd been drinking the evening before, and they started bothering the man. He told them to go away and not to bother an honest man. Then one of the guards grabbed him and called him a thief. They punched and kicked him and trampled the food he was selling, they dragged him out of the city and threw him at the side of the road. The man went up to the mountains, where he met people who believed in a different world. He joined them in their struggle against the occupiers, and when they were cut down, one by one, he could see through them all, and he could see that they were all the same, even the enemies, there was no difference between them. So he dropped his weapon and let himself be cut down.

"Two children found him lying in one of the valleys not far from Bethsaida. The youngest child didn't recognize him at first, but the eldest saw that it was their father. They dragged him away and buried him not far from where he fell."

The fingers are warm against his neck.

"There's nothing they can't kill," says Peter.

He hears the hyena again, and it doesn't sound like a cry or a howl anymore, it sounds like laughter.

They all feel heavy when they wake up in the morning. There's a smell of rot, and the sky outside is gray. Peter gets up and wipes drool from his face. Next to him, Andrew and Mary are helping two young boys up on their feet. The boys say sorry and ask for forgiveness, but Andrew just ruffles their hair and tells them to stop it, go outside and get some fresh air. Judas has fetched some water and is washing it over the floor. Jesus is nowhere to be seen. It's cool inside, but Peter's sweating. He presses his fingers against his stomach. They're cold.

"Come on, brother," says Andrew, putting his hand around him. "We've got to tidy up, it's a sorry sight in here. You're a bit of a sorry sight too, go and get washed."

After they've tidied up and helped each other to wash their faces and hands, they all sit down on benches or on the floor. Thomas tries to speak but is silenced. John wants somebody to go into the city with him to see what's happening at Passover, but Peter asks them to stay. Mary agrees, nobody gets up, and so they sit there. It's only when Peter slowly gets up to find some water to drink that Jesus appears among them. Peter has no idea where the Lord appeared from, which room or door he came from.

"Brothers and sisters," says Jesus, "we're going up to the Temple."

Peter closes his eyes, and when he opens them, he meets Andrew's gaze. His brother's standing there with his arms around Anna, and he seems younger now, as if the last few days and hours hadn't happened, as if time weren't added to his age but subtracted from it, and it's a very youthful Andrew standing there now, looking at his big brother. Peter turns toward Jesus.

"Master," he says, "we stand together, if something should happen, we'll be there. But there are guards and soldiers, they'll seize us immediately."

Jesus says, "I don't know what will happen." And then more quietly: "I don't know." And then louder: "Believe in God and believe in me."

"Listen to our Master," says Thomas, but his voice is faint, and he coughs. "Sorry, sorry," he says. Mary tells everybody to get ready, and they start to stir, hugging and kissing each other, praising the Lord.

Peter goes over to Andrew and Anna. He puts his hands around his brother and pulls him close.

"Andrew," he whispers, "if we get separated, we'll meet in Capernaum." Peter looks at him, waiting for a sign that he's got the message. Andrew nods, and he and Anna leave Peter and head out to the children playing outside. Peter stands there while everybody around him darts back and forth, their voices like insects in a jar. Jesus stands next to Peter and puts his hands on his shoulders.

"I know you follow me, Simon Peter," he says, "but this time you must follow the others if they take me."

Peter opens his mouth, but Jesus puts a hand over his lips.

"I want to be there with you," says Peter.

"No," says Jesus. "If anybody's there with me, it can't be you. Nobody should be there with me."

Jesus leans forward and kisses Peter on the cheek. He kisses Peter and walks away from him to Mary. He says something in her ear. Mary shakes her head and is about to speak, but Jesus puts his fingers over her mouth, leans forward to kiss her, and walks on, this time to Thomas. Then Mary looks at Peter, but Peter turns away, walks toward the doorway, goes out, and stands there just outside, beneath a gray sky that looks like a veil hanging over the world.

"Lord," he says, but he has no more words, so he says "Lord" again, and once again: "Lord." Others push behind him, and everybody comes outside. They crowd around, talking softly, whispering to each other, before they suddenly fall silent and stand still as Jesus steps out from the crowd. He walks among them, seeming tired, worn out. Peter doesn't know what, but something's different. Jesus doesn't stop, he walks between them, and they follow him up toward the Temple Mount and toward the Temple.

II

"What?" says Peter. "Say that again." John is sitting next to him, trying to explain how he saw Thomas and Andrew push and pull them along down from the Temple Mount and out among all the other people.

"Where are they now?" asks Peter.

John shakes his head. "Aren't you listening to what I'm saying? Don't you get it? We scattered, nobody knows where anybody is."

Matthew comes running into the stable, and Peter spins around, holding his knife up in front of him.

"It's me," says Matthew. "Peter, it's me."

"I know it's you," says Peter. "Where are the others?"

"It's Jesus, Philip, and Judas," says Matthew, breathing heavily, with sweat running down from his hair and through his beard.

"Philip and Judas?" says John.

"Just the three of them?" says Peter, and Matthew nods. Peter closes his eyes and leans back against a beam. They're hiding in a small stable, and the dry air in there makes him cough. His clothes are torn, and one of his feet hurts.

"I've got to find out what's happened to them," says Peter, spitting and wiping his mouth. Matthew and John look at him.

"There are soldiers everywhere," says John. "You can't go out there now, we'll have to wait until darkness, we've got to get out of the city."

Peter gets up to feel his foot. He can walk, but it will be difficult to run.

"Wait here," he says, and John and Matthew sit there in the hay, staring at the tall, bearded man as he leaves them.

There are people everywhere, and where there aren't any people, there are animals and walls and openings in walls and the clatter of the soldiers' armor and weapons. Peter tries to follow the flow of the crowd, but there are currents moving in different directions: one carries him along for a time, and then another carries him along again, and eventually he breaks free and walks toward the steps up to the Temple Mount, where he can see several soldiers gathered. Peter goes up to two soldiers sitting on the ground, with their helmets down next to them. He asks what's happening, and the soldiers look at him without saying anything.

"Rebels in the Temple," one of the soldiers mutters, waving his hand at Peter. "Move along." Peter stands there. The other soldier, who hasn't said anything yet, starts shaking his head.

"They all look the same to me," he says. "We could've chosen anybody, whoever they say we should take." He looks around him, but Peter's the only one listening to him.

"Who have you taken?" Peter asks.

"A rebel or a Jew," says the soldier. "Or two or more, I can't tell the difference. A few days ago, we cut down a few of them planning to storm the Temple. We surprised them while they were trying to sneak in at night. They put up a fight, quite a lively one. We hanged some of them. If it was up to me, I'd have let them tear down the whole place on top of themselves."

"Shut up," says the other soldier. "Nobody's listening to you. Who the hell are you talking to?"

"These things happen, you know, and what about you?" says the soldier, who just keeps on talking. "Have you got anybody to talk to?"

Peter stands there, looking at the man sitting in front of him. The soldier is talking out loud to himself. His hands are large and coarse, his head is shaved bare, and his eyes are small and pale.

"When are they going to be crucified?" Peter asks, unable to recognize his own voice. He needs water, where can he find water?

The soldier coughs and laughs simultaneously. "There's only one left to string up," he says.

"Shut up," says the other soldier again, who's now started staring at Peter.

"They're on their way," the chatty one goes on. "An example for you lot during this festival of yours, what is it you call it? Passing over or something?"

"Shut up," says the other soldier for the third time. "I can't stand listening to you."

"I don't care," says the soldier.

Peter turns to go, leaving while the soldier behind him is still talking out loud to himself. He pushes his way past people, trips over a goat, gets up again, and walks into a man who's holding a cockerel tightly in his hands and tells him to move. Peter steps to the side and tries to see how he can get back to the stable. He tries to spot somebody he knows, someone from their own group. He goes into a gateway, where the walls let off a cold odor.

"Lord," he says, there's that word again, he hasn't got any other words. He spits and kicks sand over the spittle. Two soldiers suddenly appear, calling him a pig, a slob, telling him to clean it up. Before he can say anything, they strike him in the throat and between the shoulders and shove him to the ground. They spit on him and move off. Peter gets up and brings his hand to his throat. It's difficult to breathe, but he doesn't dare to spit, he doesn't dare to cough. He lowers his head and tries to move along as calmly as possible.

John and Matthew greet him with an embrace. They sit together in the cramped stable and see the light fall outside. Peter holds his fingers up in front of him, they're ten cold bones with flesh and blood and skin around them, and he lowers his hands to whisper a prayer, but he can't say it like it should be said, and he tells the others that it's time to go.

"We've got to get out of here," he says.

They walk out of Jerusalem, down to the Well of En-Rogel, and sneak through the Valley of Hinnom. Peter's foot hurts, so Matthew props him up. They walk around the city walls until they get onto the road that leads all the way up to Caesarea. They turn back in the evening, but the light has gone, and the night is getting darker and darker. There's nobody to be seen, only the glow of torches on the city walls, and the outlines of soldiers at the entrance. Matthew mumbles something about going back, but he's cut off by the sound of dogs, and he starts to cry. He punches himself in the face, and Peter has to help him.

"We can't go there," says Peter. "The soldiers are there, the dogs are already there, it's too late, it's over." Matthew tries to break free from Peter, but Peter holds on to him tightly. "We've got to get out of here," he says.

The night envelops them, and they stop to rest only when daylight comes.

They walk all the way up through Samaria until they get to Capernaum and the Sea of Galilee.

Some arrived before them, others arrive later, and they all stay there.

Peter finds Andrew, who holds out his arms, and Peter embraces him.

"You came back," says Andrew. "It's the water, it calls out to us."

Peter tries to get Andrew to tell him what he saw, what he's heard, but Andrew just wants to hold on to him.

"Everything's been torn away from us, our dreams too," Andrew whispers to him one evening.

They all live in the same house. They tell each other stories about what happened in the Temple, how every one of them got away. Some women say they saw an angel who spoke to them as they walked through the night. One of them, with open sores, says that he has new wounds in his hands and around his ankles, and that he felt a pain in his legs. Thomas says that Jesus told him the secrets of his kingdom. Peter doesn't listen to them.

He only sits up and leans forward slightly when one of them starts telling of Judas's and Philip's death.

"Did you see it?" he asks. One of the ones with open sores tells him that the soldiers let him go, as they didn't want to be near him or talk to him. He found the remains of the bodies of both Judas and Philip. They'd been buried under stones that dogs had removed before they started eating their flesh. John tells them to be quiet and gathers everybody together in prayer where they're sitting, and they pray to the Lord.

It's evening, the daylight is fading, and something closes up above them where they're sitting to eat. They light oil lamps, it turns colder, but Peter stays outside, sitting on the ground, leaning against the wall, not saying anything. When Andrew and Anna put out bread and dried fish for him, he won't eat it. His hands are pale, and the others try to get him to taste the food, to get up, to say something. But only when it's time to go to bed for the night does Peter get up and say, "I'm going out to fish."

The water's black, but it glimmers. The sky sparkles. The slight rocking and the sound of the water lapping against the boat. As they set out from land, Andrew murmured next to him, "All we have is the water, it never changes."

They draw up the net, cast it back out, and draw it up again. Peter tries to move his fingers, but they're wet and cold, he can't feel them, so he leaves it. Every time the warmth comes back to his fingers, he draws in the net and casts it out.

They sit there the whole night, nobody saying anything, and they don't catch anything either.

Day breaks, and they start to row back to shore. Peter is sitting astern. He can't feel his fingers anymore, they're not dirty or white, they've taken on another color, and when he knocks his hand against the side of the boat, a soft thud is all that can be heard. He leans out over the water, he closes and opens his eyes, but nothing happens. The others turn toward him. Andrew opens his mouth to say something, but Peter can't hear him. He sees Andrew's open mouth, the eyes of the others, dark and white in the pale light of the morning. He follows their eyes and looks down at his hands. His fingers shine out at him. They shine as they crawl up his stomach, across his chest, and up his neck, resting on his mouth. Peter feels an immense warmth on his lips, on his teeth, on his tongue. The fingers caress his face; a cold fire spreads across his body.

The others in the boat speak out loud now, and their voices reach him.

"He's glowing," says one of them. "He's burning."

"Forgive me, Lord," Peter whispers. "I have a story, if you want to hear it." His fingers cut him off, covering his lips again. "No, Lord," says Peter. "I have a story, I have several, Master, don't you want to hear them?" He feels the tears running down his cheeks and into his beard, and there's something cold tearing itself out of him. "We're alone," says Peter, but his fingers carry on, stroking him before they lock together to lie in his lap like a warm jar of embers. "No more," Peter prays. "No more will you be with us. You are with us, we are alone, no more, you are with us."

The others in the boat begin saying it together, they hear Peter's words, they see how he glows, and they repeat after him: "You are with us, no more, we are alone. No more, you are with us, no more. You are with us, no more, we are alone."

7 ||| A GLIMMER OF LIGHT

Come to me and listen. I'm blind, and yet I see many things. I'm what stays in the shadows while the light falls elsewhere. Don't come with your prayers, not here. You pray for good, but good and evil are nothing to pray about. You should pray for a story to belong to, one you can believe in, one you can doubt.

Nadab is among you. You don't trust him. You don't know what's wrong with him. You don't know what he's doing, but listen to me, and I'll tell you Nadab's story.

He was hungry, he stole a loaf of bread, he was a thief.

He wouldn't admit guilt, he put up a fight, he was a rebel.

He fled, he went out into the night, he was nothing.

"Catch that thief, punish that damned rebel," they yelled. But the guards looking for him said they couldn't see anything, it was too dark. Nadab was already far, far away. And even though they didn't catch him, Nadab sighed, as he was alone once again.

He's been alone all his life, distant, always on his way to somewhere else.

There are those who say that an honest and upright man is a law-abiding man. But who decides which laws are right? Who writes the laws? You people sitting there, you know what it's like to fight for your rights. You know what it means to fight for your daily bread, for a place to sleep. Everybody says "forgive us our trespasses," but who wants to forgive those who trespass against us? Temptations will come, good won't deliver anybody from evil, you can only do that by yourselves. For yours is the kingdom, the power, and the glory, for ever and ever. You choose for yourselves which story you want to belong to. Some call you bandits, but I prefer to call you freedom fighters. You free yourselves from this mean and empty life that others sink into.

In that way, Nadab's like you.

When you met him, you didn't think he was up to much, but he has mighty powers. I can hear you wondering if this young man's too soft, if he's made of different stuff from you.

You mustn't doubt Nadab! He won't hesitate, he won't beg for mercy. He's tough, he belongs here. There are times when he might be weak too, like you can be weak. Perhaps when he's working together with others, on a farm or in a limestone quarry, perhaps he might then think about a mother, a father, and a brother, about a family. Perhaps he might wish to be bound to others with ties that the eye can't see.

But that's what you'll give him. That's how you'll keep him tied to you. No more nights alone in the wilderness, no more days spent creeping around like a four-legged animal with a tail, scratching for something to put in his mouth. Nadab dreams of what you have to offer: being with somebody. Being a part of something bigger than himself. Being one among many.

So welcome Nadab. He'll be loyal to you, he'll give everything. I've led him here, I've given him a place in the story.

But know that there is something inside him, something I can't catch hold of, a glimmer of light. I don't know everything, I don't control everything. How did it get inside him? Who put it in there?

With you, he'll become what he is, what he was made to be. I think you can take care of him, I think you can teach him about darkness and toughness, as you're tough, you believe in what you're doing. Nadab will be safe with you, that little light will be put out here.

Now! He's coming, I can hear him approaching!

You won't remember me, but everything that's been said here will lie hidden in your hearts.

Good-bye, my thieves, farewell. Take care of Nadab.

They sat there waiting for me. I said hello, but none of them answered. They seemed tired. Jehoram muttered beneath his breath, something about putting out a light, or was it flames? I couldn't hear. He looked at me strangely. Jehoash got up and told the others to do the same.

"Have you been sleeping?" I asked.

Reuben sniffed. "I don't sleep when it's dark," he said.

Jehoram grinned. "All that anger, Reuben," he said. "You should cool down, take a bath, you stink of anger."

Reuben shook his head and spat. "Damn you, Jehoram," he said. "Listen to your brother and get up."

"Nadab," said Jehoash, "it's decided, you'll be joining us." I nodded and looked over at Reuben, but he didn't say anything.

Jehoram reached out his hands. I took them and thanked him. "You belong here now," he said.

Jehoash said the same: "You belong here with us now. What we do, you do. What you do, we do."

Reuben took hold of me and turned me toward him. "Nadab," he said, "we're tough, we believe in what we're doing. Listen to Jehoash and what he says, and we'll stick together."

I nodded in agreement. "Yes," I said. "I belong with you."

That's how I became one of them.

If it had all come to me in a language clear and plain, telling me what would happen, then maybe something would've been different.

I'd met Jehoram several days before, in Beersheba, when I sat down to eat a loaf of bread and some dried figs I'd begged for. He stood there, grinning at me, half hidden behind a pile of clay, with his back leaning against the wall of the building. I asked him what he was grinning at.

"You," he said. "It looks like you've still got your mother's blood stuck to your hair and your beard."

I told him I couldn't remember my mother, but that I could remember his mother, and she hadn't had anything against my hair.

"Neither up here nor down there," I said.

Jehoram grinned even more, so I went over to him and asked if he was hungry.

"No," he said. "I've eaten." But he still took some figs. I told him my name was Nadab; he told me his was Jehoram and asked what it was like to have hair that color. I told him I didn't know what it was like. It had always been like that.

"Do the ladies like it?" he asked.

It was the middle of the day, the sun beating down right through to the inside of your head, and we were in the shade. Jehoram said he was there with his brother. His face was full of sores, red and pink cuts. His hands and his feet were covered in the same pattern, and I asked if it hurt. He said it didn't, or, he didn't know, it had always been like that. I nodded. One time when I was starved and on the run, I'd spent two days and two nights with a group of sick and infected people. They'd welcomed me. They'd given me food, let me sleep where they slept, and when I left, I shook them by the hand and thanked them. Most of them may be dead by now, as far as I know, but I didn't catch anything, so I didn't think Jehoram's sores and wounds could hurt me.

I asked what Jehoram did and if he knew of any work going. He said he didn't, as they'd just got here. They'd soon be leaving again, but he wasn't sure, it was Jehoash and Reuben who'd decide, he said.

"Are they your brothers?" I asked.

"Jehoash is," he said. "Not Reuben. Come and meet them."

I agreed. If I was lucky, they might offer me something to eat, a place to sleep, maybe some work. The farmer I'd been working for before had let me go when the fruit trees were all seen to. There were others who'd been promised work, who'd been with him for a long time, and he owed it to them to let them stay. The farmer said I could come back when it became warmer and the fruit was ripe. I was paid and given some food, but I was already out of most of it by the time I got to Beersheba.

We walked together along the edge of the city. Some children came running and started shrieking when they saw Jehoram, who swore and told me that he hid, that he spent all the damn time hiding, and he'd begun to cover himself up. First his feet, then his face, but his hands were always trouble, his cursed hands, as he called them. I took the ends of the rags and helped him, wrapping one hand first, and then the other.

"There," I said, "you can change it if it's too tight.

Jehoram fell silent, and then said, "Come on."

"This is Nadab," Jehoram told his brother. Jehoash came over and greeted me.

"Reuben's not here," said Jehoram. "He's out on an errand, some kind of thing, all kinds of things, you never know with Reuben where he might be."

"Jehoram," said Jehoash, "that's enough." Jehoash wasn't quite as tall as his brother, he had his hair cut close to his scalp, and his eyes seemed as if they were staring holes right through me. He asked what I did, why I was in Beersheba. I told him about the farmer and the fruit trees, and told him I was on my way to find something else. Jehoash asked me to join them, they'd be going in a few days.

"You'll get food," he said. "We won't steal from you, and Jehoram seems to like you." I thanked him and asked what they were doing there. Jehoram started grinning again, and Jehoash turned to him, asking if I knew anything.

"No," said Jehoram.

"Do you trust him?" asked Jehoash.

Jehoram lifted up his hands. "He touched me," he said. "He's tough, can't you see?"

Jehoash turned back to me. His eyes really glow, they do, I could feel my feet, my hands, my whole body starting to creak and crack. Jehoram had stopped grinning and was standing next to me.

"What'll it be then?" he asked Jehoash.

Jehoash told him to be quiet, and then he told me who they were, what they did.

One time, when I was younger and living in a hut with some other children, I came across a dog that couldn't stand. Both its front legs were broken, and the dog growled and whimpered as it dragged itself back and forth. Together with two other boys, I killed the dog, skinned and cleaned it, and tried to sell the meat, but it was no use. In the end we threw the rest away. Another time, I hit another boy in the head with a stick so hard that he keeled over and his legs began to shake. Jehoash's world wasn't unfamiliar to me. I've stolen from the people I worked for, I've been beaten and thrown in dungeons by guards. Nothing started or finished then. It was no rupture, I wasn't a decent man who fell upon evil. I've always known what was good. But there's a pattern, a sketch in the sand, that shows the order of everything. I'm a grain of sand in that pattern. When God judges us, I'll be ready.

After they took me in, we left Beersheba and went up to Hebron. We got there in the pale light at the end of the day, and Jehoash said we'd stop there on the outskirts so that nobody would spot us. He went into the city and came back with something to eat and drink. When darkness fell, Reuben got up.

"Nadab," he said, "come here."

He gave me a knife and showed me how to hide it under my clothing, how to hold it. When I tried to tell him that I wasn't unfamiliar with how to use a sharp blade, he told me to follow him.

"It's not unlike seeing to an animal," he said, "but animals won't beg you to stop or call out the name of the Lord. So you've got to do it quickly, no hesitation, and you've got to do it quietly. It's easy, but it goes a long way. You understand? Here, it's yours, don't lose it."

The others got up. Jehoash stared at me, tilted his head, and scratched at a dark spot on his neck.

"It's time for your baptism, Nadab. Come on, follow me."

We went into Hebron. Jehoash told the other two to wait while he led me off the road, and we stumbled and scrambled across behind some buildings. A small brood of hens started flapping about, some dogs barked.

"Get ready," said Jehoash. "Show me who you are." He raised up a hand, drew a sign in the air in front of me, sat down and picked up some stones and soil, letting them run through his fingers. Then he got up, went over to a door, and knocked. A voice asked who it was, and Jehoash answered that he was waiting, that everything was ready. The door opened, and a man stepped out. I couldn't see his face clearly. The man was around the same height as me. He greeted Jehoash and asked where it was.

"Come with me," said Jehoash.

"Wait," said the man. "Who's that?" He pointed at me.

"He's with us," said Jehoash. "He's going to show you." The man stared at me, nodded, and came along with us.

We walked out into the field there, which was cultivated. Jehoash talked quietly to the stranger. We stopped, Jehoash came over to me, took me by the shoulders, and pulled me toward the stranger.

"Show me," he said.

"So, you know where it is," the man said to me. "Tell me, I can pay you well."

I had my hands under the cloth that was wrapped around me.

"Well, are you going to say something?" the man asked. "Is he mute?"

I walked closer.

"What's this, can't you hear me?" the man said.

I pushed the knife into him. I cut him and felt him tear, felt all the warmth and wetness gushing out as he tried to say something, I couldn't hear what. I pulled out the knife, but he was still standing there.

"Finish it," said Jehoash, so I took hold of the man, turned him around, pulled his head back, cut his throat, and let him fall to the ground.

Jehoash came up, looked down at him lying there, looked at me, and said, "Good, you're one of us."

Jehoash and Reuben went into the dead man's house and took everything they could find that was worth taking. We left together, through Hebron, following the road up toward Bethlehem. When daylight began to spread, we lay down to rest.

We walked at night, slept during the day. I got used to the dark, it became part of me. I was able to walk without falling, without stubbing my toes. I saw things I'd never seen before, creatures I didn't know existed, and the faint but sharp light of the moon.

When we'd come as far as Sychar, Jehoash said it was time for some rest. He found a house for us to stay in. Reuben was away for several days.

I lay awake at night in Sychar. When my eyes closed, it was as if I were blinded. I tried to lie outside in the open air, by the wall of the house. I took a rug and a blanket. Jehoram smirked at me, but one night, while I stared up into the sky, I saw a flashing light. First it flashed red, then green, and it was moving. Soon it had crossed the whole black arc of sky I lay under. I didn't tell the others about it. When morning came, I went inside and lay down. I didn't wake up until darkness fell again that evening.

We traveled onward, back and forth, through Samaria, through Judea. Jehoash wanted to go to the coast, but Reuben didn't want to go there yet; he wanted to wait until it became warmer. They argued. We came across soldiers, but Jehoash showed them Jehoram and told them we were going to have our brother treated. They let us go, and Jehoash cursed and swore, saying that we had to be careful, we wouldn't get away so lightly next time.

One day, when we stayed at our campsite, Jehoram told me that he'd heard of a prophet who said he was the son of God.

"Imagine that," he said. "The son of God. Imagine how well he's hung." He grinned, his teeth as dark as gravel.

That was the first time. The second time was when Jehoash told us about a woman who wouldn't shut up at him. He'd finished and paid her, but she kept on speaking, and he asked her what she was talking about, and she said he wasn't listening.

"Well, that's right," Jehoash told her, "but what are you talking about?"

The woman told him she was talking about somebody who'd touched her, who had God in his fingers and God in his eyes and God in his long hair. Jehoram started laughing and asked Jehoash how hard he'd taken her.

The third time was everything that happened afterward, from when we were caught in a storm until I met Martha.

It was too late when we realized what was coming; we'd been walking in the dark and hadn't paid heed to the signs.

Clouds took away the sky and the light, a wind blowing so hard over us that Jehoram started screaming and whimpering, and Jehoash shouted: "What's wrong? What's wrong?" Reuben stood there, tugging at Jehoram and yelling at him.

Jehoash took hold of me and said, "Come on, we've got to get away from here."

I stayed close to him; we ran down a cleft in the terrain that lay there open beneath us. Jehoash turned around and looked at me, his eyes wild.

"Are we all here?" he said.

Before I could answer, Jehoram had pushed me forward, and another gust of wind made me stumble. I was about to fall over the edge, but Jehoash grabbed my hand and pulled me up.

"Come on," he said. "Don't stop, just keep up with me."

It began to rain, big, heavy drops, I've never seen such rain. It hit us like gravel, and it was hard to keep our eyes open. Jehoash called to us. I saw his back for a moment, then he was gone, then he was suddenly in front of me again. How long we walked like that I have no idea. We were underwater, walking over the bottom of the sea, a billowing darkness crushing us.

Jehoash must have stumbled upon the stable by some kind of miracle. He pulled us all in there. We fell to the ground, spat, tried to catch our breath and pull off our clothes all at the same time. Jehoram was bleeding. Jehoash knelt down over him, asking him to get up, telling him they had to clean his wounds. But neither of them had the strength to contradict or obey the other, they just sat there like that, naked in the hay. Reuben tried to take out everything he was carrying. It had to be dried, the water would ruin everything, he said, but then he gave up and lay down on his back, coughing and swearing. I fumbled about, found a spot in the hay next to Jehoram, and lay down.

When we came around and a faint light shone through the opening, Jehoash got up and said we had to get dressed.

"This is somebody's stable," he said. "We can't lie here like this."

We did as he said, shuffled over to the door, and stared out.

The sky was torn, and there was water everywhere. We were at the bottom of a valley, and streams were crisscrossing the fresh, green fields surrounding the stable. I'd never seen anything like it, and I had no idea where we were. Birds flew above us, large beasts were staggering about, lowing, and a boat stood propped up against an enormous tree root.

"Who are you, and what brings you here?" came the voice of a man heading over toward us. He was tall, with his beard and hair braided together. He clapped his hands and called to the animals, then he asked us again. Jehoash coughed and said we'd got lost in the storm.

"Yes," said the man. "It looks like you were washed ashore by a great wave. What else can I say? Come with me, we've got to get you inside, you must be hungry. I'm the head of the family here, and those clothes need to be dried. You look like fish out of water."

We followed him across the fields and over to a house made of clay and stone. He told us to come in and said we could take our clothes off to dry. His wife and children wouldn't be home yet; they were out with the animals. Jehoash asked where we were, and the man said he could show us the way back.

"That won't be a problem, I can take you. But you need to rest and dry off. How about something to eat? You must be hungry after a night like that."

He served us lentil soup with bread. We sat there eating, naked, while our clothes dried by the fireplace. None of us said much; we listened to his voice and everything he told us. He told us the strangest stories about the place where we were, the animals he tended to, how the weather could be as hard to interpret as signs from God. The weather had whipped and lashed me in the storm, but here, by the fireplace, it felt as if my skin, my hair, and my beard had been oiled and were soft again. The man gave Jehoram some rags to put on his wounds but said he didn't need to dress them.

"There's good air here, and a blessed light, it's good for you to let everything rest in the sight of the Lord." Jehoash was about to say something, but the man cut him off. "You're his elder brother, aren't you? Keeping watch over your brother, like all of us. The blood of our brothers calls to us from the earth, can you hear it?"

None of us answered, but he waved his hands at us. "Get dressed now," he said. "Your clothes are dry. My wife and children will be here very soon, and they can't see you like this."

We stayed the rest of the day, and he let us sleep another night in the stable. Jehoash said we'd have to head off the next day.

"Yes," said the man, "that's fine. I'll take you to the nearest road, so you can make your way back."

His wife made us some more food, the children ran about, laughing and shouting, even smiling at Jehoram. Reuben went to help with the animals, while Jehoash sat there with Jehoram, playing with the youngsters. The eldest child, Martha, asked me how we'd made it past all the dangers, what powers had driven us to their land. The locks of her hair hung down, there was a warm reddish color in her cheeks, and her skin was paler than I'd seen in our people.

Her mother told me not to mind Martha and what she said. "She likes stories so much, she doesn't think of anything else," she said. Martha blushed and lowered her eyes. I leaned toward her and asked what kind of stories she liked. Martha shrugged, still staring at the ground.

"Well, listen to this, let me tell you," I said, "about the powers that called us and chased us here. It was a night as black as the deepest abyss, and we walked and walked. We fought wild animals, they chased us through the valleys, howling, snarling, and growling. When day finally broke and we thought it was all over, the storm came. It was as if the sea itself came washing over us. The water was threatening to tear us apart. But you see that man over there, the one with those eyes? That's Jehoash. Jehoash took hold of us, found a rope, and tied us together. We were lifted up by the water, thrown down, but we were tied to each other and were washed all the way here."

Martha's hands hung down by her sides, and her lips moved.

"Well," I said, "did you like the story?" She didn't answer, just stood there, talking silently to herself.

"Martha," said her mother, "you must answer when Nadab asks you something."

"I'm learning the story," said Martha. "I collect them, please, I have to tell it back to myself."

I let her carry on. She was a strange child. It seemed as if her eyes were always searching for something. Her fingers were long and thin like slender twigs. She spoke to me not like a little girl, not like a grown woman. Everything she said seemed to be extracted from a hidden place.

"I've learned it now," she said. "I've got your story now. Please can I look after it until you need it again?"

"Yes," I said, smiling. "Of course, it's yours."

"No." She shook her head. "I won't take your story from you." Her mother interrupted and told her she shouldn't argue with guests or try to confuse them with words.

"Mother's stories are the best," said Martha. "She tells them almost every evening. Can you tell us about Jesus, Mother? Tell us about when you and Father met Jesus."

"Not now," said her mother. "Our guests need to rest. Didn't you hear what he told you?"

"Have you seen Jesus?" I asked.

"Yes," said Martha, her voice singing. "Father and Mother have spoken with him. They joined his followers."

"Why don't you lend me a hand, Martha?" said her mother. "Leave our guests in peace."

"But Mother," said Martha. She didn't get any further, as her mother took hold of her and dragged her away, telling her softly about being quiet and doing what she was told.

I got up and asked if there was anything I could do. Jehoash spoke up and said I could go and fetch some water. The woman looked at Jehoash, then at me, and said it wasn't necessary. But Jehoash said it was only fair and proper, they shouldn't be our servants.

"If you want to," the mother said. "If you wish, you can go down to the stream." I nodded. The woman gave me a pitcher and told me where to go. Jehoash followed me out.

"Have a look around," he told me. "That's all. Just have a look around, and then come back here."

A path led me through a small thicket and down to a stream. The water flowed silently through the rushes, flies and other insects buzzing over the surface. I was still dazed from the night before and sat down on a flat, dry stone.

Martha must have followed me. She came down the path from behind me.

"Why are your hair and beard that color?" she asked. I told her she shouldn't be there, but she just snorted and said she was big enough to make her own decisions about where she could and couldn't go.

"Mother thinks I went to clear the small patch of ground where we're going to plant trees," she said. "Do you know how long it takes for a tree to grow?"

I shook my head.

"A long time," she said. "It won't make any difference if I go to pick up stones today or tomorrow."

She went on to tell me about how she always helped her father on the land, how her days were split up, and how black the nights could be. "Sometimes I can't see anything," she said. "It's as if I couldn't tell the difference between what's up and what's down."

I told her about the time when I'd been out by the coast and had seen the night reflected in the sea. She asked what the sea was like, what it smelled like, whether it made a noise, whether the water was heavier or lighter than in the stream there. I told her I didn't know, but that it seemed heavier in a way, and that it was never still.

"You can always hear it," I said. "You can hear it whispering against the shore. If you put your head beneath the water, you can hear something pounding and groaning down in the depths."

"It can't be the same water," said Martha, lying down on her stomach with her ear to the stream. A gentle breeze blew over the fields and down to us. We saw it sketch a pattern across the water.

I asked if her mother had really met this Jesus.

"Oh yes," said Martha. "He comes from Nazareth. It's a small, poor town, Father says, up in the hills. He has long hair and a beard, and Mother says he touched her and Father."

Her mother and father had met Jesus when they'd gone to the nearest market. They'd seen him defend a farmer who couldn't afford to pay his taxes. "Give your master what belongs to your master, and give God what belongs to God," Jesus had told the guards. He put his arm around the farmer and said, "We are children of God, we need our daily bread."

After that, her mother and father had sought out Jesus and his followers. He'd laid his hands on them, and they'd been baptized with the Holy Spirit and fire.

"The Lord himself," I said, and tried to smile at her, but Martha wasn't paying attention to what I said. She went on with other stories about Jesus, stories that her mother and father hadn't witnessed, but that they'd been told. The sick had been cured, the unclean had been cleansed. A woman who sold herself had been cleansed by Jesus and walked by his side. Rebels had come down from the mountains and lay down their arms. Violent men had received the Word of God, and fire had flowed from their fingers. Children who had been abandoned, marked by the Devil, ran around Jesus's feet, with God in their eyes.

Martha was no longer speaking like a little girl. Her voice seemed to have its own life, like a snake slithering and writhing, sliding and winding. The stories Martha told were broken off at the ends and began suddenly. Sometimes she would mention a name, other times a city. At first, I thought she was trying to get everything to fit together, to suggest the clear pattern according to which the world was arranged. But it wasn't like that, no, it was different. She let her stories twist and coil, as if they were being put around me like a fortress against all evil.

I don't know how long I sat there listening to her, I can't remember.

"And Father's favorite story," Martha said, "is about a man who was attacked by a band of thieves and was left to die."

I opened my mouth but couldn't bring myself to say anything.

"It's not about Jesus," she continued. "It's a story Jesus told."

And she showed me the small stones that had made the man's feet sore. She showed me how the man had gone on anyway, how he'd wanted to find a roof for his head before darkness fell. She showed me how afraid he'd been when the band of thieves had come and taken him. She showed me how he'd been left lying, naked and beaten and kicked and torn apart, by the side of the road. She showed me how the blackness and evil had reached right up to him, in under his skin, into his aching fingers, his feet and his hands that wouldn't obey him, one of his eyes that wouldn't open, his battered mouth that had dried out and cracked. She showed me the sounds of the people who'd gone past, the people who hadn't heard him, the people who'd stared and gone on their way. She showed me how he'd shrunk and shriveled, how everything had flowed out of him, how he'd smelled, how he'd tried to call out. But eventually, somebody stopped. A stranger from Samaria lifted the injured man up, gave him something to drink, laid him on top of his donkey, told him to be quiet, just to stay alive, just to hold on, not to close his eyes.

"Father says that's what we should be like," said Martha. "We should help those who need help, we should be strong for the weak."

She fell silent. The dark locks of her hair blew in the wind.

"So," I said, "what does your father say about us?"

"Father says we shouldn't ask you what you do," Martha answered. She crouched there, her eyes drifting from me down to the ground in front of her. "He says we offer shelter to anybody who's lost or who needs help."

I said her father was a good man.

"Yes," said Martha, "but I've got to help Mother mill the grain, and Father says I've got to help tend to the animals in the evening too, while the others can go home. He says I'm the eldest and it has to be like that until my brothers are bigger, and when we come home and the others have gone to bed, Mother doesn't have the strength to tell another story."

"Your brothers and sisters will join you sooner or later," I said. I picked up some small stones and threw them into the stream. I couldn't stop thinking about Martha's story.

"Are you a good man, like Father?" Martha asked.

"No," I said. "No, not like your father. Not like your mother either." Martha was silent. "Maybe I'm waiting to do some good," I said. "Maybe not, who knows?"

"Why are you waiting?" she asked.

"I don't know," I said. "I've done some things that won't go away. Things you don't need to hear. I've done a lot of bad things. But you don't need to be afraid of me."

Martha got up and stood there, with her hands and her long, thin fingers. Her lips moved as she talked to herself under her breath.

"You don't need to be afraid," I said. "I won't do you any harm. I'm just going to fill this pitcher, and then I'm going back. You can come with me, or you can stay here."

"I'm not afraid," she said.

"Good," I said. I tried to smile, but I couldn't look at her. In spite of the rain having washed me the night before, I felt dirty. I closed my eyes, and everything became dark. It was the middle of the day, but in this darkness I could rest. Nothing to see, nothing to do, just being in this darkness.

"Why have you done so many bad things?" she asked.

"I don't know, Martha," I said. "I can't answer that. You should go now, your mother might be out looking for you. She won't want you to be here, not with me."

Martha started to walk away from me. I sat still, opened my eyes, and stared at the water, at the rushes trembling ever so slightly. After a while, I got up and picked up the jug. Martha had gone. I filled the pitcher and took it back. I didn't know what I would tell Jehoash.

When I came back, the food was ready, and Martha's mother shepherded me to the table. We prayed, we ate, and after the meal, we said good-bye. I sat Martha on my lap, thanked her for all her stories, and told her that if she ever went to sea, she should throw a stone in there and imagine that stone was me. Then I could lie there and perhaps be thrown back ashore a second time. She said that was the strangest thing she's ever heard, but I kissed her and told her I was waiting to do some good, that she should remember that.

Her father took us back to the stable.

"I'll come tomorrow morning," he said. "I'll bring you some food to take on your journey, and then I'll take you as far as you need." He blessed us and left us alone.

The stable was full of shadows, and we stayed standing outside. Jehoram shook his head and said he had a bad feeling about this.

"I'm ready," said Reuben. "Who gives a shit about feelings? I'm ready."

"We'll go back when it's dark," said Jehoash. "Can you find the way?"

Reuben nodded. "Yes, I think I can find the way back without him tomorrow too."

I shook my head. "No, no. We can't do this," I said.

"What can't you do?" asked Reuben. "Is it that little girl you like so much? I can take care of her. You can watch if you want."

Reuben smirked, and I turned toward Jehoash.

"We can't do this," I said.

"I hear you," said Jehoash. "I think you're forgetting yourself."

"They have nothing," I said. "They've been good to us, and there are small children there. This isn't the kind of thing we normally do."

"What the hell do you know about what we normally do?" asked Reuben. "You've only just had your baptism. It's time to come of age."

"I'm not talking to you," I said, trying to keep my eyes on Jehoash. "I'll go back there with you, but this isn't right. You know it's not right, Jehoash. We've been shown something here, something we've never seen. There's nothing there anyway, all they own is the soil under their feet."

Jehoash didn't say anything. He just stood there, staring at me. I turned toward Jehoram.

"Jehoram," I said, "say something. You were with those children today, they were playing with you."

Jehoram turned to his brother.

"You know I'll do as you say," he said. "I'm not the one who makes the plans around here. But I agree with Nadab."

Reuben shook his head and muttered something about everybody going soft. Jehoash sighed and looked out across the fields and up at the sky, which had begun to grow dark.

"We'll leave it," he said.

"Why?" asked Reuben. "They're easy prey!"

"Yes," said Jehoash, "but there's little to be had here. It's like Nadab says, they don't own anything."

"Jehoash," said Reuben, but Jehoash raised a hand and cut him off.

"We'll start again," he said, "but not tonight, not these people, not while we're here. We've been shown something. We must be grateful for it."

Reuben swore and said we'd become squeamish. He muttered to himself, something about his not liking to kill children anyway, they were so small, and he slept badly after things like that. Then he went and lay down in the hay. Jehoram followed him, kicked Reuben's feet, and told him to make space for one more. Reuben didn't answer and just rolled over on his side. I said I could start keeping watch, but Jehoash said we didn't need to.

"Go to bed, Nadab," he said. "We'll start everything again tomorrow."

Night came, none of us slept. Jehoash didn't even try; he sat at the door to the stable, staring out. I got up and went over to him, but he didn't look at me, just moved his legs so I could get past.

The animals out in the fields could be heard softly. A gentle breeze made my garments flap. It all glimmered up there, high above me. Jehoash said something. I wasn't listening. What was it I'd told Martha?

"We are what we are," said Jehoash.

That I'd done things that won't go away.

"We do what we do," said Jehoash.

I've done a lot of bad things.

"I don't know what it means anymore," said Jehoash.

I'm waiting to do some good.

We never returned to Martha and her family. The storm, the animals in the fields, the family, the young children, the stream, it's all just a vague memory. But something hit home. Jehoash and Reuben have begun to lead us into a new pattern.

We try to do good. We make agreements with rebels and rich families. We've guarded farms and property, monitored a stretch of road to prevent ambushes. Jehoram grins and says that we're being given food and drink and a roof over our heads to keep ourselves away. For a while we worked to track down a band of thieves and chase them out of Judea. We were paid by the head, but Jehoash said we shouldn't kill them. There was almost a fight when we came asking for the money. Another time, we were paid to take care of the security of a well-off man and his entourage while they traveled to Jerusalem. And now we're accompanying two men to the same city of peace. They're from a rich family, but they paid their own way and didn't want anybody, not even their father, to know that they'd gone, or where they were going.

But in spite of this, it's as if something or other were still clinging on to us. Reuben's starting to get fed up, and something's come over Jehoash. He doesn't like all the people who hire us. He says they give us money but don't want to be seen next to us. We're just tools for them, he says, we're just something they use to dig in the ground or to move rocks.

One evening when we were talking together, Jehoash said that it would soon be over.

"I can feel it coming," he said. "I can't hold it back."

He had laid his sword and knives down in front of him and stroked his fingers over the blades.

"I don't want to kill again," I said, and Jehoash looked up at me.

"You have to sleep, don't you?" he asked. Before I could answer, he continued: "You have to eat, you have to drink, you have to shit, you have to piss. This is like that too. I can't hold it back. I'm not somebody they can buy, I'm not an animal they can tame."

On our way toward Jerusalem, Reuben says that we're leaving a pattern behind us.

"Where we've walked, we leave a pattern drawn in the sand, an outline in the earth," he says.

"You're talking like a prophet," Jehoash tells him.

Reuben goes on: "We've got mixed up in the wrong pattern." Jehoash tells him he should shut up about this pattern of his, and they almost start fighting. Jehoram's sores are bothering him more; Jehoash says it's the warmth. Meanwhile, Reuben thinks we should go back to Sychar and take it easy for a while. He wants to visit a woman called Anna. But Jehoash says the coast and the sea air would be better for Jehoram. This makes me think about the sea and Martha, and whether she'll ever get to see the vast plains of water or hear the heavy sighing of the deep.

The two men who are with us try to get us talking. They ask Reuben about his weapons, but Reuben won't answer them.

"Come on," one of them says. He has no beard, his face is smooth, and he says they've got weapons too, they're carrying tools for the liberation.

Reuben stops and holds out a hand.

"Let's see," he says. "What have you got?" The man with the smooth face takes out a knife and puts it in Reuben's hand.

"It's small," says Reuben.

"It's big enough," says the man with the smooth face. "I'll be quick."

"You'll have to strike true," Reuben tells them. "If you don't strike true, you might meet resistance, your victim will still be standing, maybe shouting. You won't have time, will you?"

The one with the smooth face turns to the other man. "What did I tell you?" he says. "They know their stuff." Reuben is about to say something, but then he's interrupted.

"We're going to take the life of one of the priests at the Temple," says the man. "We're our people's resistance movement, and we're fed up with not being listened to. Everything's been tried, but this time they'll see how hard we can hit them."

Reuben doesn't say anything next, he just looks over at Jehoash and shakes his head.

"We'll have nothing to do with that," I tell them. "We're taking you to Jerusalem, and that's all."

"You're our brothers, you're of the same people as us," the one with the smooth face continues. "We're rising up against the occupying powers, we're the spearhead that will start the great wave washing the army of darkness into the sea."

Jehoash mutters something about everybody speaking like prophets now.

"We're all fighting the same battle," says the other man. He's missing a finger from each hand, and his eyes point in different directions. "You fight in the mountains. We're taking the war to the cities, to the rich, to the ones collaborating with the rulers."

"We've got nothing to do with it," says Jehoash. "We're being paid to take you to Jerusalem, that's all."

But then the two men say, almost in unison, "We won't say anything, we're true to God. If they get hold of us, we'll stab ourselves! God is great!"

Then they start telling us about their plans, how they'll walk up to the Temple Mount, get into the Temple, wait until they see the right one, how one of them will talk with the guards, while the other one gets going. Reuben asks who they're going to kill, and the one with the missing fingers says a name I've never heard before. Jehoash tells him to shut up.

"I don't want to hear what you're going to do," he says. "I don't want to know the name."

"He's not one of our priests," says the other man. "He's been appointed and works with the occupiers; he deserves to be slaughtered like an animal."

Jehoram starts grinning, and the two men fall silent. They don't like Jehoram being there and constantly try to stay as far away from him as possible.

"They're not listening to you," says Jehoram, pointing at Jehoash. "They just talk and talk."

"You won't survive," says Jehoash, "you won't get away. The soldiers are based right next to the Temple. They'll track you down and nail you up."

"You don't see," said the eight-fingered one. "We're carrying tools for the liberation. God is with us, even if we're not successful. We're being occupied, the army of darkness rules over us, but God's light will shine most strongly."

Jehoash shakes his head.

"Save your energy," he says. "There's still some way to go to Jerusalem."

But the one with the smooth face doesn't want to stay quiet. He says they're used to this.

"Far too many people don't want to take part," he says. "Far too many sit there, waiting for a miracle. You tell each other stories about Moses and about the prophets, but you won't listen to the Word of God, you won't let God's will happen. Your prophets will sit there, talking, they'll travel all over this holy land of ours until they disappear in the desert. We've stood face-to-face with this prince of light, Jesus of Nazareth. He's a fool. He wants to rise up against the occupiers with empty hands, open arms, and holy words. They'll tear them to pieces and nail them up. I'll tell you what the priests up there in the Temple in Jerusalem do with holy words. They piss all over them."

"Have you met Jesus?" I ask them. They both nod.

"We met him in the valley below Mount Gilboa," says the eight-fingered man. "We spoke with him and his followers. There were women and children there. You can't take people like them into war."

"That's enough," says Jehoash. "It's time for a little rest. We'll take a break here."

The two men with us stop and sit down. I walk over to Jehoash. It's silent, except for a bird singing from a nearby tree.

"Why are we stopping?" I ask. "Shouldn't we walk a bit before darkness falls?"

"Nadab," says Jehoash, taking hold of me, "do you remember what I told you that night when we were awake?"

I try to work out what he's talking about.

"Sometimes I lose my way," he goes on, "but I always find it again. I've tried to do the right thing, we've served other people, kept away from what we used to do. But they can't buy me, I can't sell us, we're not owned by the wealthy. I can't change who I am or what I am. Perhaps there have been evenings when I've wondered whether I could become somebody else. But we've tried this out now, and the more we've done, the longer we've spent doing it, the longer these two rich men's sons speak, the surer I feel. We'll go back to what we were, what we're meant to be."

I still don't understand what he's talking about.

"You said you didn't want to kill again," says Jehoash, "but we are what we are. Get ready, Nadab, show me who you are."

8 ||| A LIGHT GONE

His face was a fresh, rosy color, his eyes blue. He was beautiful, and he was the king of Jerusalem. That's why he called himself David, and all the boys in his band, his court, were called David II, David III, David IV, and so on. There were seven girls in the band, and they were given the names Bathsheba I, Bathsheba II, Bathsheba III, all the way up to Bathsheba VII. David had heard the stories from Joseph, who let them sleep in the back room facing out toward the stable. Of kings and wars, of queens and the voice of God.

Joseph called David "little one." He had no father, no mother, but he had Joseph: a booming voice, sinewy hands with yellow nails, a long, shabby beard that prickled when he kissed. David was one of the small and vulnerable ones, but he had to fend for himself. He helped out in the kitchen, cleared tables, and was responsible for sweeping the floor in the morning. When he began bringing others with him, Joseph had nothing against it, as long as they all worked and helped him run the place. There, in the back room at Joseph's place that faced the stable, was where David's short time as king began. There, in that back room, the others swore their allegiance to him, and he swore to be their king and rule them fairly.

That's why there was only one thing for David to do when Bathsheba VII came back, all beaten and torn up. Just as water runs downhill, as the sun runs its course, as fire lights up the sky, as night turns everything to darkness: he had to punish the culprits.

When they could get Bathsheba VII to talk, she told them what had happened. David held her hand the whole time, and he stroked her forehead and her cheek, even the mark of the beast that covered half of her face and ran all the way down her body. Little Bathsheba VII cried and cried, but David told her to be strong. He told her to close her eyes and think of the taste of pomegranates, how their color was as bright red as the tears of angels. He told her about the great sea and how it sparkled in the day, how it sparkled at night, how it never stopped sparkling, in spite of its enormous depth and all the unknown creatures that dwelled down at the bottom. David had never seen any sea, and he'd tasted a pomegranate only a few times, but he'd heard grown men speak of all sorts of things as he went between the tables at Joseph's.

For Bathsheba VII, a new world was opening, as this was the dream she carried in secret. That something miraculous would happen, that it must happen, that David, her king, would open, that his heart would open, that one morning she would lie in his hands and be saved. She was only Bathsheba VII, but now she was there with him, and he was there with her.

For David, this was the first time he'd seen darkness gather around him. He knew what evening and night were, but he'd never seen such a darkness as the one that was now gathering in the corners, up beneath the ceiling, indeed even around the eyes of some of the people standing near him. He wondered where the light had gone while Bathsheba VII had been speaking.

There were rules in David's kingdom in Jerusalem, the city of peace. One of the rules was to stay away from the Temple, the territory of the Temple Dogs. David recognized this, he acknowledged that his royal power didn't reach all the corners of the kingdom. The Temple Dogs had their own king, Saul, and he and David had never met. They shared Jerusalem between them.

Bathsheba VII struggled to explain why she'd gone up to the

Temple. First she said that she'd gone to fetch something up there, but she couldn't explain what it was she was fetching. Then she told them about a family who'd asked her to join them, since she was alone. Eventually, and this was the version of the story that David and all the others believed, it became clear that Bathsheba VII had quite simply been tricked into going up to the Temple by one of the Temple Dogs. The boy, who'd also had a mark on his face, a scar stretching from one cheek to the other right across his nose, had told her she was allowed. The boy gave her safe conduct. The Temple Dogs wouldn't do anything to her, as long as she held his hand. But when they'd got up to the Temple, the boy wanted to kiss and lick and taste Bathsheba VII, so she tore herself away from him and ran. She ran as fast as she could, with the boy barking behind her, and then she was caught by the Temple Dogs, who took her with them and did all they wanted and could to her. It was so painful for her to tell that David had to hold her still until her whole body stopped twitching and trembling.

He had to punish them, and he knew how. He was the king, he'd make everything right again. But he'd seen the darkness, it'd shown him what had been started. All the stories he'd been told, of kings and wars, of queens and the voice of God: there was a pattern there, and he knew it. Everything's built up, and everything's torn down. Then it'll be built up again, and the same thing will happen again. Once it'd been started, nobody could stop it.

The next day, David asked everybody to go to Joseph's and help out. If Joseph sent them away, they were to go into the back room and stay there. He took out some coins he'd been saving, which were all he owned. He went over to Bathsheba VII, kissed her, and told her it would all be over soon.

Without Joseph seeing him, David took a cloak Joseph used only when he went to the Temple, and he put it on. It was far too big, but it was clean, and there weren't any holes or wear marks on it.

When he went up to the Temple, he kept close to a father who had three children with him. He walked right behind them so nobody would think he was there alone. He followed the family some of the way, then he left them and stayed close to another family of two women and two little boys. David carried on like this, back and forth across the temple precinct, until he spotted the boy with the scar who'd tricked Bathsheba VII. The boy was sitting like all the Temple Dogs did at that time of day, kneeling down with a small bowl in front of him. David knew that they barked at each other, he knew that was their signal. If the boy barked, he'd be exposed. But the Temple Dog kept his head up, so that everyone passing could see the way his face had been cut up.

David noticed a temple guard standing some distance away, and when nobody was staring in their direction, David went up to the boy with the scar and dropped the coins he'd brought with him in the bowl. Then David ran straight to the guard, shouting, "Thief, thief, he took my coins." The guard turned toward him.

"He stole my money," David shouted. "He stole my money."

The guard moved and came over to David. "Where, boy?" he asked. "Where is he?" David pointed at the boy with the scar, who realized only now what was happening. He got up, picked up his bowl of money, and ran off, barking. But the guard was already after him. The boy disappeared into the crowds, but then another guard emerged, holding the boy tightly. The guards lifted up the boy, took the money, and threw his bowl on the ground, smashing it. They called across to David, and David went over to them. The Temple Dog they were holding between them stared at David, but before he could say anything, the guards asked David how many coins he was missing. David told them how many. One of the guards bent down and gathered up all the coins that were lying there from the smashed bowl. He gave David the ones that were his and ruffled his hair.

"Go to your father and your mother," the guard said. "Tell them that no wrong happened that wasn't righted again."

"Liar," the little boy yelled now. "Liar." But one of the guards slapped the boy on the face, shutting him up.

"Thank you," David said to the guards. "My mother and father are waiting for me, they'll be pleased when they hear how you helped me." And to the boy, he said softly, "Nobody touches my queens."

The guards took the boy with them. David knew that they would hurt him, they would lock him up, and eventually they'd throw him in the pits with the thieves and rebels. But before that, maybe even there and then, the Temple Dogs would find out, and Saul would learn what David had done, so David hurried back to his own kingdom. He ran through Jerusalem, all the way to Joseph, who yelled at him, asking him where he'd been and why he was wearing his clothes. David said sorry, but Joseph hit him and sent him out to empty and clean out where the adults did their business.

When he was finally allowed to go to bed, his band were waiting for him. They cheered and praised David; indeed, David was received as the king he was. The rumors and stories of the deeds he'd carried out had reached them all. Even Bathsheba VII got up to sing his name.

That night, David dreamed that he was standing on a plain that reached out as far as the eye could see. The grass beneath him was green, and the wind made it rustle and ripple. When he lifted up his eyes, he could see that the night was coming in over the plain like a fluttering blanket. But behind the immense darkness, he could see something blinking faintly, and he reached out his hand and said something. He woke up and couldn't remember what he'd said, or why he'd said something to the small, blinking light.

Bathsheba VII stayed with David and Joseph for the next while. Joseph didn't want to have her in the tavern, and she had to stay at the back of the kitchen, where nobody could see her. David told her everything that had to be done, and Joseph praised them for getting everything done so quickly these days. But one evening, Joseph took David aside and told him he wanted to speak with him.

"Listen here, little one," said Joseph. "I've got no problem with you having all this lot here, but that girl, the one helping out now, she's got the mark of the beast on her. I know, I know, you probably think it's weird for us men to be talking about it, but we do.

My customers can't see me having all these children here, and then one of them's got the mark of Satan himself. You see what I mean?" David nodded.

"So you understand what I'm saying, little one?" said Joseph, ruffling David's hair, kissing him, and sending him off.

That night, David couldn't sleep. He lay awake, while all the others snoozed quietly like small animals hibernating around him. It was only when morning came, and he was about to drop off, that he realized David IV was missing. He got up, woke up the others, and asked them all if they knew where David IV was. Had anybody seen David IV the day before? The evening before? Nobody could give him a clear answer, so David sent them all out looking, all the Davids and all the Bathshebas, except for Bathsheba VII.

Later, when the band had come back and explained what had happened, David was struggling to breathe. There was something in his throat, down in his body, something tight tying itself onto him, and at the same time, all that darkness flowing out of the walls, out of the eyes of the ones around him.

"Get away," he started shouting. "Away, go away, get away from me!"

The light only came back when Bathsheba VII washed his face and stroked his hair. He managed to sit up, but Bathsheba VII said he should lie down. She told him that all the others were helping Joseph, and he, their king, should just lie down. She would take care of him. While David lay there, being cared for by Bathsheba VII, he began to think through everything that had happened, and everything that had to be done. Everything that had been built, everything that had been torn down, everything that would be destroyed, and everything that would be rebuilt. Kings and wars, queens, but no voice of God yet. Just darkness.

The night before, while David had lain awake, listening to the others, David IV was lying hidden behind the corner of a building down in the Tyropoeon Valley. It was Bathsheba I and Bathsheba II who'd reported what had happened to David. They'd gone out in the morning, on David's orders; they'd searched and searched and spotted some soldiers running off in the direction of the Pool of Siloam. Several adults stood there calling out above them, as a child was lying there for all to see. The soldiers took the child, lifted him up, and carried him away with them. Bathsheba I and Bathsheba II recognized him as David IV, and they realized that he'd been killed, as his eyes and mouth were open, although he couldn't see and wasn't breathing, and his whole body was dyed and wet with all the fluids that had run out of him.

While Bathsheba I and Bathsheba II had stood there, staring at David IV being taken away from them, several youngsters gathered around them. It was the Temple Dogs, and out of their ranks stepped a boy who was a head taller than the others. It was Saul, the king of the Temple Dogs. He pointed at the Bathshebas and said to them, "Go up to your king and tell him what you've seen here today. Tell him that it was me who took one of his warriors from him, just as he took one of mine from me."

When David heard those words, darkness came, and he couldn't breathe.

"What have I done?" David whispered, lying there.

Bathsheba VII leaned over him. "My king," she said, "just lie still." David looked up at her, his eyes coming to rest on her bright red wound. It looked as if her skin there were made of something else. "It's the mark of the beast," said Bathsheba VII.

"I know what it is," said David, as he'd been told by others what had made that mark. Children who'd been left out in the wilds or left to die in the water could be found by the Devil. Then the Devil would make the child his own, putting his mark on it and sending the child back out into the world, bigger and stronger, but damaged, to show what people were in his eyes.

"Have you met the Devil?" David asked her.

"It was water that burned me," she replied.

"Water burning?"

Bathsheba VII nodded.

"What happened?" David asked.

"I don't know," she said. "I just remember that it burned."

"Who left you with these wounds?"

"I can't remember," she said. "I dream about it, it's everywhere when I sleep."

"How old are you?" he asked.

Bathsheba VII fell silent, and then she answered: "Ten."

"Ten?" he asked.

"Ten," she said.

"Come here," said David, pulling Bathsheba VII close to him. He took off her clothes, he took off his own, and he laid her down beneath him. It had to be done; this was how the king chose his queen. And Bathsheba VII was a good queen, she was quiet, apart from a slight whimper when he penetrated her. Afterward, he pushed her out from where they lay, and told her to dry herself and get dressed. He thanked her for everything she'd done, and got up.

"Where's the king going?" she asked.

"I'm going to get everything ready," he said.

The sky was gray, a cold wind was blowing, he could feel the rain coming before it fell. This was the time when they froze most, and David thought of David IV lying out there on the ground all night as he passed away. He prayed to God that David IV had been taken up to the Lord straightaway, that he hadn't been lying there crying out to his king for help.

David gave them the same orders as before. They were all to stay indoors. Only in the middle of the day, when the sun was at its brightest, could they go out into the town, and then they had to be back in good time before evening came. He helped out at Joseph's.

The days went by, and they were all the same. They had their rhythm, they had their jobs to do, they had their small duties. When all the Davids and Bathshebas were inside, David went out alone. He came back in the evening, but didn't say anything about where he'd been or what he'd been doing. He inspected his band thoroughly, checking that they were all there before they went to sleep. Bathsheba VII lay by his side now, and nobody said anything about it. He was their king, and he alone chose who would be his queen.

At night, the same dream came to him. The plain, the green grass, the storm of darkness, and the light blinking softly just before he woke. He made everything ready, as the dream was speaking to him. David was sure of this, there was a pattern ahead of him, and all he had to do was to follow the pattern.

Then, early one morning, with the night still hanging over the city, David went around and woke them all up. He told them to take everything they owned, put on all their clothes, and follow him. The Davids and the Bathshebas asked what was happening, but David told them to be quiet.

"I'll explain," he said, "but do as I say now, quickly."

When everybody was ready, David told them to follow him. They left Joseph's house and headed out into Jerusalem. They walked all the way to the city walls, where they were stopped by the guards, but David spoke to them. He told them his band were leaving and would not be coming back.

"Just let us through," he said, "and you'll never see us again."

The guards smirked and let them out.

David and his band walked for a while along the road that led all the way to Caesarea. A large group of men and women with donkeys and carts stood there, waiting for them. David went over to one of the men and pointed at his band. He spoke to the man and put a purse in his hand.

"I trust you," said David. "I've sent word to Sychar too, where somebody will be expecting them all with you. If any of them are missing, if only a single one of them has gone, you will be punished."

The man nodded, and David went over to his band. "Don't be afraid," he said, "as I'm sending you away. This man and the rest of the group will take you with them to Sychar. When you get there, you're on your own. I don't know what's waiting for you there, but you'll be safe. Don't come back here, as Jerusalem, the city of peace, is no longer a place for us. You must go out and find a new land, and that land is where you will live."

All the Davids and Bathshebas started shouting; they turned around to look back at the city they were leaving, and the Bathshebas tore at their hair and fell to their knees.

"Listen to me, as I'm your king," said David. "I know you follow me, but this time you must follow others. David II will be your leader now. He'll lead you onward and take care of you. Do as I say, and do as David II will say."

With those words, he took David II aside and whispered to him: "Listen, I've only given that man over there half of the money. I'm giving the other half to you. Give him the money when you get there, but don't show it to anybody. He doesn't know which of you has it."

David II took the other purse; David put his arms around him and wished him good luck. Then he went over to Bathsheba VII. She said nothing. She just stood still, staring at him.

"My queen," David whispered to her, "listen to me. I'm sending you away. You won't have that name anymore. You will be remade, away from all the bad things that have happened here. Your name will be Esther now."

Tears poured from her eyes.

"I want to be there with you," she said.

"No," said David. "If anybody's there with me, it can't be you. Nobody should be there with me."

David bent down and kissed her on the cheek.

"Go with these people," said David, "but if anything should happen, if you should find light somewhere, follow that light. I've dreamed about it, I've seen that it exists. It's gone now, but it exists. When you find it, then follow it. You're Esther, you're free."

She nodded at David, and her king bent down and kissed his queen once again before he left her. He left them all and went back to the city. The guards let him in, as he was alone. The band would never come back to him.

David didn't return to Joseph, as all the coins he'd given away had been stolen. There was nothing to go back to there. No, David didn't go to the home he'd lost; he went to the Temple, to the den of thieves, where Saul was sitting, waiting for him. The evening before, David had sent a message to Saul that he would come to petition for peace between them.

On his way up the stairs to the Temple, David suddenly dropped to his knees. But he got up again. "Not here," he said, walking back into a side street. He got down there and prayed to the Lord for forgiveness for everything he'd done. For the money he'd stolen, for the way he'd betrayed Joseph. For sending his band away, for breaking his ties to his queen. And he prayed for the strength to do this last thing, this very last thing.

When he went back up the stairs to the Temple, his feet carried him all the way.

The Temple Dogs were waiting for him at the Temple; everything was ready. David looked around, waiting for the darkness to come, but only a pale shimmer of day fell over him. Everything was ready, this was the only thing that was unexpected. That the darkness didn't come.

They took him to a quiet square. He didn't recognize it and didn't know where they were. That didn't mean anything. He'd gone with them, but he was with his queen. He remembered the way she smelled, the way her eyes were like a sky full of stars. He only lost hold of Esther when Saul spoke.

"So you're David," said Saul, staring at him. "You're short, how can somebody like that be a king?"

"The Lord appoints us," said David. "The Lord dethrones us."

"The Lord," said Saul, snorting dismissively. "There's no Lord here. Look what he's given us. Don't talk to me about the Lord."

"I have to go soon," said David. "You'd better say what you want to say before it's all over."

"What are you talking about?" asked Saul. "You've got whatever time I give you, and when that's over, there'll only be one king left in Jerusalem."

"They don't want us here anymore," said David. "After what we've done, we're like grasshoppers in the fields. I told them to follow me when you led me here. I said they'd find everything they want to drive out of their holy city."

Saul looked at the others and asked if anybody understood what he was talking about.

"They're coming now," said David. Just as Saul was about to cut him off, the guards stormed around them. They grabbed the young ones and threw them to the ground, pulling them by the hair and bellowing at them. Saul pulled out a knife, but two of the guards ripped the knife out of his hands and punched him so hard that he was left lying there.

David stood completely still, with his hands raised up to the sky. He couldn't feel or hear anything. Everything had been made ready. David closed his eyes and didn't open them again, even when the guards took all the young ones, King David, King Saul and his band, and led them out of Jerusalem to Golgotha, toward a pit that had been dug in the ground. There they were all led to the Lord, through a great and powerful darkness.

9 ‖ ALL WE HAVE IS THE WATER

I

My brother Simon and I had been following the Master for some time when Anna found me. We were already a small band of women, men, and children who didn't belong anywhere, whom we gave food to and looked after. I was with the Lord, his words were alive inside me. But even though I had all faith, so that I could move mountains, I was nothing. Everything was still in pieces. I understood in part, and it was only when Anna came that I was able to know even as also I am known by God.

I did all I could to be close to her. When I touched her, I swear it was as if I were no longer one person. I was no longer Andrew: I was Andrew and Anna. Her dark hair curled up, her brown eyes and little nose, her fingers so clean and cool, and her pale neck when she lifts up her hair, rolling it all up together. Even the battered ear she always hides: it's like a soft, sacred stone. She showed it to me the first evening we slept together. Her small toes that almost turn white when she washes them in water, that small mark on one leg. We belong together. I'm bound to her; she's mine.

Simon was glad that Anna found me. He still remembers the time, before we met the Master, when I left him. We had only each other, and I think he thought that if he lost me, then he lost every-thing he was too. I left to find something else, something else than what we were. On my journey, I met Anna, and that was when I abandoned her too. I couldn't find peace. I searched and searched, but my route led me back to Capernaum and the Sea of Galilee again.

Peter didn't say much when he met me, he just put his arms around me. "I won't let you leave again," he said. "I shouldn't have let you leave."

Since then, he's said that the Lord led me back to him, and that perhaps it was the Lord again who led Anna here to me.

Jesus found us by the Sea of Galilee. There are many of us in Capernaum now; he was there often. But when everybody talks about everything that happened, I don't say much. Neither Simon nor I wish to remember the evening Simon came back with our father's body, or all the mornings when the two of us waded with the water up to our knees, drawing up the net. Nobody was there then. Nor all those evenings we lay hungry and full of doubt and uncertainty. We come from nothing; all we had was the water. Sometimes I froze so much that my fingers felt detached.

When I'm with Anna, it's as if my fingers glow.

When she came back, at first I thought she was another woman, but one who reminded me of the one I'd left. There had been days when I'd seen her walking ahead of me, there had been nights when I'd heard her waiting out in the darkness. But that evening, when I came walking up the road toward Nazareth and she stood there with Orpah and little Esther, it was all like a dream. I had the sun on my back, and they were bathed in the warm light. Anna didn't say anything, she just stood there. I had to touch her, I had to be sure that it was really her, in flesh and blood.

I did all I could to be close to her those first days. I walked with her and carried the tubs when it was her turn to fetch water from the spring. I rounded up the children in the evenings and took them to the women, simply in order to see her and be with her. I sang with Judas for the children. My deep, low voice and his sharp, high voice. I did woodcutting and tried to make small animals, but I couldn't do it until some of Jesus's brothers showed me. I think Anna liked it when I carved something resembling a chick, a bear cub, or a lion cub, for the children trying to sleep.

It was a new life for Anna; it was a new life for both of us. We came closer to each other, trying to get used to the way we slept, the way we woke, the way we said our morning prayers and ate, the way we washed in the evening, and the way our hands fit together. We sat together for our evening meals, her leg against mine, fingers touching fingers, nobody noticing. The weave that binds us together now was woven at that time as we circled around and around each other.

Once, one evening when I couldn't find her and got Simon to come and look for her with me, we found her sitting cold and crying next to a pile of stones, some distance from where we were gathered to sleep. I asked what was wrong, but she didn't answer. She just got up, took hold of me, and put her arms around me. I told her to come back to the others.

"It's night," I said. "Sitting here and freezing won't get us anywhere. Come on, take my hands, and then we'll go back."

Anna told me only later what was wrong with her, why she would wake up in the night screaming and shouting, where that small, pale mark on her leg came from, and how her ear had been crushed. I'd never asked her; I had no desire to hear how she'd been hurt. But I understood that the evil she was carrying had become part of her. It wasn't something that would go away, it wouldn't disappear, she carried it with her every day, and it throbbed and beat and pushed away at her every night. Anna told me everything because it was the only way she could cope with carrying it and holding on to it. Transforming it with her own words stopped her wounds and memories from turning into an illness setting into her skin, her blood, her bones. They just stayed small scars, small signs that evil won't triumph, signs that the Lord God has given us a body to live in, to be alive in. Painful and heavy, soft and light.

As we were joined together, so our stories were also joined together. When I told her about our father and how Simon and I lived alone, it was Anna's tears that came falling. When Anna told me about her sister, Ruth, and about her other men, I was the one who became furious. But Anna didn't tell whole stories. They were broken off at the ends, they began suddenly, they never ended, they just kept on going, and I couldn't understand what she was telling me. Sometimes she might mention a name and say that it was number two, or three, or five. One time, she told me about Ruth and how they'd taken care of each other, how she sometimes still thought her elder sister was out there somewhere, living a happy life. Sometimes Anna might be singing, and as soon as the song ended, she told a story about how Ruth had taught her the song, where it had happened, and what the weather had been like then. Everything was told separately, and everything was connected. Or rather, I wished that everything were connected. I wanted to hold Anna tightly, shake away all the bad things, and let her see the brightness of day that always lies waiting behind the darkness.

Now that I've grown older, I've realized that every one of us has so many stories. It's up to us to understand how they come together; it's impossible to see the pattern. I try to understand, Anna tries to understand. But everything moves, like the desert sand in the wind.

There were so many of us, I couldn't keep track of all our stories. I once heard somebody telling the story of Clopas of Sepphoris, who was close to Thomas. It was said that the reason he was missing fingers from his left hand was that his shield made of weak planks had been shattered by a soldier in fighting up in the mountains. His fingers had been cut right off, but Clopas had killed the soldier and got out of it alive. Now he was here with us, minus four fingers and a little wiser for it, as Simon used to say. Simon had little time for people who took up arms. I said he should show respect for those who'd laid down their swords and shields to follow the Master.

"A little smarter than they were before," said Simon, "still doesn't make them very smart."

One time when we were camped in the valley below Mount Gilboa, we noticed a group of people approaching us. They were carrying weapons, and some of us feared they were a band of thieves. But when the group reached us, they greeted us and said they came in peace. The small group's leader introduced himself as their commander.

"What you see in front of you now are only a few of us, but there are many of us," he said. "We're like the shadows: our numbers only grow when the great, strong sun shines more weakly."

"And when it's night, then there are none of you. You disappear into the darkness," said Simon. "You're welcome to be here with us," he continued, "but please put your weapons away."

"If that is your wish, we'll lay down everything," the commander said. "But that won't be easy for us to do, as what we're carrying can't be separated from our hands like any tool you can put down at the end of the day. Ours are tools of liberation."

"Well," said Simon, "you can liberate yourselves over there, and when you're finished, you're welcome to sit with us."

Then the commander became annoyed and asked if this was the prophet he'd heard about. Simon told him that he wasn't a prophet, and that we didn't want to have weapons where we were.

"It is the Prince of Peace we have among us," Simon continued. "If someone were to see us with weapons, that would be another reason for enemies to come after us."

The commander nodded, turned to his group, and told them to lay down all their weapons. Simon gave Mary a signal, and they went off together to find the Master. But he was nowhere to be found, and nobody knew where he'd gone. Mary thought he'd gone off alone, like he sometimes did. Simon asked me to take somebody with me to look for him. Just then the Master emerged from the descending evening darkness and walked into the growing light of the bonfires.

"Lord," said Simon, "there are rebels here, and they want to talk with you."

The Master called for his closest followers, gesturing at me to come too. The rest carried on preparing things for the night. Our evening meal was being made, wood was being gathered, prayer groups were being formed, and the sick were being seen to and cared for. It was decided who would keep watch through the night.

We sat down together and shared the leftovers we'd kept from the day before. The rebels ate all they were given, but none of them spoke. The Master turned to the commander and asked him why they'd come. What did they want?

"We've heard stories about you," the commander said. "We've heard what you've done, what you've said. We're both fighting against the same powers, against the army of darkness. I've heard that you're the Prince of Peace, so I've come to you to find out more."

"The Prince of Peace?" said the Master, turning toward Simon and the others. "Have you heard that one before? The Prince of Peace, I haven't been called that before, have I?"

A few people sniggered, but the Master apologized and said he didn't mean to make fun of them. Then he told them who we were, and what we were doing. When the commander started asking questions, the Master let Thomas, John, and Mary answer. He sat still, listening. Simon drew in the sand with a twig.

"You can see for yourselves the way our people are being killed, the way the occupiers and those who collaborate with them are pillaging the country," the commander said. "They're beasts, monsters, destroying everything that honors God and our own history. We'll be like livestock to the slaughter if we don't resist them. So I say that we must stand together and fight. We must stand together and drive them into the sea."

"Lay down your weapons," the Master said. "Then we can stand together. If you want to join us, we'll welcome you."

The commander fell silent. He took out a small leather canteen, drank from it, and then spat behind him.

"We've always borne arms," he said. "None of our people became kings without bearing arms, and none will become kings without them."

"Where are those kings now?" the Master asked. "Where's their kingdom?"

"Where are you after such a long time?" the commander replied. "Where are you now, out here in the wilds, with no crown as far as I can see, surrounded by whores and lepers."

Several of us started to protest, and I was about to get up, but the

Master silenced us. The commander hadn't finished. He looked at all of us, and then his eyes fixed on the Master again.

"Who are you?" he said. "You're just yet another band of people dreaming about wandering through the wilderness. You're still dreaming of Moses. It's time to wake up. I don't want to be there watching when the enemy comes after you."

"Where will you be then?" Simon asked, making me jump. Simon had been sitting there quietly the whole time, and this was the first thing he'd said. "Where will you be when they come?" he went on. "Will you be up in the mountains, in caves, will you be sitting there, carving your own rules into stone tablets?"

"Who are you?" the commander asked. "Who is this?"

"This is Simon Peter," the Master said. "He's one of the people closest to me."

"If he's close to you, then I'll let this rest, but what kind of a way is that to speak to us? We've been fighting, we are still fighting for our people. We're fighting for God, we don't want foreign gods or enemy banners. Do you know how many we've lost? Do you know how many have fallen in our struggle?"

"But what for?" Simon cut in. "What did they die for? What happened to them, how can you add something after their deaths?"

"I can't add anything," the commander responded. "That's up to God, but I can honor them, I can keep the struggle going, like we do every day."

"And then you'll die," said Simon. "You're no heroes. There are no heroes, only people. In this world, you can only be a person who carries on, or a person who's torn away."

At this, the commander got up, and all the men with him got back on their feet.

"Listen to what our Master's saying," said Simon. "Lay down your weapons. The army of darkness is so great that it will consume you all."

"Peter," said the Master.

Simon got up and looked at the Master. "I'm finished here," he said. "Lord, I don't want anything to do with these people, they want war, they're living off the same deaths as the soldiers and the guards in this land."

Then he left us. I got up and followed him. I heard them go on speaking behind us.

"Simon," I said, "wait, what's wrong with you? How can you talk to them like that?"

Simon stopped and turned toward me. He didn't say anything and just stood there, looking at me. When I went over to him, he took hold of my shoulder and pulled me close to him.

"Little brother," he murmured.

The rebels gathered together. They were to stay the night with us before we parted in the morning. One of them came toward us. He seemed older than the others and had a stick that he prodded in the ground ahead of him. When he reached us, I could see that his eyes were gray and white, like a fish's eyes.

"Greetings, Simon Peter and Andrew," he said. "I'm blind, and yet I see many things. I wish to talk with you, Peter, if you have time for an old man."

Simon greeted him, as did I. The old man passed his hand over Simon's face, and then mine. Even if he was blind, it looked like he was staring straight at us.

"I'm what stays in the shadows while the light falls elsewhere," he said. "You were harsh to them, Simon Peter."

I stared at the old man's hands: they were pale, his skin was blotchy. How old was he, and how was he able to travel around holding weapons? Simon seemed to be wondering the same thing.

"You've lived a long life," he said. "What are you doing with a group like this? How did the commander and his men talk you into it?"

The old man didn't answer, he just smiled faintly, and then said: "You mustn't be so hard on them, think about all their sacrifices."

"It's not the right way," Simon told him. "It won't lead to anything other than more sacrifices and more loss. If armed groups win out, or if the rulers carry on in their way, our land will be destroyed."

"How do you know?" the old man asked. "Maybe it's the only way."

Simon began to protest, but the old man waved his stick, and Simon stopped.

"Listen to me," said the old man. "Listen to me, Simon Peter. I can't get close to your master, I won't even try, this is as close as I can get. You're here in front of me. I'm going to tell you a story. I've tried to be someone who changes the world, I'm still trying. Did you believe yourself when you believed your master? I say that doubting or giving up is natural. I'd like to have a word with you. Could we be alone for a minute? I'm hardly ever sure, I'm doubting even now. Can you believe that? I give you my word."

The old man's voice was like a soft incantation. I tried to open my mouth, but it was caught shut. Even Simon was quiet and didn't move. I stood there, still in Simon's arms as the old man spoke to us. What his story was about I can't remember. It's almost gone, it was never for my ears. I remember only his voice, it was everywhere, and him talking about Jesus's death. It felt as if something were climbing inside me, into my mouth, down my throat, and I couldn't do anything about it. I was about to retch, I was having trouble breathing. How long it lasted, I don't know, but after a while, the old man fell silent, and Simon moved.

"Get away," Simon told him.

"You know how it'll end," the old man said, lifting up his hands and holding them out to Simon. "Take my hands," he said.

"You can't," said Simon.

But the old man was so close, he took Simon's hands, held them in his, and Simon immediately began to shake. I had to hold him up as he was starting to collapse, and I struck out at the old man, making him lose his grip on Simon.

"Little brother," said the old man, turning to me.

"Stay away," Simon whispered, and the old man stared at him with his pale eyes. He tilted his head and said, "It's happening again, what is this? Where is it coming from?"

Then he began to leave us, not walking back in the direction he'd come from, but out into the night, talking away to himself. I was about to shout, as my voice wasn't caught any longer, but Simon stopped me.

"No," he said. "Let him go." And then he collapsed on the ground. I couldn't hold him up.

"Simon?" I said. "Simon, are you there?"

I knelt down and put his head between my legs.

"What happened?" said Simon.

"He touched you," I said.

"Andrew," he whispered, "don't tell them about him. Will you promise me? None of the others should hear about this. We won't spread what he's trying to make us think. Don't tell anybody what you heard about Jesus here this evening. Promise me."

I couldn't put into words what had happened. The blind old man had gone, and I was already struggling to remember what had been said. Now, several years later, it's only a vague memory. Sometimes I think it must have been a bad dream. But I did as Simon told me. I've never told anybody about it.

"It's coming," Simon told me softly. "It will happen, as the old man said, all of it. But we'll make it into something great, something beautiful."

"Simon?" I said, but he hushed me, holding a finger up to his lips. Then he pointed up into the sky. I looked up there and felt something tap on my face.

"Rain," I said.

"Andrew," Simon whispered, "my little brother. You're grown now. You've found Anna. I'm telling you this so you'll remember it. Are you listening?"

"Yes," I said.

"Everything they've been saying this evening, everything they're trying to make us believe. That's how they got Father to join them, that's how they left him to die."

Later that evening, when I was with Anna again, I asked her to be quiet. I asked her to listen to the rain and the way it spread out everywhere. I sat down next to her and put my face against her hair.

"What is it?" she asked.

"Do you remember what I said that evening about the rain?"

"You will be the rain," she said.

"I will be the rain," I said, "that nobody fears."

As I lay awake that night, I saw for the first time Simon get up in the dark and walk off, away from us. I followed him. The sound of him ahead of me, stumbling, stopping, and then the way he started speaking. At first I thought he'd met somebody, that they were talking to each other, but I gradually realized that he was alone. He was talking to himself. His voice came murmuring through the night, telling stories about our father, about what happened to him. I went back and lay down. I couldn't sleep. I tried to look up into the night, trying to draw a pattern between the stars. I only shut my eyes when I heard Simon coming back.

Those rebels left us alone after that. We were welcomed by people who didn't practice violence, the ones who worked and lived under the Lord's countenance. We kept meeting new people who wanted to follow the Master. They were good times; I remember them fondly.

But things changed. Something or other came over us all. It's difficult to put it in words. I might see something moving out there where the ground meets the sky. When I blinked, it was gone. Other times I might hear sounds from up in the clouds, but there was nothing there. We didn't sing as much in the evenings anymore. Several of us were whispering that they were waiting for us, that soldiers would come in the night.

When we were going through Samaria and were approaching Judea, we were met one day by some men working in a field. They were thin, and they looked sick. We hadn't seen so much of it in Galilee, but people here were worn out, frightened. They complained of the taxes levied by the occupying powers, they complained about bands of thieves. They told stories of soldiers yelling at their doors in the morning and taking all the men who were home, young and old.

Simon appeared sad at that time. He would be awake at night, and I would get up in the dark and find him among the trees. He sat there talking to himself. His hands started to tremble: he tried to hide it, but I'm his brother, I noticed it. I spoke to Anna about it, and she said we were all frightened.

"That's what it must have been like for our father," I said.

"Don't say things like that," said Anna. "Don't let that story come back to us now."

But she didn't say any more. We put our arms around each other. That was the only way I could get to sleep. I dreamed about the water, about our hands being so cold. Then I woke up and tried to spot Simon, but there was nothing other than the night and the embers of our small bonfire. We didn't know then that Simon would be the one to lead us onward, that Simon's trembling hands would fill us with warmth.

II

Every morning, after our prayers, Mother tells me that I'm not a little boy anymore.

"You're the eldest here now, Simon," she says.

Every evening, Andrew asks me to tell him a story. Our father has been gone for several days now. He's up in the mountains, I know because some of the other children told me everything. So many of them went, and none of them have come back yet. But I saw soldiers today, on their way back where they came from. I haven't told anybody, not even Andrew, but I think that means it's over. Father can come home. I'm going to go and tell him, as we've hardly got anything left to eat.

Everything's black, and I try to find the door without waking up Andrew or Mother. It's as if I'd been put in a sack and dropped down to the bottom of the lake. Father's told me that they used to do that, in the old days. They'd take all the children who weren't any use, put them in a sack full of stones, row them out onto the lake, and throw the sack into the water. That's why we don't have a boat, he says, it's got nothing to do with being rich or poor. You don't know what the fish in the depths out there have been eating.

When I get outside, it's brighter. It's not light, it's not black, it's just night. I thought it would be quiet. I've heard the night before, I've been out with Father, drawing in the nets. But that was down by the lake. It's different here. There are sounds everywhere.

Mother won't say anything about Father. She has trouble walking on her feet, so recently I've been helping her back and forth to the spring. I tell her that I can fetch water myself, without her, but she won't listen to me. "It's for your brother," she says, "for Andrew's sake, so he'll think that everything's the way it should be."

I have to get Father back. I know what to say. Mother's ill, Andrew and I are hungry, we don't have any food. And if he doesn't already know, I can tell him about the soldiers, that I've seen them, that they were heading back.

I know the way by heart, how the path twists and turns up the mountainside. When I was younger, I went up there once to help bring in the sheep. We ran after them, shouting and whooping. I asked Father why we didn't have sheep of our own. He said that all we had was the water, and he seemed neither sad nor happy as he said it. It seemed that was just the way things were. Sheep are sheep, and water is water.

I fall over several times, but I don't get hurt. No cuts or gashes, I'm all in one piece. Mother always tells me to be careful. If Andrew or I get cut, even a little bit, the cut might grow and drain us altogether.

I walk and walk, feeling the ground rise up beneath me. I'm on my way up now. My hands help me to find the way. The moon's shining, so I can see where I'm going.

When the path starts to level off, I can hear animals. I stop and wave the stick I'm carrying. If they should come, I'll be able to see them in the moonlight. The advantage isn't theirs. Father's always told me that. Whatever you can see doesn't have the advantage. That's how we catch the fish in the shallows.

I keep walking on, and I see peculiar, large trees sticking up from the ground where the grass grows. On the flats, before the mountain rises again, woods have risen up now that weren't there before. I stand in the moonlight, looking at the woods. That's where all the animals are. They snarl and howl, letting out all kinds of sounds. They stand up on two legs, trying to climb up the strange trees. I feel myself holding on to the stick so tightly that my fingers hurt. I can't go any farther. This is the only way I know, over the flats that have now turned into woods with wild animals. I don't want to go back: Mother will realize what I've done and will lock me up. I'm not going back without Father.

Morning comes. I've been sitting there, watching the light that began as a small, red strip, and that became a whole day rising up above me. The wild animals are quiet now. I climb down alongside the rock where I've been sitting, and I start walking toward the unfamiliar woods. I dreamed of the woods, and they called to me.

As I approach now, I can see stakes and planks thrust down into the ground, splintered, red, damp. There's a stench. Some of the animals snarl. I hear something buzzing, humming away, and there are people hovering everywhere, I recognize their faces, the buzzing, I know who they are. None of them are saying anything, but there's that buzzing. Dogs and hyenas have ripped off bones for themselves, one of the poles is bent, there's just a torn-off hand hanging there, buzzing. I know who they are. I walk on, walking through the buzzing, I'm right among them. They're a forest. Fingers, feet, noses, nails. Hands, hair. The birds squawk, I've never seen birds like them, I've never heard such sounds. They're eating ears, eyes, cheeks, and lips. Some of them fly above me, and I ask them if any of them know where my father is.

"Father, father," they squawk. "Who's your father?"

I tell them who my father is. Do they know where he is?

"Father, father," they squawk. "Follow us, follow us," and I follow the birds. They show me the way through the woods. A face blinks its eyes at me, some fingers move.

"Follow us, follow us," the birds squawk. And there's my father. He's hanging far, far up.

I shout out to him: "Father, father."

He smiles. "Simon, my boy," he says. "I knew you'd come. Listen, the pole they've fixed me to isn't dug into the ground properly. Can you see it? Just give the wood a bit of a shove, and be careful not to get splinters in your hands."

So I push, leaning my whole body against the pole, which starts to tip over, and then it falls to the ground with a crash. I go over to my father, who's still smiling at me.

"Thank you, Simon," he says. "Thank you for coming to get me. Take my hand, take hold of it, that's right, and then pull, come on. Yes, that's right, that's it. Then the other hand, the same again. Give it a really good pull, pull it there, that's it, yes, come on, there we go. Then there's just my feet left. You see they've been fixed with the same nail, so maybe you think it'll be easier. But no, my lad, it's worse, because the nail's hammered in harder, and we've got to pull it out through two, not one, but two bones! Hit it, son, who'd have thought it? But come on, hold on, get that stick of yours, that was smart of you, that's my Simon, yes, always ready with the right tools. That's it, come on, there, now they're free. But the nail's still stuck in my feet, it just came free from the wood. I'll lift my feet up like this and put them on this stone here, and then you hit the other side of the nail. Just like you do when you're going to reuse a nail. That's right, you learned it from me, didn't you, you can tell your mother that, that you learned from your father. Now, take hold of me, help me up. We'd better get home so your mother won't be too afraid, she's always been so nervous. We'd better get down from this mountain, we don't belong in the mountains, my lad. I've told you that before, do you remember when we went along to help bring in the sheep? You liked it, I remember how much you liked it and asked if we could get sheep. But I tell you, son, we don't belong in the mountains, I was wrong, I was. An old man spoke to me, he told me he was blind, and yet he saw many things. He said he was what stayed in the shadows while the light fell somewhere else. He said I should try, said that I belonged in the mountains. I had to do what he said, I had to see if there was something here for us, something that would set us free, but he'd sent me off on the wrong track. All we have is the water, I can see that now, the water's all we have. Don't let anybody fool you, my son, there are people who'll tell you all sorts of stories just to trick you. They start sweet and then, before you know it, they leave you with a bitter and bad taste. If anybody like that comes to you, tell them to go, be true to the Lord, follow the way he's shown you. Stay by the water, then nobody can touch you. Nobody can touch us, only God can pass judgment over us. Only God leads the way, and he's given us the water."

10 ⫴ FOUND AND LOST

Ruth found her little sister on the floor, whimpering, with one hand over her ear. She took it as a sign that things had finished with Aaron, that a new era would begin now. It would just be the two of them again.

Anna tried to hold back her tears as Ruth leaned over her, but her tears came pouring, and she could not look at her sister.

"It doesn't matter," said Ruth. "Just cry. It'll stop. Everything stops, and then we start again."

One of Anna's ears had been battered. It looked red and tender, twisted and stuck to her hair. Her face didn't look too bad, just one eye was swollen up and closed, and the skin on one cheek had been grazed. It was only when Ruth undressed Anna that she became worried. Anna's neck was swollen, and she breathed heavily and moaned when she moved. There were black, blue, and yellow marks all up her back and down her sides. Ruth felt her, trying to see if there was anything loose, anything that wasn't as it should be. But she couldn't find anything and told Anna to lie still.

"I'm going to get help," said Ruth. "I'll find somebody who can see to you better than I can."

"I don't need it," Anna said softly. "Don't go, I don't need any more help, I need you."

"It's fine, Anna," said Ruth. "Just lie down here. Aaron's not coming back. He's finished with you. It was Aaron, wasn't it?"

Anna nodded. She looked at Ruth, and then at the door. A chill wind blew straight through the back alley to them. Some birds landed on the ground outside, and Ruth bent down to Anna again and kissed her on the cheek.

"It's all right, I'm here with you," said Ruth.

Anna got better, but nothing could be done about her ear. Ruth noticed that Anna always covered it up, and she thought that whichever man would lay his hand gently on that ear must love her little sister. Anna could never deal with the way men left her. It was as if she always had to be destroyed, as if the world had come to an end, every time she was abandoned. Anna was hurt, beaten, smashed to pieces. Only to get back up again and start something new with a new man. How many times could she stand it?

Ruth, on the other hand, was much more used to the ways of the world. "I know the score, and when you know that, it's not so easy to fall and get hurt," she used to tell the men who came to her. She wanted to teach this to her sister, but Anna wouldn't listen. It was as if she were waiting for someone, for somebody or other who would come and touch her like nobody had touched her before. Ruth shook her head when Anna spoke about these beliefs and waiting and being touched. How could you make brothers or sisters listen to you, how could you get them to see what's best for them? Ruth would do anything so that her little sister could live a good life.

When they talked, Ruth always stressed that Anna should look for love in a man who respected her. No more than that.

"No more than that?" said Anna.

"It means a lot," said Ruth, "a man who respects you and won't hurt you. A man who's with you, who comes back, time after time. A man who stays, who gives you children, who builds a house, who prays to the Lord with you."

"That is a lot," said Anna.

"It's no more than other people have around here," said Ruth, "but it's a lot more than we've had. You can't go around thinking that any man who comes to you is a good man. The ones who come to us have lost their way, and all they want is to think, just for a short while, that they've found the way home."

Ruth never told Anna that she thought that the two of them had also lost their way. She was afraid that her little sister wouldn't be able to stand living like that, wandering about aimlessly. If there was anything Ruth could do as a big sister, it was to nurture and maintain Anna's belief that somebody would come. The belief that the two sisters were the constant, and that there was somebody out there searching for someone like them.

When Ruth found Anna with her ear battered, lying on the ground in her own home, she began stitching up what had been torn apart. She took care of her little sister, sat by her side in the evening and washed her in the morning. She told her stories she remembered from when they were small. She said things that were meant to help, to do good, such as:

"It's over now, something new and better can begin."

"Maybe it was for the best, he was bad, and now he's no longer here with you."

"God is with us, he can see us, he won't let us be destroyed."

"I'm your big sister, I'll look after you, our love is strong, love that will save you."

"You'll be healed soon, and everybody will see how beautiful you are."

"Somebody else will come along, somebody good."

"Everything will grow, and soon you'll have forgotten who he was and what he did."

Ruth really thought that this would be a turning point. She didn't want to see the cuts and the swelling and the marks as traces of evil. No, Ruth thought that this time, finally, they meant liberation. Being torn apart, destroyed, only to get up again and be put back together for a new life. Anna wanted to listen to Ruth, letting her words lead her through the world and into the arms of a good man.

But the little sister didn't do as her big sister did.

Only a short time passed before Anna met a man called Reuben.

He frightened Ruth with his stature and his pale, rough hands. The way he ignored Ruth, as if she weren't part of Anna's family, not her sister, nothing but dead to him. One time she came to see to Anna, Reuben was sitting on a stool at the door, drinking from a small pitcher. She stopped, but he didn't say anything to her; he just lifted the pitcher up to his lips and stared right past her.

"Is Anna here?" she asked.

He shook his head, turned around on his stool, and looked into the house behind him.

"Where is she?" said Ruth.

"Big sister," he said.

She was about to say something, but he waved her away, telling her to go.

"She's just gone for a walk," he said. "I'm waiting for her."

Ruth didn't want to wait there with him. Anna might have gone to the marketplace, or to the well, maybe she was there.

"I like her," Reuben said suddenly. "Don't think you can do anything about it."

"I just want you to be good to Anna," said Ruth.

"Good," he said. "I'll be good." He mumbled something, and then abruptly got up. Ruth was startled and stepped back. But he didn't care about her; he just stood there, trying to get his balance, before turning around and going inside the house.

It was around that time that Ruth met a man she thought would be hers. It wasn't like all the other times. This time was different. He'd come to her at the market and asked whether she'd help him to keep an eye on some fruit and olive oil he was selling. To thank her for her help, he gave her figs and olives and said that she could come back the next day if she needed work. After a few days like that, he told her that he was living there in Sychar, but only for a short while. Soon he'd be going back to Gaza, where he came from. He asked her to join him, to leave everything and start a new life there. Ruth didn't tell this man that she wanted to take her sister with her. And she didn't tell Anna about her new love and his wishes. Ruth couldn't bring herself to tell this man that she wanted to take her sister with her. But neither could she see how she could explain all this to Anna.

It was a strange time, and Ruth was constantly torn between the happiness she'd found and the difficult situation she'd ended up in. She told herself that she had to go to Anna and tell her what was going to happen, tell her that she was going to leave, that they'd be parted from each other. That her big sister had been found.

Still, Ruth couldn't bring herself to go to her. She didn't want to meet Reuben again either. He reminded her of men she'd been with too. The sort of men who could hit you on the face just as suddenly as they might scratch at their hair. But Anna was still in one piece anyway, Ruth thought, and she was still surprised at that, as the first times she'd met Reuben, she didn't think he had it in him to show feelings or love. But she gradually came to think that there was something delicate about the way he spoke about Anna, something reassuring about the way he hung around her house. After what Aaron had done to her little sister, Ruth was happy, in a way, that Reuben was there to look after her.

But Ruth was wrong, and when she realized it, she cursed herself and her own cowardly, failed dreams.

It happened when she least expected it, on a day nobody would remember. The sky was gray, the wind was blowing, sudden gusts making people rub their eyes or spit and cough. You could smell the rain, and her man was nowhere to be found. Ruth returned to an empty house, with only a few things left. A chipped dish, a frayed rug with holes in it, a pair of slippers that were as stiff and hard as planks of wood. Ruth immediately realized what had happened. She realized that he'd gone, she knew that she'd been abandoned. She didn't go about asking questions or searching for answers, she wouldn't let questions slip into her mind. That's the way of the world.

She went to the well. The damp smell of the water and the hint of scent from the flowers had been blown away. There was no birdsong to be heard, only a soft rustle of bushes and twigs and something beating, going *thump*, *thump*, *thump* in her ears, inside her chest, down inside her stomach. Ruth got up and walked slowly back to the town. She wanted to see Anna, she wanted to hold her sister. The words Ruth said, everything she came up with to keep Anna on the straight and narrow, it all had to be said now. She had to say it loud and clear, so that everything would be fixed and cling to it. So her world would again be a place to belong, a place to be tied to.

But when she arrived at Anna's house, it was empty. There were small, dark stains on the floor. Ruth knew what it was even before she brushed her fingers over it and smelled it.

"God," she said, "dear God, don't let him take my sister."

Ruth stopped some children who were running past, knocked on neighbors' doors, asking them if they'd seen anything, if they'd heard anything. Eventually, a woman who lived nearby said that Reuben had come to ask for help. He was carrying Anna, her leg was broken, and the bone was sticking out. Ruth wanted to know where they were going, where they'd gone.

"I don't know," said the woman. "I told them to go to the old man who lives over on the flats toward Shechem. He's helped us before."

Ruth asked where that was, thanked the woman, and went off straightaway. She didn't know what to think. Reuben had saved Anna, he'd carried her alone to get help. But what had happened? Had Aaron come back? Had Anna fallen and hurt herself? Or was it Reuben, who'd then regretted it and wanted to make everything right again?

"Oh God, dear God," she whispered to herself. "Take care of Anna, take care of my little sister, I beg you, please, dear God."

When Ruth found the way to the little house where the old man lived, she was met by Reuben, who didn't want to let her in at first. He said she should go away. Ruth hadn't seen him like this before. He stared straight at her, grabbed her by the shoulder, and pushed her away from him. His eyes were red, and his hands were stained with Anna's blood.

"What have you done?" asked Ruth. "Where is she? What have you done to her?"

"He's going to heal her," Reuben said. "He's promised me. Just go, get away from here."

"No," said Ruth. "I don't want to go, I want to see my sister, I want to be with Anna, let me in."

"Didn't you hear me?" said Reuben, grabbing her. "Go away, she'll be fine, but you've got to get away, leave this place, now."

But Ruth wouldn't listen to him. She tried to tear herself free, she started screaming, then Reuben held her close, begging her to keep quiet.

"Just let her in," came a voice from inside. Ruth stopped screaming and stood still, but Reuben was still holding on to her.

"Go," said Reuben. "Leave now."

"Come in, Ruth," said the voice again. Ruth escaped Reuben's hands and stooped as she went through the low door.

Anna was lying on a mat. One leg and foot were bound in rags, and next to the mat was a dish of bright red water. An old man sat on the ground, stroking Anna over the head. He turned toward Ruth; his eyes were a grayish white.

"Big sister," he said. "There you are."

Ruth stayed silent, looking at Anna, then at the old man, and then back at Anna again.

"I'm blind, and yet I see many things," he said. "I'm what stays in the shadows while the light falls elsewhere. I'm going to heal your sister. She'll be able to start all over again."

"I'll look after her," said Ruth. "She has nobody else but me. I have nobody else but her."

"You don't have each other anymore now," the old man said. "She was given to me."

"She hasn't been given to anybody," said Ruth, going over to Anna and kneeling down by the mat. She took hold of Anna and tried to pull her up.

The old man got up and stood facing Ruth. It seemed as if he were staring at her, but his eyes had no power. The old man smiled. "Reuben," he said, "it's a good thing you're here."

Then Ruth suddenly felt Reuben grab hold of her, lift her up, and pull her toward him. One of his hands was over her throat, while the other held her hands together.

"Anna was going to fall and be destroyed," said the old man, "just how women like you fall. But when Reuben broke her leg, he chose to do good, to lift her up and run around trying to find help. He wanted to save her. He came to me and asked me to make her well again. You're surprised at that, I bet."

Ruth tried to speak, but Reuben told her to keep her mouth shut.

"No, no," said the old man. "Let her talk, it doesn't matter. It's already decided what will happen anyway."

"Let go of her," said Ruth. "Let us go."

"She's free," said the old man. "Reuben's made sure of that. I would've preferred her to stay what she is, a woman like you. A woman who'll fall, be destroyed, disappear, rotting away in the arms of everybody tearing her apart. She was on her way there. Maybe she'll be something else now, or maybe she'll fall back into the same pattern. But Reuben and I have made a trade. He did good when he came begging for Anna's life. I'm asking him to do evil again, so that I won't lose him, so that Reuben won't leave my story."

Ruth tried to tear herself away, but Reuben held her tight.

"He's not going to let go of you," said the old man. "And do you know why? He's not letting go of you because he's got to do something bad, now that he's done this good thing for Anna."

Ruth felt herself trembling. She pushed both her feet hard against the floor, trying to stand still.

"Don't do it, Reuben," she said. "I'm her sister, you don't need to do anything. Just let us go."

"You don't understand," said the old man. "I have to say this over and over again. Reuben did something I wasn't expecting when he saved your sister. He pulled himself out of the story I'd prepared for him. So I have to get him back and get rid of the good he's done. He can have Anna, as long as he goes back into his own story. That's why I'm telling him now: take Ruth, and do what you normally do."

Reuben tightened his grip on Ruth and dragged her out of the little house. The gray daylight shone in her eyes, and she was about to scream, but Reuben held on to her mouth and hit her on the head. First once, then again, and again.

She came around, and everything was dark. She tried to move, but her head hurt so much. It was difficult to get up, the ground was rolling like she'd seen the sea roll.

"You're awake," said a voice.

It was Reuben: he was sitting there next to her. Ruth filled with fear and began scratching at the sand.

"What was it you told me that time?" he said. "You said that I should be good to her."

She reached up to her head. It was sticky and stung when she touched it.

"I am what I am," he said. "There's nothing that can be done about it. But I won't touch her like that again, I promise."

"Reuben," she whispered. Her mouth was so dry, her head was pounding, her feet cold.

"Here," said Reuben, reaching down toward her. He was holding a small leather canteen in one hand and let the water run into her mouth.

"Thank you," she murmured, trying to sit up, but she couldn't. "Am I going to die?" she asked.

Reuben crouched down next to her. "Yes," he said. "I'm doing this for her."

"I can't remember," said Ruth. "Where's Anna? What happened?"

"I want you to know that I'm doing this for her," he said again.

"Take care of her," she said. "Look after her."

Reuben said he would.

"I'll send light," said Ruth. "If you don't look after her, I'll send light."

Reuben nodded and passed his hand over her face. He let his fingers glide over her forehead and down over her nose and mouth. Ruth felt his warm skin, and she kissed him. She kissed his sticky fingers.

"God is with us," she whispered, "and he can see us, and God's love will save us, and I'll be healed soon. Somebody else will come along, and everything will grow again, and soon you'll have forgotten who I was, and soon you'll have forgotten what they did."

Reuben lifted his hand and stood above her. Ruth closed her eyes and took a deep breath.

11 ||| IT WON'T GO AWAY

We're near the end, and yet something new is beginning.

When I stutter and get stuck, Naomi doesn't say anything. She just tries to hold my gaze. But I look away, close my eyes, clench my fists. My whole face tries to be like my hands, trying to grab onto words and throw them out. When I eventually finish, Naomi says, "Jacob, don't fight against it." I feel myself going into a rage. What does she know about fighting? What does she know about not being able to say straight out what seems plain and clear?

I try to remember Jesus's words. I try to remember my father, the way he always sat there, waiting for my words to come, the way he spoke with me. And I try to bring back what I think is my mother, as she appeared to me in a dream, with glowing hands.

We've been traveling for a long time, and I've become thin. I've been scratching myself, along my arms, and down on my feet. Naomi wraps me up and says I shouldn't scratch. She says I must fight against it, and I tell her I can't remember what she wants me to fight against, and what I shouldn't fight against. She calls me a fool but doesn't let go. She just strokes my face, kisses me, and says it doesn't matter how I behave.

"I'm still yours," she says. "We belong together."

We're traveling to spread the word of Jesus. People welcome us, but there are also some who are afraid and don't want to be seen to-gether with us. Lately I've been having trouble talking to strangers; I don't want to call on families or knock on doors anymore. That doesn't make it easy for Naomi. When she goes alone, few people let her in. A woman without a man, and with a face that makes chil-dren hide.

It was Naomi's suggestion to go to Capernaum. It's where Jesus stayed when he was in Galilee, and both Peter and Andrew have spoken of how they spent more time in the water than on land when they lived here. A place where we could start over again, Naomi thought. We could meet other people, pray together with them, visit the synagogue where Jesus used to teach. I could get some rest.

When we arrived, I sat there, staring out at the lake, while Naomi looked for somewhere to stay, a place to sleep. I took off my san-dals and put my feet in the water. It was like stepping into another world, cold and clean. I remembered how my father always began the day by praying for water to wash in. Every morning, a new start. We were a wealthy family, and my father had close ties to the rulers. Occasionally, when he was with me in his last few years, he men-tioned that he didn't like the way the country was being run. I think he trusted me, I think he knew that I'd do the right thing. When he died, I gave everything away to my brothers. I built a new life based on the model Jesus laid out for me.

Now I'm afraid everything's falling apart. I don't have my father's strengths, I'm not the Master's chosen one.

Everything changes, everything shifts its shape. I wake up in the morning full of faith, I praise the light coming in everywhere, the new day arriving. And then I lose it; it slips through my fingers, it slips away from me. In the evening, I try to hide, I wrap myself up in blankets, I talk to myself. I try to remember all the good things. Like when my father took me to see Jesus. But more and more often, I think of my journeys up the valley where the river Jabbok runs, into Hananiah's country. Hananiah comes to me in my sleep, out of a dark, empty cave. His head has shriveled, and another voice rises out of it. It's Jesus talking from its dark mouth, and I wake up, scratching myself.

There are a number of us here in Capernaum. Some are afraid after what happened to Jesus. Others have had their faith strengthened. There are so many stories going about, stories about his life, about everything he did. But I don't want to tell them what he meant to me. It doesn't feel right to talk about it anymore. All these tales, it would take several lives to fit in everything they tell. It won't be long until we start arguing about what was true. It won't be long until we make new laws, new rules, to set the boundaries of what's the right way, the true faith.

We're staying with a family who own a small house just by the synagogue. Their children aren't afraid of Naomi: they run around her legs and argue about who gets to sit on her lap when she sings to them. I can easily talk with these little ones, but when I try to speak with the adults, then I start to stutter and get stuck.

Every evening, I sit together with Naomi. She tries to get me talking. She won't give up, she wants me to say something, say anything, just carry on and not fight against what's inside me. I tell stories from when I was a child, from when I was with my father. Like the time I decided to run away and live alone up in the mountains. My father spotted me sneaking out of the house. He stopped me and asked where I was going. Then he asked if I had any food with me, if I'd taken something to wrap myself up in when it got cold. I showed him everything I was taking, and he nodded. "Good, that's good, son," he said. But how would I find the way? I pointed and told him which way I was going, which route I'd follow. "That's good, Jacob," he said. "You're very thorough." Then he bent down, lifted me up, kissed me, gave me a hug, and wished me a pleasant journey.

Naomi asks me how far I got before I turned back. I tell her that I didn't go, I decided I'd rather be with my father, and Naomi laughs.

"But why did you want to run away?" Naomi asks me.

"My brothers were tormenting me," I say. "They all thought I was sick, that I was possessed, things like that. I don't know. I remember my father, but not everything."

"There you go," says Naomi. "That's it."

I look at her.

"You didn't fight against it," she says. "You didn't get stuck."

I try to tell her that doesn't mean anything, but then it all gets stuck again. My whole body struggles and strains.

"You mustn't let it control you," says Naomi.

I tell her to be quiet, and I try to sit still, even if all my small sores start itching.

"It doesn't matter," says Naomi. "You're not evil, I don't care what other people say, or what you think yourself. You've not been marked. Jesus touched you, he took it all away."

I shake my head and say that there's something that's changed. I don't know what, but something led me to that cave that day, to the one-eyed man and Hananiah's skull. Naomi says it's not true, there's nothing evil guiding us.

"Nobody has that power," she says. "Not since Jesus touched us."

But I don't believe her. There's something different here in the world, something different in us. It was able to grow in Hananiah and his followers, and it's growing in me.

Sometimes we walk together down to the shores of the Sea of Galilee. Sometimes I go there alone. I tell Naomi that I want to be in peace, that I need to think.

There's another kind of life there, another kind of rhythm. The fishing nets, the fish colored and shaped by the water, the children waving and calling to the boats heading out, and standing there when they come back. Sometimes I see young men who couldn't get a place on the boats, standing there casting nets from the shallows. I keep away when they come back ashore, as I don't want to get talking to anybody.

This morning I've got up while it's still dark, while Naomi and the rest of the household are still sleeping. I go down to the lake, past all the houses in the town, watching the boats heading out toward the depths. An elderly man is sitting by some stones a short distance away, staring at me. My eyes are still sleepy, and I go down to the shore to wash my face. I glance over at the old man, who's still staring at me.

When I get back to the house, Naomi's sitting there, waiting for me. She tells me she had a strange dream. I try to listen to what she says, but I can't. I look down at my hands. They're soft. My father spared me from hard work. I was trained in his profession, I was his firstborn, I was to take over and manage everything we had, everything that became mine. But my father led me down a different route, without even knowing it. He wanted to get rid of the evil inside me, so he took me to Jesus. Now both my father and Jesus are gone. It feels as if a whole lifetime's passed since the day the Master laid his hand on me.

"Jacob," says Naomi, "you're not listening."

"I can't follow anymore. It feels as if it's all over."

"It's not over," says Naomi.

"Yes, it is," I reply. "If it's not over, what is this, then? What are we doing? We're telling people about how he came back, but I didn't see any of it. I wasn't there when they caught him, I wasn't there when they killed him, hung him up there, I wasn't there when he rose again."

"Be quiet," she says. "Don't talk like that."

Naomi takes hold of me. She pushes me over, and when I get up, she shoves me again, pushing me up against the wall and hitting me on the chest. But there's no strength in her, and after a while she gives up and leans against me.

"Don't say things like that, Jacob," she whispers. "You have to believe, like I believe in you. If nothing else, then believe in me, stay here with me."

When evening comes, we join the family we're staying with for a gathering at the synagogue. The moon's up, bonfires and torches have been lit, and all the followers of Jesus in Capernaum are there. Naomi talks to another couple who were in the far south of Judea before they came here. They're older than us, and they turn out to be

Andrew, Simon Peter's brother, and his wife, a woman called Anna. He says they're planning to go to the coast and take the sea route to Lycia and Asia. I don't say very much, but Naomi tells them about when we both saw Jesus for the first time.

"I remember it," says Andrew. "That day, we couldn't understand why he wanted to stay there."

He looks at me, and his eyes narrow as if he's trying to remember something.

"Were you the one who went up to the Master that evening?" he asks.

I nod.

"What did you talk about?"

I look at Naomi, but her eyes won't look at me.

"Quite a few of us were wondering about it," says Andrew. "I remember Simon felt hurt because the Master told him to leave him."

The woman called Anna smiles, as if there were something funny about that story that the rest of us don't know. That's when I feel that I can't take it anymore. If they're so strong, if God is in us, in our fingertips and toes and tongues, then they can see and hear how Jesus's power has run out in me.

"Uh, uh, uh, uuuh, uuuh, I t-t-trii-triii-triiied," I tell them, "to sss-sss-ssspeak with him ab-ab-abooout it."

Andrew opens his mouth to say something, but Anna puts her hand on his. Several others around us have stopped talking. Naomi looks at me, her eyes, they hold me steady.

"He d-d-didn't ss-ssay anything, b-bbb-bbb-bbbut then uh, uuuh, uuuh, I saw he was t-t-t-trying, he was t-t-trying to speak, b-b-bbb-bbbut h-h-he c-c-c-couldn't. He wuh-wuh-wuh. He wuh-wuh-wuh. He wuh-wuh-wuuh-wuuh-wuuh-waaas like m-m-meee. He had th-th-the s-saaame, th-th-the same th-th-thing you see n-n-n-nooow. B-b-b-buuut e-e-e-everything he said wuh-wuh-waaas nnn-nnnn-nooo yu-yu-uuuuse. B-b-because the e-e-e-eeeevil iiis s-s-stiiill, stiiillll. Here, in mmm-mmm-meee."

Andrew gets up. He looks at me and Naomi.

"There are many of us," he says. "Many of us who were there, who heard everything he said, whom he touched. But it's never been easy. Even my brother, Simon Peter, has been full of doubts. I saw him wandering about sleeplessly at night while the Master was still alive. I don't understand everything the Master told us, nor everything he did. I'll say only this to you, Jacob, so you know. We're alone, but he's here."

I don't have the strength to speak. It feels as if my legs had been walking all day. My neck hurts, and I try to breathe calmly and quietly. Somebody starts singing nearby, and several others join in. I don't have the strength to look up. I just sit there staring down at the ground. I'm alone, he's not here.

The next day, Naomi goes down with me to the lake. We don't say much, just walk along the shore. The boats are out on the water, some men casting their nets in the shallows. The sky's gray, a cool wind blowing the water, making small, white-capped waves. It looks like many people are busy salting the fish that's come in. A group of children run away from Naomi, but she just smiles at them. Then she stops and asks if I know him. I don't know what she's talking about or whom she means, until I look up and see the old man from the day before. He's coming toward us.

"I don't know who it is," I say. "He was here yesterday too."

"Maybe he recognizes you from when you lived and worked with your father," says Naomi.

I don't answer her, just staring at the old man coming over to us instead. He's broad shouldered in spite of his age, and his hands appear huge. His eyes are sharp, and he's tall.

Naomi says hello to him, and the old man is clearly surprised when she speaks instead of me. He stares at Naomi's face, but then turns his eyes to me.

"I've heard of you people who follow Jesus of Nazareth," he says. "I've heard that you're different."

Naomi tells him she isn't quite sure what he's talking about.

"I'm an old soldier," he says. "I'm a Roman, and when I was young, I worked for King Herod the Great. That was long ago now."

Naomi looks over at me. I've already taken her hand to pull her toward me.

"Why aren't you saying anything?" the old man asks me. "Can't he speak?" he asks Naomi.

I ask him why he's been following me, and what he wants. He stares at me.

"I've never heard anybody talk like that," he says.

"What do you want from us?" Naomi asks him.

"I want to save something," he says. "Not everything was lost that evening when your master was born, and not everything was lost when they killed him in Jerusalem. I thought you'd run away when you heard what I used to be. But you were alone, and I thought that it would be easier to talk to a person alone than to a whole group."

Naomi seems nervous and looks around her. But there's only us there, some children, and the fishermen who haven't gone out on their boats. The old man holds my gaze.

"There's nobody else here," he goes on. "Nobody lying in ambush, I'm alone. Look at me, I'm old, I'm dressed in rags. I only want to speak with you."

"Who are you?" Naomi asks him. "What are you doing here?"

"My name's Cato," he says. "I was there, in Bethlehem, when your lord was born."

When evening comes, Naomi goes to the synagogue. She wants to tell the others about Cato and what he's told us. She wants to see if Andrew would like to meet him. Cato stays with me, and we sit by the small house, wrapped up in blankets that the family's let us borrow. The wind isn't blowing anymore. Cato points up to the sky and says there was a star that night, shining so brightly.

I look up, and everything's black. When Cato asked Naomi what happened to her, she told him the whole story. I've heard her tell it before, but it was as if the story were different this time. I don't know why, but it was as if I'd forgotten parts of it. Cato was moved by the way Naomi opened up to him, a stranger. He took one of her hands between his.

"We break each other into pieces," he said.

Then he told his own story. It was difficult for him; he stammered and had to start again, not sure which parts he remembers and which he's added in retrospect.

He told us about that night in Bethlehem, years ago. All the houses they'd gone into. All the small children he and the others had killed. I thought of the children in the family we were staying with now. Cato told us that they took the lives of boys even younger. They did what they were hired to do.

"I've done other things too," he said, "but this is all I wanted to tell you. I was there. There were a number of us, we did all we could, but your prophet still got away. I'm glad he did, I think that if he'd been one of the ones we killed, then there'd be nothing left of me."

When Naomi asked him why he'd come to us, why he wanted to tell us this, Cato fell silent. He said he didn't really know. He'd been going over it in his mind for a long time, what he was and everything he'd been.

"I don't have much time left," he said. "I've lived longer than many. I've always believed in what I was doing, I was one of the best. But when I became older and they no longer had any use for me, I was given a new life. I've traveled around, and when I meet people like you, I try to tell them about what I did that night. It's always been with me, it won't go away."

Cato's quiet now, staring up into the sky. It feels strange, but I like sitting here with him. I don't want to meet the others. I don't know if I can stand being with them anymore, it only makes me think about everything that's gone.

"Has it always been like this?" Cato asks.

I turn toward him.

"The way you speak," he says. "Has it always been like this?"

I nod, but tell him not always. There was a time when it had gone.

He lets me finish, and then he continues: "And then it came back?"

I'm about to say something, to tell him that Jesus got rid of it, but he shakes his head.

"Maybe it won't go away," he says. "Maybe it's a part of you."

I tell him that it's not a part of me. It's a sickness, something that's been put inside me.

"But it changes," he says. "I can hear it now. It's not getting stuck as much as earlier today. You can control it yourself." I stare at him. "Maybe it's not something inside you, Jacob, maybe it's the way you are. The way you speak, that's you."

I tell him I'm not like that. I tell him that I was like him, tall, my father's firstborn. I spoke with Jesus, I was full of his power. I can be another person, I was another person. But now I'm nothing, I've lost everything, I can't hold on to it.

"That's doubt," says Cato. "It's a part of us. And just like there's doubt inside us, there's evil inside all of us too. It's a part of everything we are. We have to live with it, fight it so it doesn't take over. I let it take over, but you've always fought it, you haven't let it consume you. You've got to keep on like that, Jacob. We must make it a part of all the good we do."

I tell him it's not like that. I say, "It's something else, it's been put inside me."

Cato falls silent again.

"You can't know this," I tell him.

"It doesn't matter that much what I can or can't know," he says, "but I believe in it. It's how I try to carry on. Something lured me in, something called to the evil in me, and I obeyed. I chose that story. But I've chosen something different now. I don't want to be a part of the story that was made for me anymore."

His voice almost turns into a murmur, but he looks at me and smiles.

"It won't go away, Jacob," he says. "You speak the way you are. We're transformed by what we do. Not by what we think, not by what other people tell us. Jesus gave you what I'm telling you now, didn't he? He gave you the courage and strength to be somebody else. He didn't take away what makes you twitch, what makes your words get stuck. He got you to do it yourself. He showed you how you can live with it."

Somebody comes toward us; it's Naomi, moving through the dark with a candle in her hand.

"Jacob," she says, "Cato, they want to see you."

Cato gets up. I stay sitting down.

"Are you coming?" Cato asks me.

I shake my head.

Naomi is about to say something, but Cato puts a hand on her shoulder.

"He'll be here," he says. "When we come back, he'll be waiting for you. He won't go anywhere."

Naomi looks at me, and then she comes over, kisses me on the cheek, and strokes my bald head.

"Come on," she says then, and Cato follows her. They walk through the evening air with the small candle flickering like the wings of a bird.

We stay in Capernaum. Neither Naomi nor I want to leave. We move to a house at the edge of the town, together with another couple who have traveled around too. Cato is taken in with all the rest of us who believe in Jesus's words and life. In the morning, while the night is still hanging in the air, I walk down to the harbor and meet Cato. We look at the boats heading out, we stroll along the shore. Sometimes we talk to each other, while other times we don't say anything. Cato tells me about the times before he became a soldier. He talks about things he doesn't want to see again, and says that's the way it must be. He says that nobody will find him here, but he found his way to us.

Our mornings together do me good. Something's loosened. When the words get stuck in my mouth, I try to let it happen, not to change it, not to fight against it. I tell him about my father, about our journeys. I tell him about the time when Naomi and I met the one-eyed man, and when I was lured into the cave. I no longer dream at night. I close my eyes when I go to bed, and when I open them, it's daylight.

One morning, Cato and I join a boat going out onto the water. The whole world moves, the lake is heavy and alive, like something lethargic pushing us out. We help to draw up the nets, and the fish look as if they're all joined together like a glittering, shimmering blanket.

When Cato falls ill, and Naomi and I take turns sitting by his side, he often talks about that morning. About the lake, about the boat, about the fish. One evening, when he's hot and sweating, he says that he'd like to be wrapped up in a blanket like that, a glittering, shimmering one.

Cato gets better, but it takes him a long time. He looks even older, and his skin is pale in the sunlight. I hold him as we walk down to the harbor, but he usually just wants to sit peacefully. There's a large tree by the house where we live. I've made a small, simple bench there for Cato to sit or lie on during the day, in the shade of the branches.

Naomi and I have decided to travel onward. It feels like I'm ready again. If I get stuck, I'll try to leave it. I won't fight against it. Maybe the people we'll meet will find something reassuring and genuine in what we are: a woman with a battered face, and a man who stutters and stammers when he talks. We're still equal in the eyes of the Lord, we're still embraced by his love.

The evening before we go, Cato falls ill again. I tell him to sit still and try to drink more of the water we've boiled for him.

"Listen to you," he whispers. "Keep talking to me, Jacob."

So I talk to him, about the Sea of Galilee and the waves that suddenly rise up and then can suddenly disappear. About the first time he came to us, about the evening when we sat there, wrapped up in blankets, talking to each other.

"It's a good story," he whispers. "Isn't it? I've saved something now. Not everything was lost."

12
MARTHA'S STORY

One time, long ago, there was a little girl called Martha. She was often out working in the field. She was the eldest, and until her brothers were big and strong, she had to go along to help her father. Now they've been working all day, and her father's hands and feet are dirty. Martha's dirty too. Her fingers hurt. But it's evening now, and they'll go home soon. Then her mother will tell her a brand-new story.

Martha likes evenings very much. She likes evenings better than mornings. When darkness falls and everything's hidden in the black of night. When her brothers and sisters are crawling around her, and everybody's warm and cozy. When her mother sits down and starts telling a story.

Martha knows several of the stories by heart. Sometimes, when they're all out in the field, Martha tells stories. Again and again for her brothers and sisters. There are six of them: Jehoahaz, Joseph, Jacob, Jehu, and Omri. And Martha.

"Tell us one of Mother's stories," says Joseph. And Martha tells them.

She tells them about the time the sun and the moon swapped places. She tells them about the hyrax that wandered all the way from the sea into the desert and back again just to find its baby that had got lost. She tells them about the bear that lives in a cave up in the mountains. She tells them about the snake and the lizard, always arguing about who's smartest. And when Martha tells these stories, she can hear her mother's voice inside her.

One evening, it's been a long day and Martha's so tired. She and her father are out in the field until darkness creeps in. Martha's been cutting and harvesting flax stalks. Her fingers hurt so much. Her father says it all has to be finished before the autumn rain comes. Martha misses helping her mother mill the grain.

While she's standing there, she sees a group of people over on the road. They're wrapped in filthy clothes and are walking so strangely, as if on tiptoe. Suddenly, one of the group turns toward Martha. His nose has gone, his teeth shine white from a large, red gash. It looks as if he's smiling at her. Martha screams, and the man turns away. Martha's father comes over to her and lifts her up.

"They're ill," he says. "They're not dangerous. We've had people like them in our home."

Martha's father holds her and kisses her hair, and the group vanishes into the night.

Her father takes her home, where her mother and siblings are waiting. It's dark now. The light from the oil lamp falls around them like a soft blanket. Martha's mother puts her on her lap and starts telling a story. It's a beautiful story about a grasshopper who tries to play music even though one of its wings is broken. Martha closes her eyes, trying to forget the face with the white teeth. She feels her mother's warm fingers around her.

The next day, the sun comes up, tearing apart the darkness. Martha's father tells her to stay with her brothers and sisters this morning. Joseph asks if they can play hide-and-seek; all the others shout "yes" and look at Martha. Martha smiles, and off they run.

Jehoahaz sits down behind a rock, and Joseph lies down flat by a bush. Jehu has almost finished counting, and Martha runs over to the pile of rocks by the field. Her father's standing some distance away, he waves to her, and Martha waves back. The stones are still cool from the night before. She sits down to hide, stroking her fingers over the cold stones. She doesn't notice that nobody's shouting or laughing. The stones are almost soft. Everything's fallen silent.

Then she hears Joseph crying. Martha runs out from behind the stones. All her brothers and sisters are sitting over by the thicket behind the well. It looks like they're talking to someone. But their father's out in the field, and their mother's gone down to the stream. And why is Joseph crying?

When Martha gets over to them, she sees a man sitting in the thicket. He's old, his eyes are a grayish white, pale. He smiles, and says, "I'm blind, and yet I see many things. I'm what stays in the shadows while the light falls elsewhere. You must be Martha. Big sister Martha."

"Why's Joseph crying?" Martha asks him.

The man is still smiling as he turns toward Joseph.

"I told Joseph a little story," he says, "but I don't think he liked it."

Martha puts her arms around Joseph and strokes his hair.

"Joseph told me that you like telling stories too," the man says.

Martha looks for her father, but he's nowhere to be seen.

"Listen to me when I'm talking to you," the man says, and something in his voice makes Martha feel cold. She looks at him.

"Have you got a story to tell me?" the man asks.

Martha shakes her head.

"Well, I've got another story," the man says, "and since you're all gathered here, you can all hear it."

"We don't want to hear your story," says Martha.

She puts her arms around Joseph and signals all her other siblings to leave.

"Your mother and father aren't here," the man says. "I could take one of you and leave, never to return."

Martha feels like she's freezing now, and something's pressing right at the top of her stomach. Joseph won't stop sniffling.

"Or we could make a deal," the man continues. "I'll tell you a story, and then you can tell a story, Martha. If I make you cry, then I win. But if you can get your brothers and sisters to stop crying and to smile, then you win."

Martha nods.

"Good," says the man. "I've got a story I've been saving for you."

"Far, far away from here, there's a lake so black, so black. And out in the middle of that lake is an island. Every summer, children went out to that island. Their parents rowed them across the water and waved good-bye when they left. The children taught each other songs, they made each other food. And when the summer was over, their parents came to get them. Nobody knew exactly what it was, but the children used to be different when they came back from the island. It was as if they'd been filled with a strange light."

"But what's light without darkness? What's the morning sun without the black carpet of night?

"One day, a father went out to the island. He wanted to check if everything was all right out there. What he didn't know was that there was a snake in the boat. A very bad snake. When the father's boat came alongside the island, the snake bit him, and the father fell down dead. The children who came to see what had happened were also bitten. The snake went across the island and bit everyone it found. Nobody really knows how long the snake went on like this. But when the first adults went back out to the island, it was totally silent. There was only the sound of the waves, and the wind in the trees. They found none of the children alive."

"The grown-ups couldn't understand it. Then they found the snake. The snake told them everything. How he'd sneaked onto the boat. How he'd bitten all the children. How he'd writhed and slithered.

"'But I'm a snake,' he said. 'I'm doing what snakes are supposed to do.'

"And the adults agreed. A snake is a snake. So they threw him away, and then they went home, without their children."

The man starts smiling, raising his hands up in the air. He looks at Joseph, at Jehoahaz, at Jacob, at Jehu, at Omri, and then back at Joseph. Joseph is crying, and Jehoahaz is reaching his arms out toward Martha, saying, "Mommy, Mommy." Jacob tries to look away, while Jehu and Omri stare down at the ground.

"Right, Martha," says the man. "Now it's your turn."

Martha closes her eyes. She can hear the man smacking his lips, she can hear him breathing. Martha closes her eyes even tighter, and then she can hear her mother's voice. She can hear the giggling of her brothers and sisters as they crawl and roll around her in the evening.

"Come on," says the man. "I want to hear my story."

Martha opens her eyes.

"It's not your story," she says. "It's ours."

And then Martha begins.

"Far away from here, there's a lake so blue, so blue. And in the middle of that lake is an island. Every summer, children went out to that island, with flowers in their eyes. Their parents gave them a hug, let them go, gave them another hug, then let them go again. 'Take care of each other!' they told them. 'We'll come and pick you up in a few days!'"

"The children waved back, trying not to smile too much. As they were so excited. They were looking forward to hearing their own soft voices soaring like birdsong between the trees. They were looking forward to teaching each other songs and holding each other's hands. Those days on the island were like a summer breeze. Warm and light, soft and good."

"But a snake made its way out to the island. One day, there he was, flourishing his tongue.

"'Ssss,' he went. 'Ssss, ssss.'

"The children could see that this was a poisonous snake.

"'Dear snake,' one of the children said, 'what are you doing here?'

"'Ssss, I'm here to warn you,' said the snake. 'You must be careful of the wolf.'

"'Wolf? What wolf?' the children asked him.

"'Ssss, you must be careful of the bear,' said the snake.

"'Bear? What bear?' the children asked him.

"'Ssss, you must be careful of the snake,' said the snake.

"And then he slithered straight toward them."

"The children ran off. Some of them hid among the trees. Some hid in a little cabin. Some tried to swim away in the water, but they had to give up and turn around. And there, at the water's edge, the snake was waiting for them.

"'Ssss,' said the snake. 'Come to me.'

"But just then, out from the woods behind the snake came a soldier called Cato. He was carrying a sword, and with one blow he cut the snake in two.

"'Come ashore,' Cato shouted to the children out in the water. 'Come out, come out,' he shouted to the other children hiding among the trees and in the cabin.

"And the children came flocking to Cato, they put their arms around him, and he put his arms around them."

"'Dear children,' said Cato, 'I heard your screams all the way from where I was, so I stole a boat I found at the water's edge to come out here.'

"'But you're from the army of darkness,' said one of the children. 'Why are you saving children like us?'

"'I've been waiting to do some good,' said Cato. 'I've done so many bad things.'

"'Why have you done so many bad things?' the children asked him.

"Cato didn't answer. But they all saw a tear run down one side of his face. Cato dried the tear and said, 'I don't know, I heard a story, a bad story, and I believed it. It was so long ago.'

"The children took him by the hand and said, 'Come with us and tell a good story, stay with us.'

"So the children and Cato went across the island, and their voices soared like birdsong between the trees."

"No," says the man. "That's impossible."

Martha's holding on to Joseph, and Joseph's holding on to Jehoahaz, and Jehoahaz's holding on to Jehu, and Jehu's holding on to Jacob, and Jacob's holding on to Omri. None of them are crying anymore. They stand there with their eyes open, smiling at each other.

"How?" says the man.

"We're going home now," says Martha.

"No," says the man. "Stay here."

Martha leads her brothers and sisters toward the house.

"Stay here," the man shouts behind them, but his voice is faint, so faint. They walk away from him.

Martha doesn't turn around; she just says, "Go, go." And suddenly their father appears. He lifts up Joseph and Jehoahaz and asks Martha what's happened. Martha turns around to point at the man, but there's nobody there anymore.

That evening, Martha can't get to sleep. She lies awake until after her mother's told her stories and put the light out. She lies awake until all her brothers and sisters are breathing calmly and softly. It's not evening anymore, it's night. And Martha can feel that she doesn't like evenings best anymore. Everything gets so dark. What if the light never comes back?

13 ||| THE GREAT FIRE

Over forty years have passed, there's been an uprising in our land, and rumors are spreading that Roman troops are heading toward Jerusalem. Over forty years, all that time, and I can still see Nadab in my mind's eye. His red hair and his beard. His whispering voice that last night, the way he said my name, "Jehoash, Jehoash," the way he fell out of the darkness. Sometimes he turns up in my dreams, covered in fire. Other times we're all there, the whole band of us. Like we were before everybody was taken away. Like I was before I was caught.

Dear God, I know you've shown me mercy, I know the gift I've been given. You read my heart, you see my soul.

My master, the one who owns me now, won't show me any mercy if he reads this. But he's old, I'm older, and the time we have left here in this world is short. He took me out of a life of devastation and violence. I was brutal and swift, more fierce than the wolves in the wilderness, flying like the eagle hunting its prey, my judgment and pride laws unto themselves. But now I'm powerless and still as the fish of the sea, until the Lord God drags me up with his hook.

Before my time is over, I want to ask what isn't in my power to answer. When will God claim his right and bring us his kingdom of justice and peace? When will God's kingdom come?

Everything that's happened recently has made me think of Nadab again. It's strange, as the time he was with us was short. But he was a sign, I can see it now, he was carrying within him everything that would follow. Something was working through him. In a way, he sacrificed himself for us. What he did that day in the Temple didn't set prisoners free, he didn't come storming in with an angel's sword or spear. He just spoke, he fought his way through so that he could speak out. Maybe there was nobody apart from me and my brother, Jehoram, who heard and remembered what Nadab said that day. But it changed us, I'm sure of that. It even changed Reuben when we told him everything, even as tough as he was. Nadab's words changed everything for me.

I think that Nadab was full of justice. I think he died in peace. And now, now there's nothing left. Nothing of him or of Jesus of Nazareth, after all these years. But his followers have grown in numbers, they travel about, I've met some of them myself. They all tell stories about how Jesus was taken down from his cross, how he was carried to a cave. And there, in the cold rock, is where he's said to have risen again and left his tomb.

I'm the only one left of those of us who took down Nadab. I'm the only one who can smile about it all now. But stories like that, where good doesn't die, I think they bring his followers together. The same way stories bring us all together. When they tell each other about him rising again from the realm of the dead, some of them start wailing, pulling at their hair, or tearing off their clothes. Others fall silent. Others still are filled with rage and call for them to fight. But there are also many people who don't follow Jesus, who've barely heard his name, who've been fighting against the ruling powers for a long time. They have something else, other stories, pulling everything together.

Recently, there have been more cases of assassins, knife murderers turning up everywhere, even in the Temple. When I was young and was with Nadab, I met two young men who were on such a mission. I couldn't understand who they were then, I couldn't understand what they were thinking. I knew little of how our people lived, and I was one of the very people who were destroying things. But everything's changed. I can see that the young men I met then were signs of what was to come, of how everything in our land would change for the worse. Their thoughts, their clear aims, and blind faith all spoke to the brutality and extremes that have only grown since then. I don't know whether Nadab could already see this then, but there was something working through him, something pulling at him when we killed those two young men outside Jerusalem. Maybe he wanted to do some good, to do as he thought Jesus would've done. Maybe he'd just had too much of all the bad things we did. I have no way of knowing, but the way everything's turned out, seething and bubbling like a pot of boiling water, makes me think more and more that Nadab and Jesus could see the warning signs and wanted to raise our attention to what was coming.

Now, when I hear these stories about Jesus, it strikes me that they're never complete. They're broken off at the ends, they begin suddenly, they never end, they just keep on going, and sometimes I can't understand what I'm being told. Sometimes they mention a name, sometimes several, but the names make no sense to me. I just hear Nadab, I know that he must've heard many of the same stories. About how they shared a meal, how they were all gathered together. About how Jesus chased away demons. About how he rose again and came to them in the evening, while they were walking along. I've tried to join it all up, to get it to fit together, but they're different stories, I can see that now. There's no longer one Jesus, there are several. I know that the leading followers want to make one story, and they're struggling to hold on to this single story. They're struggling to make us see the clear pattern according to which the world is, and was, arranged. But I'm so much older now, my time will soon be over, there are so many stories. It's impossible to see any pattern. I don't try to understand, I just try to see. I don't have the knowledge to put everything together. And even if such magical, devout knowledge were to exist, everything would still be moving about, like desert sand in the wind.

Let me tell you about Nadab, or let me tell you how I remember it now. He was a criminal when I met him; I was a criminal, we all were. He lived by my side, we killed, we stole, we looted. We came looking for violence, we advanced as a group, we scoffed at those who believed in something bigger, at those who took orders from other men. We derided every city that was built, sneaking in and out, fleeing from guards and soldiers, sweeping on like the wind, and then we were gone.

But Nadab heard the stories about Jesus, and he tried to share it all with us, in his own way. I didn't understand, I couldn't then, but now I'm trying. Nadab went into Jerusalem with us. There we lost him. He went to the Temple and caused a riot, he talked about Jesus, and then he was caught and killed. He was a man of violence, but he died for a belief. He died for something bigger than himself, bigger than the Temple and the Holy Place in there, bigger than the immense empire to which the occupying forces have annexed this land. It's a belief they can't wash away.

Even if Nadab's gone, I say that he lives on.

And what about me? I'm still alive, and whoever lives through everything must see everything too. I was the one who took Nadab down from the cross. I helped to carry him to the cave. I sat by Reuben's side when he passed away. I was there when my brother, Jehoram, was killed by the guards of the man who became my master and owns me now. And those first words I heard from my new master are the ones that became the life I've now been living for many, many years, but that will soon be over: "The Lord God will let you live, for you shall be my servant."

So I was dragged back, kicked and beaten, and taken on as an apprentice by my new master. I taught myself to read, to write, to count. I learned, every day, how to follow my master and observe everything that happened around him. When the evenings came, I was to report on what I'd seen, all while the man who owns me listened and nodded.

Don't think that this was an easy task; don't think that I was given a new life with no drawbacks! No, it was never forgotten where I came from, what I was. Even though I was given food, I didn't sit at anybody's table. Even though I was given a roof over my head, I didn't sleep well at night. The other servants wouldn't talk to me. My master's mercenaries would walk out of rooms when I walked in. Nobody wanted anything to do with a former murderer, a thief. In spite of this, I taught myself to read, I taught myself to write, I taught myself to count. I was dressed in good clothes, and I washed every evening. But I was still something my master had dragged in from the wilderness.

It's not my story I'm telling, neither is it Nadab's story. I want to tell the story of what's stirring in our land as all the cords are stretched back as far as they'll go.

These have been painful years for our people, painful years for this country. It's as if a sickness had come over us, and we'd started eating each other. We've had a drought that's destroyed our harvests, but the rulers still demand their taxes. I've been told of people who have nothing to eat, of children who fall asleep never to wake up. Our land has been afflicted by bands of thieves, more of them now than when I was young. People calling themselves prophets are popping up like weeds after the rain, and people follow them. People are getting together to protest, they're doing it here, in Jerusalem, they're doing it out there, in the other cities, and in the wilds. And every time, they're suppressed and persecuted by guards and soldiers. The procurators have been harsh rulers, not least Cumanus and Felix. Last year, around this time, there was an uprising. The priests and the other rich families support the present rulers, enlisting and paying their own soldiers to collect taxes and duties, and to take care of security.

None of those who've been in power have done anything to change all of this, and now it's too late. Everything's coming to an end now.

I'm telling you all this to try to understand why all this brutality's emerged and why the young are so angry. They're like the two men we killed so many years ago, the ones we were supposed to accompany to Jerusalem, and who were so blinded by their faith. Just like them, a number of the youths of today have a burning desire to spread chaos, an irrepressible will to go through with everything, and a belief that means they don't fear death. These assassins, whatever name we give them, whatever we call them, are only a symptom: the desperation and heartlessness that this sickened form of governance has brought about. When nobody can see what to do, when everything you do is attacked, when all other means are used up, that's when desperation thrives.

I went with my master to the Temple one day and saw one of the killings myself. We were walking together, with me at the back of the group, when we heard the screams. I ran up, as my master wants me to see and observe everything. A man from one of the rich families had been stabbed in the side, underneath his armpit. He was already dead, and people were running around, shouting. That's their tactic: to creep up to traitors in the crowds, kill them, be the first ones to create panic, and then disappear. This is their way of showing that none of the powerful or wealthy are safe.

They kill, and they spread fear. But look at our country. Look at how a few benefit from the suffering of the many, look at how the Roman Empire is forcing its gods on us. Look at how the leaders, and those who collaborate with them, are suppressing us and blaspheming God. These young knife murderers are assassins, but what if the rulers are turning us into assassins? What if the priests and the well-heeled, holding out one hand to the people and the other to the rulers, are the ones creating all this violence? I think Nadab found some eternal truths in the little he heard about Jesus, and then he chose to follow it. All the way to his death. I think these young people who are causing havoc now are doing the same thing. But while Jesus spoke peace and acted in peace, these people talk of violence and act though warfare. While Jesus let himself be captured and killed, these people strike back.

I struggle to condemn them, even though I can see that the path they're leading our country on will lead to loss.

Look at all those who've been killed, look at all those who, unarmed, prayed peacefully for a little glimmer of light in the immense darkness. Where are they now? Look at how they were suppressed, hunted down, and killed! What's left, I ask you, what's left?

In my darker moments, I think that Nadab and Jesus failed. They couldn't stop what's come over us now. They couldn't get us to see how everything would turn out. Perhaps we humans are doomed never to stop before it's too late, perhaps we'll never see the truth or the evil we're doing until the shouts and screams have subsided. Perhaps violence and war are forces that give us meaning and purpose.

I have no way of knowing that. In the same way I know nothing about dying, as I'm still alive. But I do know something about living a life with evil. I've lived in an occupied country, surrounded by an army of darkness. I've been a thief who stole and killed. And I've been somebody who walked hand in hand with those who collaborate with the enemy. What does that make me? Am I evil? Will everything I touch become evil, or can I still do something, if not the work of the Lord, then something that can help the Lord's light of justice to shine?

This is my last spark I'm offering, all I have left in this world now. I don't know whether it will make any difference. Maybe this world won't take any notice of me, maybe everything I've been will be forgotten before this year is over. Maybe the world will go on and on, for several thousand years hence. Maybe men will still be sitting up in the mountains, dressed in rags, covered with beards, with weapons in their hands, fighting against a superior force, against an army of darkness, with no hope but to meet the Lord in Heaven. Tonight, tomorrow, in a thousand years, in two thousand years. When will God's kingdom come to us?

Nadab's waiting. My brother, Jehoram, is waiting, and Reuben. Even the people I've killed, the people I've seen killed. They're all waiting.

But before I'm taken by the Lord: see if my words, the words of an old man, might reach you, might reach all of you, and give you some of the strength that gave Nadab his courage, some of the strength with which Jesus filled the world. For I tell you that not everybody will grow as old as me. I've seen many things. That's why I'm writing this, why I'm begging you to listen to an old man: come together and pray for strength. When somebody wants to make you kill for a good cause, when somebody wants to make you kneel to banners and temples, come together, lift up your hands and shout out against injustice. Fill the streets and take back Jerusalem, take back our land. Don't let the people in power carry on, and don't let brutality and violence be the only ways of showing resistance. Don't let people with blind faith or total power control you. Pray for strength and shout out against injustice. The Lord God will be with you.

The man who owns me won't show any mercy when he reads this. But Jerusalem, the city of peace, will fall. My master and those like him have played their role in a regime of violence and devastation. They've created men who can't see clearly, men who'll take up arms to fight for our ways, for our land and our God. It's as if we've all become more fierce than the wolves in the wilderness, flying like eagles hunting their prey, our judgment and pride laws unto themselves. We will fight, and we will fall. As even all of us united can't stand against the tools of Satan: the army of darkness, the Roman troops. They'll subdue us, they'll render us powerless and still as the fish of the sea, and haul us in with dragnets. There'll be nothing left. They'll even raze the Temple to the ground.

Dear God, I haven't shown any mercy, and I've been given the gift of a long life. I was nothing, and worse. You read my heart, you see my soul.

All that time, and I'm still here. My gray beard, my thinning hair. My voice is just a spark of the great fire, and as I was lit in the darkness, so shall my flame be put out one evening.

ACKNOWLEDGMENTS

I would like to thank my partner, Tale, and my family for all their support, not least my father for all the books with which he surrounded himself, and for letting me sit on his lap as a child while he was marking essays. I would like to thank my friends and colleagues for taking time to listen to everything. Thank you to the theologians who read through the manuscript: Ståle Johannes Kristiansen, Iselin Jørgensen, and Marianne Bjelland Kartzow. Thank you to Anne Audhild Solberg for kindly reading it too. Thank you to everybody at the Norwegian publisher, Aschehoug, who believed in me and encouraged me, and to everybody who read the manuscript. I would especially like to thank my editor, Benedicte Treider, for the patience and respect with which she treated me and this book.

REFERENCES

"He said he lights a beacon for everyone in love," Andrew went on, *"for everyone who's walking around in circles, unable to find the way. He said he lights a beacon for all love that's lost, lighting a path through the night to the promised land."* —in chapter 5, "The Black Bird," is based on excerpts from a poem titled "Kalypso" (Calypso), by Åse-Marie Nesse.

"You know when it rains, when the whole sky comes falling down? The next time the rain comes, and if I'm not here, if you're without me, then I will be the gentle rain falling on you. If you're in the rain, I will be the lucky droplet running off your nose. I will be the water you catch in your hands. I will beat on the roof over where you sleep. I will be the gentle rain that nobody fears going out into. I will be the crowns of the trees, making puddles for the children. I will be the gentle rain that sends you to sleep. And then I will rise up through the dream, like a shaft of rising sunlight." —in chapter 5, "The Black Bird," is based on excerpts from the poem "Jeg vil være det rolige regn" (I would be the gentle rain), by Lars Saabye Christensen.

For Bathsheba VII, a new world was opening, as this was the dream she carried in secret. That something miraculous would happen, that it must happen, that David, her king, would open, that his heart would open, that one morning she would lie in his hands and be saved. —in chapter 8, "A Light Gone," is based on excerpts from the poem "Det er den drau-men," by Olav H. Hauge, translated by Robin Fulton as "It's the Dream."

But even though I had all faith, so that I could remove mountains, I was nothing. Everything was still in pieces. I understood in part, and it was only when Anna came that I was able to know even as also I am known by God. —in chapter 9, "All We Have Is the Water," is based on excerpts from 1 Corinthians 13 in the New Testament.

"Did you believe yourself when you believed your master? I say that doubting or giving up is natural. I'd like to have a word with you. Could we be alone for a minute? I'm hardly ever sure, I'm doubting even now. Can you believe that? I give you my word." —in chapter 9, "All We Have Is the Water," is based on excerpts from the poem "The Book of Lies," by James Tate. Parts also appear in chapters 2 and 5.

He took me out of a life of devastation and violence. I was brutal and swift, more fierce than the wolves in the wilderness, flying like the eagle hunting its prey, my judgment and pride laws unto themselves. But now I'm powerless and still as the fish of the sea, until the Lord God drags me up with his hook.

and

We came looking for violence, we advanced as a group, we scoffed at those who believed in something bigger, at those who took orders from other men. We derided every city that was built, sneaking in and out, fleeing from guards and soldiers, sweeping on like the wind, and then we were gone. —in chapter 13, "The Great Fire," are based on excerpts from Habakkuk 1:6–15 and Habakkuk 1:9–11, respectively, in the Old Testament.

My voice is just a spark of the great fire, and as I was lit in the darkness, so shall my flame be put out one evening. —in chapter 13, "The Great Fire," is based on excerpts from the poem "I dag og i morgon" (Today and tomorrow), by Olav H. Hauge.

Lars Petter Sveen was born and raised on the west coast of Norway. He is the author of four books, and has received outstanding praise for his first two: the collection of short stories *Driving from Fræna* and the novel *I'll Be Back*. Among other awards, he has received Tarjei Vesaas's Debutant Prize, awarded each year to the best debut author in Norwegian, and the Per Olov Enquist Prize, for a Nordic author demonstrating great artistic value and potential. He was chosen as the featured writer at the 2013 Nynorsk Festival, and was named one of Norway's ten best authors under thirty-five by *Morgenbladet* in 2015. *Children of God* is his first book to be translated into English.

Guy Puzey is a lecturer in Scandinavian studies at the University of Edinburgh, Scotland. He has translated work by a wide range of authors, especially from Nynorsk, the lesser-used of the two official written standards of Norwegian. He was shortlisted for the 2015 Marsh Award for Children's Literature in Translation for *Waffle Hearts* (published in North America as *Adventures with Waffles*), his translation of Maria Parr's *Vaffelhjarte*.

The text of *Children of God* is set in Warnock Pro.
Book design by Rachel Holscher.
Composition by Bookmobile Design & Digital
Publisher Services, Minneapolis, Minnesota.
Manufactured by Versa Press on acid-free,
30 percent postconsumer wastepaper.